QUEEN OF THORNS AND ROSES

BLACK ROSE SORCERESS, BOOK 4

CONNIE SUTTLE

Subtle demon
Connie Suttle author
subtledemon.com

Published by:
SubtleDemon Publishing, LLC
PO Box 95696
Oklahoma City, OK 73143

Cover art by Renee Barratt @ The Cover Counts

To Walter, Joe, Larry, Lee, Dianne, Sarah and Mark.
Thank you.

ACKNOWLEDGMENTS

As always, this book is the result of collaboration. If it weren't for the support of my editor, my cover artist and my beta readers, it would be less than it is. All mistakes, as usual, are mine and no other's.

About the Author:
Connie Suttle lives in Oklahoma with her husband and a conglomerate of cats. They have finally banded together to make their demands, which has proven disconcerting to all humans involved.

You may find Connie in the following ways:
Facebook: Connie Suttle Author
Twitter: @subtledemon
Website and Blog: subtledemon.com

High Demon Series:

Demon Lost

Demon Revealed

Demon's King

Demon's Quest

Demon's Revenge

Demon's Dream

God Wars Series:

Blood Double

Blood Trouble

Blood Revolution

Blood Love

Blood Finale

Saa Thalarr Series:

Hope and Vengeance

Wyvern and Company

Observe and Protect*

First Ordinance Series:

Finder

Keeper

BlackWing

SpellBreaker

WhiteWing

~

R-D Series:

Cloud Dust

Cloud Invasion

Cloud Rebel

~

Latter Day Demons Series:

Hot Demon in the City

A Demon's Work is Never Done

A Demon's Due

~

Seattle Elementals Series:

Your Money's Worth

Worth Your While*

~

BlackWing Pirates Series

MindSighted

MindMage

MindRogue

MindMaster*

~

Black Rose Sorceress Series

The Rose Mark

Rose and Thorn

Black Rose Queen

Queen of Thorns and Roses

Other Titles from SubtleDemon Publishing:

Malefactor

Transgressor

Underhanded*

by Joe Scholes

*Forthcoming

CHAPTER 1

N *y-nes*
Kyri

"There are three of us. How do you suggest we teach the entire population to read, write and follow a new set of rules—all at the same time?" I demanded.

North wasn't speaking to me. I was barely speaking to him. His back was turned toward me as he gazed out a window in what was left of Kaakos' suite.

Garkus ignored both of us in favor of showing the few who still lived inside the city how to clear ground and plant seeds. The seeds he'd scrounged from the kitchen—beans, corn and such, that hadn't yet been used as food.

At least it was late spring, and if the ground were willing, we might see results—unless the soil and air were so toxic that plant growth was no longer possible.

I watched as North's shoulders drooped, letting me know I'd hit a sensitive spot with him. "I was hoping we could bring teachers and such from Az-ca."

"After you rendered their King helpless? *Those* people from Az-ca?"

Sherra would make his life miserable—and mine, too, if we even suggested such a thing.

"You say she's smart," he whirled to face me. "What if there's a way to reverse this?" he tapped his chest in frustration. "I wasn't intending," he stopped before saying something else.

"Intending what?"

"I thought we could unite the country—like it once was." He turned his back to me again.

"You thought you could walk right into Az-ca, take over where you left off centuries ago, and everybody would just fall in with your plans. Is that it?"

"I didn't count on her—never saw her in all my divinations."

He meant Sherra. An unseeable. He'd divined Thorn II, just not his Queen and partner. "So. You wanted to take over after practically destroying their current King—who was a very good King, and before that, an excellent Commander of the army. That's a hell of a way to get Az-ca's population to adore you, isn't it?"

"I can offer them peace," he began.

"Except you can't. Kaakos is still alive, remember, and he'll be coming for you—of that I have no doubt. You know it, too, and you can't take him on without Thorn's army at your back."

"I thought we could work together—Thorn and I. That he'd see the reason in it after a while."

"And, as he's currently powerless, what choice would he have?" I sniped. "Except he has the strongest Queen you've ever seen at his side, and she certainly won't fall for that bullshit."

"I could be his right arm. His power," North turned to argue with me.

"It's not the same, and you know that."

"It's what I'm willing to offer."

"Go ahead. I want to hear what Sherra says when you say it. Frankly, the only reason you're still alive is that you and he are connected."

"You think she can kill me?" He snorted and turned his back to me again.

"You saw what she was doing with that army—she'd have taken Kaakos down and his palace with him, if you hadn't done what you did and distracted her. She kept him inside this place. He'd be dead, if you hadn't decided to pull Thorn's power away."

This time, I watched him stiffen. He knew it just as I did. Had he left things alone, we wouldn't be having this argument, now. Had he not interfered as he did, Sherra and Thorn II would be happy to send troops and teachers, I think.

Instead, Kaakos was still alive, and that meant he was a hidden threat to anyone who thought to stand against him.

Like his bastard son, Thorn I didn't think any woman was good enough to do the job—not when a man was available.

Both those things—his son and his attitude—had ruined our relationship centuries before.

Not much had changed between then and now.

"How—is he?" His voice was quieter, now.

"Depressed. Not eating. Refusing to leave the palace. That's how he's doing." I received regular mindspeak from Doret—there was no sense in attempting to contact Sherra. I was too ashamed to try, actually.

You should have told her the moment North pulled you away from Kaakos' clutches, a small voice taunted me.

Yes, I should have. I'd told Doret, but as neither of us wanted to inform Adahi, we'd kept that secret from him and everyone else.

Now we were left with the aftermath of that malformed decision.

"Will it do any good to write her a letter, asking Az-ca to stand with Ny-nes for a common purpose? She can hate me as much as she wants, and he can, too, but until the threat of Kaakos is eliminated, neither Ny-nes nor Az-ca will be safe."

"Feel free," I tossed a hand in the vague direction of Az-ca. "Just be prepared to have your ass handed to you."

"It's what the diplomats of old would do," he said. "The enemy of my enemy, and so on. We can send the letter—and Jubal, at the same time."

"You think returning a traitor to Az-ca is a peace offering?"

"His execution belongs in the hands of Az-ca, not Ny-nes. If I thought I'd receive a civil audience, I'd go myself."

"You try that," I said. "To see how far you get."

"What about approaching the army Commander?"

"Armon? He'd be waiting with Sherra at his side. You have no idea how close she is to him and much of the army."

"Then I'm back to writing a letter, or contacting her in some way, to request a civil audience with the King and Queen."

"If I thought I'd be welcome, I'd go, just to watch them take you down a peg or two."

"If they accept my request, feel free to accompany me."

Secondary Camp

Armon

"Wend and Marc have been permanently assigned to the King," I sighed as I took a seat beside Levi for our midday meal.

"I suspected as much. Sherra wants somebody who actually cares about him to stay at his side during the day, whenever she can't be there."

Levi looked grim. Misten, who sat across from us, looked pale. Caral was at the palace more often than not, as was Cole. Sherra called them in frequently, to act as assistants and advisors.

Thorn would only speak if compelled, nowadays. I can't say I blamed him; I'd be furious and seeking revenge against the one who'd removed my power.

Except Thorn's life was now tied to the one who'd stolen his power to begin with. I worried that the King would let it affect him in adverse ways, and that eventually, he'd shut himself off from all of us.

Doret and Barth acted as liaisons between the Crown and the Council, thank goodness. I felt Sherra could blast someone if they asked the wrong question at times. Sherra and her dreamwalker had modified the shields around all the villages already, to watch for Kaakos' arrival.

She was sure he'd come eventually.

After hearing some of the story from Doret, I imagined Kaakos would go for his father and Kyri first, then come after Az-ca afterward.

"Hard to believe that Thorn the First has been alive and plotting all this time, isn't it?" Levi nodded his thanks to Caral's sister, who set plates of food in front of us.

"It's infuriating," Misten hissed. "That fucking piece of—I don't have a good word to describe what he is and what I think about him."

Levi and I stared at Misten—I could count on the fingers of one hand how many times I'd heard Misten swear.

"Well, it's what I think," she sniffed.

"We think the same, it's just—different, hearing it from you," Levi said. "Not that we're complaining," he held up a hand. "You're free to speak your mind whenever it's just us."

"I know. I wish Caral were here. We haven't had much time to ourselves since—well—you know."

"We know."

"I don't know how Sherra is able to deal with all this," she added. "I'd be crazy by now."

Levi and I looked at one another. We were worried that Thorn would be the one to follow that path.

Very worried.

As for Hunter, he could feed himself, now, but he'd not attempted to speak, and still stared blankly into the distance most of the time.

We'd been so close to eliminating Kaakos, when Thorn I decided to pull his stunt and fuck it up.

Sherra had punched him in the nose, breaking it. I wanted to do much worse than that. Like her, I had to quash those thoughts, as any violence against the one who'd named himself North was irrevocably tied to Thorn and his continued existence.

"In all my life, I'd never imagine anything like this was possible," Levi said and stabbed green beans with his fork.

"That's the honest truth," I agreed and started eating.

~

King's Palace
　　Sherra

"How much faith do you have in your shields around the villages?" Pottles asked. She and I were having lunch at the outdoor table in the garden.

"They'll do what they did when I was alerted to Narvin's presence at North Camp. I don't know whether they'll actually hold Kaakos back if he's determined, but I'll know when and where, if all goes as planned."

Ever since I'd returned from Ny-nes, she and I had carefully skirted the subject of Kyri and her former lover, North.

I hadn't yet heard how they'd separated centuries ago, but I really had no desire to do so. It was understood that Pottles stayed in touch with Kyri—I would have in her place. Besides, we needed to know if Kaakos came back to Ny-nes, bent on killing his own father.

Kerok's life could depend upon that outcome. I let my shoulders droop with a sigh as I considered the King of Az-ca, who was now so deep in depression he would hardly speak to anyone.

I'd already asked Barth to begin gathering information to add a new law—forbidding blood spells of any kind in Az-ca. That's how we'd come to this impasse with Kerok and the former King of Az-ca, whom he was named after.

After considering another mindspeaking of *fuck you, North*, I decided against it. If he didn't know already how I felt about him, then saying it again would likely be ignored.

A part of me felt sorry for Pottles, because she was caught between two angry people that she cared for.

Another part of me was angry with her, too, because she knew things she should have told me long ago—that North was alive in Ny-nes. That Kaakos was his son. Perhaps she'd been right about Kaakos' mother being a whore, but I didn't really want to hear that story, either.

Not now.

They'd damaged Kerok. They'd damaged our relationship. Az-ca still had a King—in name only. Nothing I could do or say would convince Kerok to return to his study and begin working again.

Rumors abounded that Kerok had been injured more seriously in Ny-nes than anyone had reported, and those wounds kept him away from his desk and Council meetings.

Only a handful understood that his power had been stripped away by a man who should have died centuries earlier. At first, Pottles said the Council asked about the King. They'd stopped after only a few meetings.

"Fuck." I dropped my fork onto the white tablecloth covering the table. I had as little appetite as Kerok did on some days.

"We didn't know what North was planning," Pottles sighed as I turned my head away. "That doesn't absolve us of guilt in any way for not telling you, but it's what I have."

"I need to be somewhere else for a while." Without telling her where I was heading, I *stepped*.

"Nothing's changed," I told Armon as we watched battle exercises at Secondary Camp. It was Armon's idea to be fully trained and ready, should Kaakos bring the war to our doorstep again.

Only this time, we were training everyone who could be trusted and had the talent to form flying bubbles, to attack from the air.

Armon had asked me about Kerok and Hunter while I stood beside him on the training grounds, my arms crossed tightly over my chest to keep my anger in check. That's when North's mindspeak came to me.

I need an audience with you and King Thorn, he said. *It concerns our combined futures.*

He'd said it fast, so I couldn't interrupt.

And if we deny the meeting? I didn't hide my mental contempt.

You know Kaakos won't be satisfied until I'm dead, he replied. *That, obviously, will affect the King. I wish to visit under the flag of truce, to determine how we might defeat this threat together.*

I wish I could say that this is too little, too late, I snapped back. *You should have said this to me months ago, rather than waiting until you failed to kill Kaakos to suggest it.*

I understand that, now. Adahi always said I was too full of myself. He was right.

Well, it's convenient for you, I suppose, that he's really dead this time.

You won't believe me, but I wish that weren't so.

You're right—I don't believe you.

When will be a good time to bring Jubal to Az-ca for sentencing?

Bring him tomorrow. It's as good as any other day.

Might we sit down for a midday meal with you? Food is rather plain and difficult to find in Ny-nes.

I'll tell the kitchen to prepare more plates—two or three?

Three. Perhaps four, if Kyri brings someone with her.

I'll be waiting at the outdoor table. I have no idea whether Kerok will consent to see any of you. I'm only seeing you because your life is tied to his. I fully expect Kaakos to devise a way to kill us all, now that you've given him more motivation than ever to do so. I'll have guards waiting to take Jubal to the lockup.

Is there anything else you'd like to tell me—or Kyri? he asked.

I expect full disclosure on any plans to combat the threat Kaakos represents. If you know where he'd go to plot his next moves, I'd like that information, too. There are many places he can strike and cause far too much damage. That doesn't include the deaths of innocents, either. I want every scrap of information you and Kyri have.

I didn't add that Kerok and I should already have it—it would have made a difference, I think, in recent events. Especially the part where North planned to steal Kerok's power. Now, every time I saw that ring on Kerok's finger, I felt burning anger.

We'll give you the information, North agreed. *It's only fair that you have it.*

I didn't waste my energy yelling at him in mindspeak. Nothing would change if I shouted at him—mentally or in person.

Realistically, I knew that Kaakos had to be found and dealt with, and North had to be kept alive in the meantime.

I wished for Adahi, then. Perhaps he'd have a solution to this blood spell that connected Kerok to North. If not, he'd be sympathetic, at least.

We'll arrive tomorrow at midday, your time, North said and cut off his mindspeak. Just as well; I was done talking to him anyway.

"Message from the palace?" Armon asked as I released a slow breath.

"No. Message from the fucker in Ny-nes," I said. "He, Kyri and Garkus are meeting me for a midday meal tomorrow, to discuss dealing with Kaakos and keeping himself alive—for Kerok's sake. That's the only reason I listened to him."

"I'd prefer to be in that meeting," Armon growled.

"You're invited, as is Barth and a few others. They're bringing Jubal with them—I'll send him to the lockup and determine what to do with him afterward."

"You know what needs to be done to a traitor," Armon said, turning back to the training exercises.

"I think I'd like to ask a few questions, first. He saw Kaakos firsthand, remember? I want information, any way I can get it."

"Understood and agreed, my Queen."

"Good. I'd like you to be there—Barth, too, when I question him."

"I'd like to break North's nose again. No—I won't do it. Unless you ask, that is."

"He has twice the power he used to have," I pointed out. "I don't know what that could mean if he's attacked. I do know Kaakos got away from him, though."

"Kaakos pulled power from who knows how many, and killed them to do it, so he could accomplish that feat," Armon grunted. "He destroyed his warrior-priests, his servants and his army, too."

"And that's why I worry about innocent lives," I said. "He could be looking to tap into the population of Ny-nes again. That's terrifying."

"He could strike anywhere. Are they sure he doesn't know where Kyri's City or Cole's village is?"

"A question for tomorrow. We can move people here, but I don't know whether it would be any safer."

"Who does he hate more?" Armon asked. "You or North?"

"I think North, but there's no real guarantee of that. He's had centuries to build the hate against his father. On the other hand, I'm a woman, and he really hates women."

Armon's jaw worked after I made my pronouncement. He wanted to say something, but held it back.

"Go ahead—you can say anything to me, Armon," I sighed.

"I'd like to say that doesn't make sense, but nothing about Kaakos makes sense. What I really want to say is that his power should have been removed the moment they realized he was dangerous, and that was probably when he was in his teens, if not younger."

"A powerless criminal is certainly much easier to deal with than a powerful one," I agreed. "I don't know when they figured out he was a menace to everyone, but I believe you're right about this. They may have held off, since he was the King's son."

"I don't give a damn who his father was. He's a fucking sociopath."

"No argument from me on that," I said.

~

Kerok

Anger and depression. Those two emotions were now the entirety of my life. I'd never been without my power. Even as a small child, it had been a part of me; I merely hadn't employed it until I was taught to do so.

Too many times I gazed at the ring on my finger, tempted to remove it and send myself and the one I was named after to oblivion. That would ease my pain.

A part of me still worried about what that would do to Sherra and Az-ca. As for the psychotic fool who'd done this to me—it would feel good to deprive him of his life as mine drained away.

Lately, my thoughts strayed to that scenario more often.

Sherra tried to tell me what was happening in the outside world.

She asked questions. Wanted to know how I wanted something done. *You are the King*, she reminded me gently. *You hold the power in Az-ca.*

I remained silent. I had no power, because someone had callously stripped it away. Had Adahi known the ring would do this to me? If so, he'd played his part so well that I never suspected.

Adahi's dead, I reminded myself. *Hunter may as well be.* Whatever Kaakos had done to him was obviously irreversible. He could barely feed himself.

"Tea," Wend placed a cup at my elbow as I sat in the garden, not far from Grae's burial spot. I didn't bother to thank her for the tea, or even acknowledge that she was there.

They were getting used to my silence. Like Hunter, perhaps, I was imprisoned in my own skull and might never venture out again.

"Thank you, Wend," Sherra had *stepped* in while I was mired in self-pity.

"Want tea?" Wend smiled at Sherra.

"I'd love tea. It's so dry at Secondary Camp, right now."

Wend produced a second cup and poured from the pot on her tray. "The troops are doing so well in the new exercises," Sherra said, her eyes searching mine. She hoped to start a conversation with me.

I wasn't in the mood to hear how troops, who still held power, were doing. I should have asked after Armon, and how he was holding up after our recent losses in Ny-nes, but I didn't. That question was long overdue, and I really didn't want to know anyway.

We lost elite troops in Ny-nes, a small voice reminded me. *Shut up*, I growled at it.

"Armon wants to give the elite troops a name for their squad, and raise their pay so the others will have something to strive for," Sherra said when I refused to speak. "I think it's a good idea, but we don't know what to call them."

"Can we call them eagles?" Wend sounded excited. That meant she and Marc, who were members of the elite corps, would be called eagles, too.

Eagles were scarce where we were, and almost mythical, until you saw a rare one flying high overhead.

According to Sherra, they weren't quite as uncommon near Cole's village, but sightings were still rare. "I think that's something to consider," she said, "Only I think they should be called the *King's Eagles*. I'll mention it to Armon when we see him tomorrow."

Had I been myself, I may have been pleased with that name. As it was, I turned my head away from Sherra and Wend's excitement. They could call the troops whatever they wanted. I reminded myself that in my current condition, it no longer mattered.

"There's ah, something else," Sherra said, sounding subdued, now.

"What's that?" Wend asked.

"We're having visitors at the midday meal, tomorrow. Kyri, Garkus and uh, North, are bringing Jubal in, and they want to uh, discuss what to do about Kaakos. We know he'll attack; we just don't know where or when he'll strike first. They owe me information, too, and they promised to answer our questions."

That's when I snorted my anger. "You had no business consenting to this meeting without consulting me, first," I snapped at Sherra, before rising and stalking toward the side door of the palace.

I didn't have to treat them with anything other than contempt when they arrived, and I intended to do so.

Besides, plans could be made to deal with the other traitor coming. The one who'd stolen from me what couldn't be returned.

Yes. I'd see what could be done about him.

Indeed.

CHAPTER 2

*S*herra

"At least he spoke," Wend hunched her shoulders.

"I expected some reaction." At that moment, I wanted to find a quiet place to lick my wounds. With the way things stood, that wasn't an option.

Kerok no longer had any desire to govern Az-ca. I'd already escaped to Secondary Camp once today. Twice would get the palace talking, and soon enough, there'd be more turmoil among the people than I could handle.

"Queen Sherra," Briar raced toward me, sounding out of breath. My thoughts immediately went to Kerok—had something happened after he went inside the palace?

"Hunter spoke," Briar huffed, coming to a stop in front of me and holding her side as if it pained her. "He's asking for you."

"Wend," I whirled toward her. "Call Marc and see to the King. I'm going to Hunter now."

I didn't waste time running, as Briar was forced to do. I *stepped* directly to Hunter's suite, where I found him sitting up in bed and blinking.

13

"Hunter?" I rushed toward the bed and grasped one of his hands in both of mine.

"It's not what you think," he rasped. "I'm Adahi, Granddaughter. In Hunter's body. His mind is too damaged to do anything for himself."

"We can't tell anyone about this," Armon paced at the foot of Hunter's bed. "I'm still coming to grips with it, and how it's even possible."

I'd told him about Kerok's reaction to the news of our guests coming the next day, and like me, Armon knew that Kerok probably wouldn't react well to the news of Adahi's survival and Hunter's problematic existence.

Or non-existence, in this case. Every movement to feed himself had been Adahi's attempts to make Hunter respond to his caregivers. Nothing had worked unless Adahi forced it to happen.

In essence, we'd mourned the wrong man since the accident, although Adahi admitted that he'd only come back to himself recently. His power was so depleted from helping me against Kaakos, that he'd become just as helpless as Hunter.

"I may be able to extricate myself," Adahi said softly, his voice sounding like Hunter's.

"No," I held up a hand. "Please, no. We must come to grips with this, and Kerok is already in an unsteady place. This—will you agree to act as Hunter, at least for a while?"

"I can, I suppose. If you ask it."

"We can cover any mistakes or lapses with his injury and recovery," Armon sighed. "It may take a while to rehabilitate the body, you know —he's been in that bed for a while."

"If it will help you, Granddaughter, then I am willing," Adahi confirmed.

"It will be an enormous relief," I told him. "The way things are, and with Kaakos' survival looming over all of us, I need information only you may have. There's something else, too," I began.

"I know he's alive and calling himself North," Adahi growled.

"Doret, thinking she was doing Hunter some good, has talked much in the past weeks. I know what he did to Thorn—your husband and current King. I had no knowledge of it, I swear."

"Oh, I can believe that," I waved away his concern. "It hit us in the face, too, and left us with a powerless King who is drowning in misery from it."

"Do you still have your power, Adahi?" Armon thought to ask.

"It grows stronger every day, but is still weak. I am adapting to inhabiting this body, and drawing energy from it to feed my power. I think, now that I'm officially awake, that things will move much faster in that respect."

"Good. We may need you to stand with us against Kaakos, when he comes."

"I was thinking the same thing," Adahi confirmed.

"From now on," I said, rubbing tension-forming knots on my forehead, "you have to answer to Hunter's name. Once we walk out this door, tonight, your name will be Hunter. We will call you nothing else aloud. Is that understood?" I turned to give Armon a hard look.

"I fully agree," he nodded.

"Understood, Granddaughter," Adahi allowed a sigh to escape Hunter's lips. *I will still call you that in mindspeak,* he added silently.

And I am grateful, I replied.

Ny-nes

Kyri

"Soobi, I want you to come with us," I told her.

"Afraid," she said, backing away and shaking her head. I'd found her in the kitchen, searching for food to prepare for tomorrow's breakfast.

"When you arrive, you'll see they are much like us," I cajoled. "They eat, they laugh, they talk. The food will be quite good, too. You'll get fresh vegetables you've never tasted before. Fruit, too, I think."

"North?" She was very protective of North. He'd healed her, and she'd never forget that.

"He'll be fine," I said. "He has some explaining to do, that's all."

"We safe?"

"Yes. Quite safe." At least I knew that much—Sherra would be sympathetic toward Soobi, if I knew her at all.

Besides, it would be good for those in Az-ca to see the real people of Ny-nes, instead of Kaakos' controlled army and warrior-priests. Leave it to the sociopathic brat to kill all those people just to save his own skin. I didn't mind that they were gone—I merely had issues with who had done it and the way it was done. Blood spells were an abomination; North and his son should have realized that long ago.

Forcing my thoughts away from subjects that led down a sinister path, I turned to the fact that Soobi and I needed suitable clothing to wear to the palace in Az-ca.

~

Sherra

I felt so ill at the impending visit that breakfast was nearly out of the question. Instead, I had buttered bread and tea, hoping it wouldn't add to the upset. A visit with Adahi was also on my morning schedule; I wanted to check on him to see how he was progressing with his exercises, now that he was awake.

I was hoping, too, that Hunter's apparent recovery would bring Kerok out of his withdrawal, but only time would tell.

"Caral, did Kerok read the note about Hunter's waking?" I asked, after entering my study and finding her there ahead of me.

"I don't think he read anything handed to him yesterday—not after he was informed of the visit."

She wasn't willing to say North's name, or Kyri's for that matter. Her inflection on the word *visit* was more than heavy. I'd held myself back from doing the same, but only because it might set a bad example.

"I think I'd like to see North before lunch," I said. "To make sure he knows how things really are."

"I'd like to meet with him too, but only to put a stake through his heart."

"That will kill Kerok," I reminded her grimly.

"I know. But it's fun imagining it."

"I can't argue with your logic."

"Why don't you ask him and the others to come early and meet with you in private, then? Armon or Levi can back you up if needed, and provide notes later, if you want."

"I think I can get by with you and Cole," I told her. "Armon and Levi can visit with Hunter while I'm speaking plainly with our guests."

"That sounds like a good idea. I'll send mindspeak to Cole. What time do you want this fiasco, er, meeting to take place?"

"An hour before the meal, if possible. I'll send the invitation now."

North? I sent to him. *Kyri?*

We're here, Kyri answered immediately.

I'd like a private meeting with both of you before lunch.

What do you want Garkus and Soobi to do while we're meeting?

He can show Soobi around the King's garden, I said. *With Barth.*

You're not threatening us during that meeting? North spoke for the first time.

I'm laying out—plainly—how things stand between us.

That could take more than an hour.

Then come now. I'll have it set up by the time you get here.

Kyri

I gazed levelly at North. We thought the same, most likely. Sherra didn't like meeting with us and wanted nothing to do with us, and she wasn't one to mince words; not since Thorn's depression and withdrawal.

"You'll be lucky if she doesn't blast you where you stand," I snapped at North and stalked away from him to find Soobi.

Kerok

"I don't remember much—just flashes of consciousness," Hunter worked to move his hands as he spoke. His voice sounded rusty and unused, as was expected. His hands, once so lively as he talked, now struggled to move at all.

I understood that on some level—my power felt almost within my grasp at times, until it was bled away by the bastard who'd stolen it. It was like dying of thirst with the water bucket in sight, but sitting just beyond your reach.

"The physician says perhaps six or eight weeks of prescribed movements, and walking, of course, to bring your strength back. Then you may consider whether you wish to take up your old duties," Armon said. He and I sat on opposite sides of Hunter's bed, while Levi occupied a chair beside the door.

"Thorn? Will you not talk to me? I heard about what happened," Hunter spoke hesitantly to me. "Doret has told me all sorts of things while she imagined I was beyond understanding."

"Hunt, I don't want to discuss it," I snapped. Then, feeling horrible about that, I apologized. "I'm sorry," I told him. "This is just—too much at times."

"What about—the one they call North. Is there no way to reverse this?"

"He says no. Sherra insists that there must be a way, but nobody has come up with anything." I shoved my chair back and stood, angry and ready to leave. Speaking about the bastard and what he'd done to me always put me in the foulest mood, and here I was, forced to have a civil lunch with him and his minions in only two hours' time.

"Thorn, I don't know if I can rise from this bed, and if I do, I can't say if my power will return, either. Please, let me cling to hope—for both of us," he begged. "For my sake, and for Sherra's and all those who love you."

"Hmmph." I stalked out of Hunter's room, feeling sorry for myself.

How long would those people love me when I was like this, and without my power?

My father would have called me a fool, I know. He'd have pointed out that his power had been withheld from him, because he ruled Az-ca.

Letting my shoulders droop, I walked toward my suite in a black haze of anger. So many things had been wrong—not just about that law, but others, too.

Laws precipitated by that evil who'd named himself Kaakos.

And by the evil that spawned him, whom I'd been named after.

Fuck you, Thorn, I sent, knowing the mindspeak would only rattle inside my own head.

~

North

My head jerked up as the words penetrated my skull. They'd come from Thorn II and no other. I was finishing up in the bathroom before *stepping* to Az-ca with Kyri, Garkus and Soobi.

Was I the only one who could hear Thorn's mindspeak now, because we were connected and I siphoned his power? Somehow, his words, shrouded in despair and black anger, terrified me.

"I can't think about this now," I told my image in the mirror, my words sharp and with an edge of fear to them. "I have to speak with his Queen, to see what she wants."

My mind struggled to inform me of my greatest mistake in this, and one that I hadn't considered throughout the long years I'd planned my attack. In all that time, I hadn't seen Sherra or her abilities, and I hadn't imagined this—that suicide by one would kill both of us.

~

Affa-Gannis
  Kaakos

It helped that I knew the geography of the world before the End-War. Therefore, I knew where the highest elevations were, and where there could be people still living who'd accept me as the god I should be.

They'd also have no idea that I'd left Ny-nes lying wrecked behind me—they'd see me as the coming of their prophet, long expected.

I'd see if there were enough to fight my war against the one who'd fathered me—and against the filth in Az-ca, who'd helped him in his attack against Ny-nes.

Especially their bitch queen.

"I escaped you and defeated you," I spoke to the bitter winds from atop my perch on a mountainside. At least it was green farther down, and I'd already seen a few birds flying. That meant I'd chosen well, and there would be food somewhere.

"Here is the genesis of my new army," I whispered. "I must plan my entry into this world carefully, so they will willingly—and blindly—follow me anywhere."

~

King's City

Sherra

When North, Kyri, Garkus and a woman named Soobi landed in the garden, I waited for them at the nearby table. I'd asked to have tea delivered for this preliminary meeting; Garkus and the woman could walk the gardens after they drank their tea.

Garkus and Soobi were more than pleased as they sat while Briar poured for them. "Honey?" Briar asked Soobi, whose eyes grew so round at the offer of the sweet that she couldn't speak for several moments.

Briar smiled and gave her a generous portion of honey before turning to Garkus and the rest of us. As yet, I hadn't met North's or Kyri's eyes; I was too angry with both.

"I'm ah," North cleared his throat. I jerked up a hand to stop him from speaking. I wanted no apology; I couldn't believe any of it was sincere. I also didn't want Soobi to see an argument between someone she idolized and a stranger whose only merit thus far was offering honey with tea.

"The garden is lovely," Kyri sighed. For a moment, I wondered what words Adahi would have for her, were he able to sit here with us. She had no idea that he'd survived in any way, and I didn't intend to tell her. If Adahi wanted it, he could let her know himself.

"King Wulf loved it," I said, deciding that the former King was a safe subject. "He made sure it was tended with care, as he could see it from the window of his suite. I believe it was a welcome respite for one who was trapped inside the palace most of the time."

"Trapped?" Soobi turned to me.

"By his duty to Az-ca," I explained. *How much does she understand?* I sent to Kyri.

She understands well enough; she has trouble expressing herself at times. Lack of education, you know.

I sighed and hunched my shoulders. How many other Soobis were trapped in Ny-nes, with little hope and the same lack of education?

"I'll take Soobi through the gardens, now," Garkus rose and held out his hand to Soobi. Surprised, she accepted and rose from her seat. She'd finished her tea quickly; she probably hadn't had anything like it in a long while.

Once Garkus and Soobi were away, I turned to Kyri and North, not bothering to hide my anger. "Kerok is nearly suicidal, you lumbering ass," I hissed at North. "You know what will happen to you if he gets away from us and makes an attempt? I have someone watching discreetly all the time, and he hates it."

"I ah, received his mindspeech earlier. The blackness of his mood did not escape me," North's words were dry.

"Well, it doesn't escape me either, because I see it every day," I snapped. "He can't bring himself to rule as he should, and there are far too many things that need his attention. At least Kaakos was forthright in his intention to destroy Az-ca. So far, he has failed. You, however, have achieved that goal in his stead, with your fucked-up method of revenge."

"I ah," North began again.

"You will not rule as King here. Ever again. I'll burn the power out of you before I'll let that happen. Your past choices have worked against you, North, and you should be smart enough to realize that by now."

Kyri's mouth now hung open. I meant what I said, though. I'd burn power out of North myself if he even suggested moving into the King's palace. That was Kerok's place, and I'd die defending it.

"I see you've considered this carefully," North rubbed the back of his neck, his eyes downcast.

"Every fucking day since you did this to him," I replied. "And if I find a way to undo this filthy spell," I said, "I will do it immediately. I have no care what happens to you when I do it, either, Thorn the First. You should be dead, like everyone believed. My first concern, now and always, is Kerok."

"Should we bother staying for lunch?" Kyri asked, toying with her empty tea cup.

"Yes. We will discuss how to defeat Kaakos when he returns, and he will return, thanks to North. That's what the lunch meeting is for. This preliminary meeting is for me to tell you how things are in Azca, with its King and its Queen."

~

Kerok

The moment I'd learned that Sherra was having an early meeting with the one who'd stolen my power, I commanded Marc to take me to the garden and hide us behind a mirror shield so I could listen. Marc was reluctant, but I was his King and he obeyed.

Yes, I wanted to stab North through the heart the moment I saw him. That was until Sherra began to speak, and what she said to him should have blistered his ears.

What she said about me, well, I knew the truth of it when she spoke it. When she threatened to burn the power out of him, I knew she'd do it without a second thought, she was so angry.

Would she find a way to undo the spell, as she said? Until now, she'd accomplished near-miracles, handing Az-ca new ways to defend itself and new methods for its army to employ to fight our battles.

Could she do it?

I was afraid to hope. I watched her now, from a short distance, as she glared at North and Kyri, her shoulders stiff and set, determination evident in every tense muscle of her body.

She hadn't let Az-ca down. *Wouldn't* let Az-ca down.

As I had done.

Had North stolen more from me than my power? Had he also taken my sense of responsibility and my will to live?

Sherra, can you hear me? I sent to her.

Her head jerked up immediately—she'd heard me. *I am coming to join you now. Let North bluster as much as he wants. We will find a way to defeat this spell.*

Together.

<h1 style="text-align:center">CHAPTER 3</h1>

herra

Get up and bow, you cretin, I snapped at North, who scooted his chair back and stood as Kerok and Marc approached.

Kyri stood, too, and both dipped their heads to Kerok, as they should. They owed him. They owed Az-ca. They may not have survived their war against Kaakos without our help and our sacrifice. We'd lost good men and women in that battle, and thanks to North, it was all for naught.

"I trust that Jubal has been delivered to the lockup?" Kerok frowned at North.

"He has been delivered, as requested." North remained standing, as did Kyri.

"Good. Take your seats. We have plenty to talk about," Kerok growled. I went still. The King of Az-ca had returned—with a vengeance.

Briar, have more tea sent, I silently told her.

"Garkus is showing Soobi the gardens," I told Kerok. *She's a former slave to Kaakos, and deserves care and an education,* I added silently.

"Soobi can be trusted?" He lifted an eyebrow at me, then turned toward Kyri and North.

"Very much so." Some of the tension in Kyri's shoulders relaxed. "She is more than grateful for her ah, healing and her freedom."

"What about Garkus? Is he still the same, impetuous man I knew? The one who can cause more trouble than he's worth?" Kerok didn't hold anything back. I ducked my head, feeling a small amount of guilt; my dreamwalker was responsible for sending Garkus to Ny-nes and giving back his power.

"He has learned to curb some of that," Kyri shifted uncomfortably.

"After he almost got us killed," North deadpanned.

"He's responsible for many deaths," Kerok said. "That's why he's welcome to return to Ny-nes with you, when you go."

"Exile?" Kyri asked.

"Better than the penalty he'll receive should he stay here. Many on the Council lost friends and loved ones, because of Garkus' reckless acts. He escaped his trial once. I won't be this lenient again."

A hardness had entered Kerok's voice; one I'd seldom heard before. "May we join you?" Cole had arrived, bringing Hunter with him.

I have to call him Hunter from now on, I reminded myself. One slip of calling him Adahi could destroy too much to put right again.

"I don't have much strength," Hunter admitted as Cole helped him onto an empty chair beside Kerok's. "But I have questions, and my voice is improving."

"Hunt, it's good to see you," Kerok told him. "Let us know if you tire; I'll have you returned to your suite."

"I've been there enough, lately," Hunter mumbled.

"Ask your questions, Prince-heir," North dipped his head to Hunter.

"Tread carefully, North," Hunter hissed. "I have no love for you and would as soon see you dead. Only the danger to the King's life and my current weakness prevent me from writing the decree demanding your power and your head."

Kerok, who'd frowned at North as he spoke, now turned toward Hunter quickly, surprise in his eyes and countenance.

Kyri drew an audible breath at the obvious threat while I blinked at Hunter. He was serious in this. Adahi's former friendship with North had been destroyed, with no thread of it left to save.

Only North had no idea who this really was. He thought it was Hunter, as did Kyri. Neither would learn that secret unless Adahi chose to tell them himself. Besides, I agreed with him. North had committed a terrible crime against Az-ca, bringing harm to its king.

"Do you have anything, other than demanding my head?" North asked dryly.

"Kaakos won't attempt to take Az-ca on his own," Hunter snapped. "He'll look for new slaves to do his bidding. Where do you think he'll begin his search?"

"Only Az-ca, Ny-nes and Kyri's City still exist," Kerok began.

"No." Kyri held up a hand. "That isn't true. Others have come to me—from places far away. A few can tell you their stories, King Thorn. Of where they were and how their people treat those among them who are born with power. Other places may still exist that have welcomed the ones born with power in their midst. Those have not cried out for help and I haven't gone looking for them."

I hadn't heard this before, but I'd suspected. A few people I'd seen in Kyri's City didn't bear a resemblance to other people I'd seen before. I didn't understand why until now.

"He'll begin looking in places where there is a religion he can exploit," Cole said thoughtfully. "It's how he controlled Ny-nes."

"Food is coming," Briar set a tea tray down on our table. "Your other guests are arriving, my King."

"Ask them to join us here. They need to hear this discussion," Kerok sighed and shook his head.

"There are only a few places remaining where Kaakos may be able to convince them that he is a god," Kyri snorted. "He'll run to them first."

"Do you know anything at all about these people—the ones Kaakos will target?" I asked.

"Only that once he convinces them, they'll be as bad as Ny-nes' army in every way—perhaps worse."

"Will they have weapons? Kaakos left all that behind in Ny-nes. We destroyed as much as we could."

"I have no doubt that he will find other weapons elsewhere. If not where he finds his army, then he'll take them away from whomever and wherever he finds them."

"Like we moved vehicles and such." I watched as Kerok's fists clenched and unclenched—as if he were remembering the power he'd had to do such things.

North didn't miss the gesture, either, and turned his head away. I hoped guilt ate at him; he deserved it.

"Should we go looking for him—where you think he could be?" I demanded. "I'd rather face him alone, than with an army at his back."

"It's worth some serious thought," Cole agreed as Armon, Caral and the others arrived. Another table and more seats were brought out for them while we suspended our discussion.

Food was served after that, so we waited until the table was set and the servants had retreated to continue.

"Where do you think Kaakos is?" Kerok spoke first, aiming his question at Kyri. I held my breath as he cut into his fowl while waiting for her answer. He needed to eat; his appetite had been missing almost as long as his power.

"In a mountainous region far to the east," North answered for her. "Low-lying areas will be flooded, the same as they are, here. Higher elevations will hold any survivors, and that's where we should look."

"Why haven't you gone looking for Kaakos already?" Armon demanded.

"Because we need your help," Kyri's eyes dropped to her plate. So far, she hadn't touched her food. "We need teachers and guards for the people of Ny-nes. We need a hand-picked, elite force to go after Kaakos, and we mustn't leave Az-ca unguarded."

"Therefore, you need the assistance of Az-ca's King, and his army," Hunter said. His hands shook badly as he attempted to lift his fork. Unobtrusively, I reached out to place a hand on his arm, to feed him power. The shaking stopped and Hunter dropped his eyes.

Thank you, Granddaughter, he sent to me.

His hands steadier, he lifted his fork and began to eat.

❧

Kyri

Doret hadn't come to the meeting or to join us for the meal. I wondered if she were that angry with me—or with North.

Doret? I sent hesitant mindspeak.

I'm having lunch with Barth, Soobi and Garkus, she replied. *Soobi is overwhelmed as it is, so we're talking to her in the kitchen while we eat. Besides, I really don't want to hear anything North has to say.*

Too bad; you should have seen Sherra put him in his place, and then watch Thorn do the same. North is barely speaking, now.

Thorn is cooperating?

He is. I believe that was Sherra's doing, after she told North she'd find a way to undo the spell if it killed her.

Good for her. I hope it kills North instead of her, though. What will Thorn do with Garkus?

He's sending him back to Ny-nes. It's better this way; Garkus burned his bridges with the King.

I know. At least they're not taking his power away. He may need it if Kaakos returns.

We may be going after Kaakos. Sherra certainly wants to. We think it's better to go looking for him than waiting for him to arrive with another army dredged from somewhere else.

What does Thorn say?

He hasn't said anything yet, although I can tell he's considering all suggestions.

Then Sherra worked a miracle, getting him involved in this.

I hope it lasts.

So do I.

❧

Armon

What happened? Thorn is actually participating in this conversation, I sent to Sherra.

Not sure, but he came blazing into this mess with a purpose, and I don't want it to go away. Marc is here by default, but I don't mind that.

He'll hear things he wouldn't have before, I pointed out.

Then you'll have to tell him this isn't information to spread among the troops. Not yet, anyway.

I will. Once a plan is put together, we can go from there.

"We have to know where to set our feet," Thorn argued, drawing me away from my private conversation with Sherra.

"We need a general location," Sherra countered. "We can take floating bubble shields and lower them as needed to do an initial search."

"We still need a reference point for our safe arrival," I said. "We don't want to land in the center of Kaakos' new home and begin a fight immediately, when we may be unprepared and at a disadvantage."

"Agreed," Sherra nodded to me. "That's why the bubble shields have to be mirrored, and our arrival quite high in the air, to avoid forced contact."

"Some of those areas are quite mountainous; it's why they're still inhabitable," North said. "The air will be quite thin, too, and may cause a hardship if we go much higher."

"Blasts don't work well in high places, because of the thinning air," Kyri said. "We have to breathe to employ power. The thinner the air, the weaker we are."

"I've watched Sherra put out a blast-fire by placing a shield over it," Thorn said. "What you say makes sense."

"When do we begin our search?" Cole asked.

"An army isn't trained overnight, but Kaakos will move quickly. We should begin soon, I think," Kyri replied.

"We still need a focus point, to *step* our shields," Sherra said.

"I'll consult with a few from my village who can describe their former countries," Kyri offered. "Perhaps they can give Sherra information."

"That would be helpful," Sherra conceded.

~

Sherra

"I'll return in two days," Kyri said. "I have to talk to them first, so they'll know what's happening."

"Very well. Another meeting in two days, and then we plan our search for Kaakos," Kerok stated flatly. "During those two days, I will consult with my General, troops will be chosen, and the *King's Eagles* will be flying."

North's head jerked upward at Kerok's words. Perhaps his widened eyes revealed his thoughts in this—regarding the one now fully in charge of this operation.

King Thorn II had taken command. North would be nothing but a subordinate from now on, and he may as well get used to it.

Pottles, they're ready to go, I sent to her. *Bring Garkus and Soobi to the garden.*

On our way.

There was something else I needed to do before Garkus left—unless he didn't want it. I'd never changed his complexion back to its original state. The decision would be his whether that changed.

Barth arrived with Pottles and the others; Kyri dipped her head to Barth. I understood then that she'd been in contact with Pottles, and Pottles had likely told Barth why he'd be needed in two days' time.

"Garkus, I can reverse your disguise," I began as he turned to me. "If you want."

He looked down at his pale-skinned hands for a moment, before meeting my gaze. "I want to be myself, good or bad," he shrugged. "I know this was to save my life before, but I hope to change things now."

"All right."

I reached within myself to find the proper power to change him back. Soobi gasped the moment he became his normal, dark-skinned self.

He smiled crookedly at her. "I'm the same man," he told her, holding out a hand. "I just look different."

Soobi hesitated for a moment, then placed her hand in his. "I'm pleased to meet you, Soobi," Garkus displayed his famous grin. Soobi smiled back.

Kyri released a pent-up sigh. *She'd worried about this, I could tell. Soobi was only one person, too. How would the rest of Ny-nes treat Garkus?*

"We have work to do," Kyri said. "Soobi, I'll take you and Garkus to my village. There are people we have to speak with."

Pottles and Barth helped Hunter back to his suite after Kerok asked me to walk the garden with him. Yes, I felt nervous and on edge. This was unsteady territory, and I worried that he'd fall back into his black mood.

We'll talk later, Armon informed me before sending everyone else back to the palace. I understood that he, Cole, Levi and Caral would have a drink in Caral's office and discuss our meeting.

Kerok and I needed to meet with them, too, but for now, he wanted to walk the garden.

At first, I walked beside him, neither touching nor talking as Kerok set our pace. "Sometimes, I forget," he said after a while.

"Forget what?" I said before warning myself to tread lightly.

"How privileged I am. Or how lucky."

"What?" I stopped walking and turned to face him.

"I know how I've been since Ny-nes," he waved a hand dismissively and turned his head away. "I won't say that I'm not still bitter and angry. I won't say that I won't have dark moods again, because I probably will. As long as that filth holds my power, I'll feel that way, I'm sure. What I need to do," he turned back to me, then, "is focus on what I do have, and what I can still do."

"What I need to do," I told him, reaching out to take his hand, "is focus on how to reverse or destroy the spell that took your power away. Together, we have to devise our plan to destroy Kaakos before he can raise another army against us."

He turned my hand in his, until he could see the black rose tattoo. Raising it to his lips, he placed a kiss there. "Shall we join our friends, then, and begin our discussions? We have much to decide, and many people to protect."

~

"Is there an extra glass or two?" Kerok said as we walked into Caral's office. Armon and Levi stood quickly as we walked into the small room.

"We'll find some," Armon said, pulling another chair toward the desk. Levi did the same, so Kerok and I could sit.

"We were discussing how to locate Kaakos," Barth said as he poured a glass of wine for Kerok first, and then one for me. "We think that Sherra and I may be able to find his trail together, using some of our combined divination techniques."

"How much range do you think you'll have together?" Kerok lifted his glass to drink.

"I don't know—that's the thing. We have no idea how far away he is right now, or how far our divination will reach. That means experimentation, I think, until we know for sure. A map of these ah, places would help tremendously."

"Do we have any maps—of how things were before the End-War?" Kerok asked.

"Hunter would be the one to know that, and he's currently asleep," Barth sighed. "I think this trauma has caused some changes in him, too. Nothing bad," Barth held up a hand, "just slight differences. I worry his memory may not be as sharp as it once was."

I lifted my wineglass, then, hoping to hide my shaky breaths. If Barth did a divination on Hunter, he could learn things I'd prefer he didn't.

"I'm grateful he's awake and talking to us," Kerok stated flatly. I nodded my agreement and took another sip of wine.

"Very well, we'll ask Hunter about maps when he wakes, and if we have anything at all, we'll study those until Kyri comes again. She appears to know a great deal about these other places." Kerok's mouth dipped in a frown. He hated not having required information.

"There are always the catacombs," Armon suggested. "If there's nothing in the library."

"The person who'd know what is in the catacombs was Adahi, and he's gone," Kerok growled.

We have to speak with him the moment he's awake, Armon sent.

Yes, we do.

Kerok

"Briar, will you have someone come in to clean and air out my suite?" I asked when she arrived with a new bottle of wine for us.

"Of course," she dipped her head. "I'll have it done right away."

"Thank you."

Her smile made me think of a rising sun for a moment. *How morose had I been, that asking someone to do menial labor was taken as a blessing?*

Armon, do not let me fall into that black pit again, I sent to him.

I will make that a priority, he replied. *I'm pleased to know your mindspeak still works.*

At least something works, I replied without humor. *We'll talk soon about progress with the troops. Are there any among the latest batch of warrior trainees who would make a good fit with the Eagles? We have holes to fill.*

I believe there are, and you're right, we do have holes to fill.

"Sherra?" I turned to her, then.

"What do you need?" she asked immediately.

"I think we should pay a visit to Ny-nes, or at least our diviners should. Now is the time to find any of their children born with power, then decide whether to train them or dampen their ability so they can't use it. Untrained power can turn deadly."

"I'll ask Pottles to come," Sherra said.

"Yes, Doret would be a good choice to discuss this venture," Barth agreed. "And you are correct, my King. Who knows how many young ones there have power and require assistance?"

"We may have to remove them from Ny-nes," Doret walked into the room. "The superstitions those people have won't die overnight, or even in a decade. Their children will still be in danger from the remnants of Kaakos' twisted religion. There is one thing that may gain us access to these parents, however, as much as I dislike saying it."

"What's that?" I asked.

"They consider North a healer, as he has used his power to heal among them. Soobi is one of those who's benefited from his efforts. He may have to approach these people on our behalf to convince them to let us do divination."

"Damn," Armon swore.

"His legend is spreading throughout Ny-nes," Doret informed us. "He has formed a bond with the people, and they'll trust him if they trust anyone."

"The truth is often problematic, is it not?" Barth sighed.

"And becoming more so every day," I grumbled. "How quickly can you and Sherra experiment with your divinations?" I asked Barth.

"We can start tomorrow morning," Sherra said. "I'd like to question Jubal after this meeting is over."

"I will accompany you," Barth told her. "I wish to learn what transpired while our traitor was in Ny-nes."

"Perhaps we'll gain some insight into Kaakos' spells," Sherra said.

I turned sharply toward her. She was looking for ways to undo North's hold on me already, and Jubal could become a key component in her search.

After all, Kaakos was North's son, and could have very similar talents.

Blood spells, I reminded myself. He'd used a blood spell to take what he had from me. Sherra was wise to keep Jubal alive for now. We had much to learn from him.

～

Sherra

A crowd wanted to attend Jubal's questioning. Wisely, Kerok asked them to stay within a mirrored shield while he, Barth and I approached our prisoner.

"Come to kill me, bitch?" Jubal's accusatory curse was hurled at me as we entered his cell.

"You will reel in your temper and withhold your disrespectful words in the presence of the King and Queen," Barth snapped at the small, wizened man lounging on his bunk. "You remain alive by the grace of the Queen alone."

At least he'd been forced to bathe and was given clean prisoner's garb before we arrived. Still, the stench of Kaakos' power was about him, and it made my skin crawl. "I've placed a shield about him, to keep Kaakos out," I sighed after performing that task.

Jubal's head jerked up, his eyes widening in surprise. That surprise gave way to skepticism. "Hmmph. You think you're special, don't you?" He turned his head away again.

"I think you're a misogynistic traitor," I replied. "One stupid enough to be caught in the snares of Ruarke and then Kaakos. Tell me, how was your life in Ny-nes, Jubal?"

He clenched his fists and refused to reply.

"Well, you won't need to talk to give us what we want to know," I went on. "Barth and I will do a divination, and if you don't sit still for it, I'll have someone hold you down."

"What then?" Jubal still refused to look at us.

"It depends on your usefulness," Kerok replied. "Convince me to allow a traitor to keep his life. Cooperate fully, and I'll ask a physician to provide medicine for the pain in your leg. Now, will you hold still for the divination, or shall I call for the guards to ensure it?"

"I will be still for the divination," his consent was sullen.

Be careful, Sherra, Kerok warned as Barth and I approached Jubal to place our hands on him.

I will. I intend to protect Barth, too, if needed.

Thank you.

"I'll go first," Barth offered. I nodded and watched as he placed his hands on Jubal. Then, as I normally did, I placed my hands on Barth.

Images flashed through my mind—images from early in Jubal's life, when his escort died in their first battle together, and he came away from it maimed in body and mind.

Then, images switched. He was contacted by Ruarke while speaking with his neighbor. Ruarke offered gold. Jubal, who'd been spilling his complaints to his friend, readily accepted, and was snared for life.

Then, another switch.

To Kaakos.

Jubal had cringed before the ultimate traitor, as Kaakos performed his spell, forcing Jubal to act as his eyes and ears in the field and send mindspeak of his priests' activities. He'd been searching for the healer.

For North.

I could easily see in Kaakos then that he had no idea of North's true identity at the time.

I saw other things, too. Some of which I'd suspected; others I hadn't. Kyri had attempted to train him when he was young—very young. North had begged her to make the attempt—to teach him how to handle the power with which he'd been born.

When Kyri finally agreed to train the boy, he was already a troublemaker, and his mother was dead.

By his hand.

CHAPTER 4

"Did Kyri know Kaakos killed his mother?" I demanded. Pottles gaped at me from across the table. At my request, she'd joined us for dinner and was now hearing something she hadn't known.

"I think that's a no," Kerok frowned as he cut into his pork chop.

"I wouldn't have seen those things in Kaakos without Sherra there, and it was ah, disturbing," Barth grimaced.

"Everybody thought she ran away, so she wouldn't have to deal with the boy any longer," Pottles admitted. "She didn't have power. She was a dalliance with the King, and when she became pregnant," Pottles shrugged.

"So he provided for her and the boy, until he discovered the boy had talent?" Kerok lifted an eyebrow.

"Yes," Pottles said. "Exactly. North didn't have anything to do with the woman once she became pregnant and an inconvenience, so he hid her away in a village and sent a monthly stipend. Until the boy began to cause problems. North assumed Kaakos' mother took off with another man, to be honest, and the villagers informed the monthly messenger that the boy was wandering the village alone and causing trouble."

"How old was he, then?" Kerok asked.

"Seven."

"He should have burned the power out of the boy then," I snapped. "Kaakos not only murdered his mother in secret, he set houses on fire. The fires are why the message was sent."

"Hindsight," Pottles mumbled.

"Hindsight we're still paying for," Armon observed, "With our lives."

"I know. Kyri knows it, too. He was born with a warped mind. I suppose he finally had enough of his mother's whining and did away with her, then began forming plans to kill his father while Kyri taught him how to accomplish just that."

"What was his true name?" Kerok asked. "I know it wasn't Kaakos."

"Thornson," I said. "Barth and I saw that, too. He hated the name. Couldn't wait to be rid of it."

"So that's why we weren't told the name before. It would give away the entire thing." Kerok was angry, now.

"Oh, he may have told you if he'd managed to take down Az-ca, just before you died at his hand. He's very vindictive, you know," Pottles snorted.

"I'd say once an enemy, always an enemy of that one," Barth said. "Sherra and I witnessed the fury in him; fury from centuries gone and still it felt fresh."

"It was bad," I agreed. "Twisted, evil, whatever you want to call it. It made me ill to see it in him. I can't help but think it would have been a hundred times worse if we'd been touching him directly, rather than seeing this through Jubal."

"I'm not surprised you needed the filter Jubal provided," Pottles' shoulders sagged. "I'd be terrified to touch him myself."

"I saw what happened to Jubal when his escort died, too," I said. "He fired a blast too early, when he knew an enemy bomb was on the way. His escort had a shield up to protect from the bomb when he fired his blast. She dropped her shield to allow his blast through, so they wouldn't be fried by it. She couldn't get another up in time to deflect the bomb. All this time, he's been telling himself and everyone else that it was her fault, when the opposite is true."

Kerok chewed thoughtfully for a few moments as he considered my words, before nodding his understanding. "We'll keep Jubal alive for now, in case we need to revisit things with him," he declared. "Have we found any old maps here in the palace from before the End-War?" Kerok changed the subject.

"You won't find those," Pottles sniffed. "Ruarke's father burned them after Ruarke faked his death. My sister had been studying them; they were still in her room at the palace. The King sent a blast and burned the entire suite to cinders."

"That's—unfortunate," I said.

"He was a fool," Pottles huffed. "I only had a few things left to remember my sister, and the King wouldn't listen when I tried to tell him that Ruarke was behind all of it."

"An unfortunate event in our history," Kerok shook his head. "Food's getting cold. Please, eat."

"Stay, Sherra," Kerok said after dinner was finished and we'd ended our discussion. The others took their leave, while I remained sitting at Kerok's side.

"I ah," he began. "This isn't to slight you, or upset you, but I'm not sure that bringing you back to my suite right now may be a good idea," he blurted. "I don't sleep well anymore, and I could disturb you. You need your rest, and," his voice trailed off.

"I understand," I placed a hand over his for a moment, while my brief hopes died a swift death. "Let me know when you feel otherwise, Kerok."

I walked out of the dining room with as much outward dignity as I could find, while inside, my heart bled.

Kerok

How could I explain that the fire—the heat we'd form together when we were connected, was no longer within me—that the experience would never be the same because North had robbed us of that?

Instead, she'd stiffened slightly, told me she understood and then walked out without a backward glance. I may as well have slapped her and told her she was no longer desirable to me.

Besides, I had to catch up with Barth—too many things had slipped my notice since my return from Ny-nes, and my sleepless hours could be put to better use. I intended to read records of Council meetings, proposed laws and anything else that should be attended to by the King.

For now, I couldn't say whether my pride and lack of power could ever be set aside well enough to share a bed with my rose again, unless a way were found to make me whole.

You won't be the one suffering from that withdrawal, a small voice reminded me. Shoving that bit of guilt aside, I sent mindspeak to Barth.

∼

Sherra

When people are hurting, they tend to lash out, I recalled one of Pottles' early lessons as I removed the top half of my uniform and tossed the shirt over the back of a chair inside my suite. I'd reminded myself of that lesson often, whenever Kerok had lashed out at others recently.

Now, I was the one wishing to do so. I wanted to shout at Kyri in mindspeak for allowing a sociopathic boy to retain his power.

I wanted to scream at North, for not seeing his son's tendencies for himself when he asked Kyri to teach him.

I wanted to slap Jubal for blaming his troubles on his innocent escort, who'd saved his life by doing the best she could in a situation he'd caused himself.

And I wanted to shout at Kerok, while I wept at the inequities life had handed me. "Sherra, what are you doing in there?" Pottles knocked on my door. Flinging my shirt on so I wouldn't answer the door half-naked, I opened the door to find her standing there, a worried frown on her face.

"I'm drowning in self-pity," I answered truthfully. "What do you want?"

"This wasn't your choice—to come back to this suite?"

"No," I shrugged in helpless frustration. I wasn't in the mood to explain to anyone how I felt about my current situation.

"I should have known," she sighed and shook her head. "I'm sorry I bothered you."

"When did she know?" I demanded before Pottles could walk away.

"Who? And know what?"

"Kyri. When did she know that Thornson—Kaakos—was a sociopath? Did she ever have the idea that his power ought to be removed?"

"Kaakos has always been a sly one," Pottles made a sour face as if that helped her remember things. "All that was before my time, too, so I have to rely on Kyri's version of things. She says that by the time he was eleven, he'd begun to show his true colors. Animals tended to die around him, and other things happened, that he pretended were mistakes. He always promised to do better, so she'd keep teaching him."

"He was learning all along and letting his evil out when he could cover it up?"

"That's what I think."

"That's pretty much what I saw in the divination. I just can't understand Kyri's inability to see all that in him."

"She wanted to believe otherwise, and so she did. He was only a boy, and she was determined to teach him better."

"A powerful boy, with evil intentions," I sniffed. "That power should have been snuffed out quickly. He would have caused trouble, still, but at least he couldn't have fought his way out of Az-ca after he'd been found out and charged with murder and arson."

"So. You saw that, too, eh?"

"Hmmph."

"I believe Adahi advised North to dampen the power in the boy while Kyri taught him. North refused."

"And here we are."

"Yes. Here we are. Had Kaakos not ensnared Ruarke, perhaps he would have shown the King his true colors and been sentenced for his crimes. Instead, Ruarke killed my sister, faked his death and went running to Kaakos the moment he could. Bastards, both of them."

"You never talked about him—Ruarke's father—before tonight," I said.

"Stupid ass," she muttered. "Believed Ruarke was the reason the sun rose and set. Wouldn't listen to me; blamed my sister for his death—I was done with him when my sister died."

"Like Kyri was done with North."

"Both headstrong, those two. Both convinced they were right. They've been pulled off their high horse, I think, and they finally, fully, understood that today."

"How are Anari and the boys?" I asked, changing the subject.

"They're helping train the new warriors in shielding and a few other things. It's good for them and a real confidence boost. Armon and I agree that these warriors will be better trained than any I've seen for a while, and they'll be able to shield themselves while firing their blasts before we're done with them."

"At least there's some good news in all this," I said. "And once we get new pods together who can combine blasts, Kaakos should start to worry."

"Worry? He's too much of an egomaniac to believe anyone can stop him for long."

"Then maybe someone ought to teach him the finer points of fear," I said.

"I'll leave that to you. Good-night."

I shut my door as Pottles walked away. At least I wasn't awash in self-pity over Kerok's dismissal any longer. There were other things to worry about—more pressing matters to contemplate—than being turned out of the King's bed.

~

Kerok

"How long before you can resume your duties?" I asked Hunter the following morning. I'd requested that he have breakfast with me; Caral *stepped* him to the garden table, where two plates of food were being laid out.

Like a coward, I hadn't invited Sherra. I'm sure she was still upset after my announcement the night before. I should have known that Hunter wouldn't let that go, however.

"Where is Sherra?" he asked, once he was seated comfortably at the table.

"Answer my question first," I said, feeling like an ass for doing it.

"Perhaps in two weeks. Maybe more. My mind is clearing, you understand, but convincing the body to cooperate after such a long time is a different story. Cole and Doret have offered to help me with exercises during the day."

"Good. I'll be pleased to have your counsel again. I've gone over the records of Council meetings since the war in Ny-nes. There are several things that need our attention."

"Where is Sherra?" he repeated.

"Sherra, ah," I floundered.

"You haven't brought her back to you, have you? Not really, as a warrior should with his rose."

"I fucked up last night, Hunt," I admitted, scrubbing my face with a hand. "I told her I wasn't ready, only, well, I fucked it up."

"When will you be ready?"

"I'm not sure I will ever be, unless I get my power back."

"Is that what this is about?"

"Some, yes. Maybe more than some."

"So. To salve your pride, you harm your rose."

"I told you I fucked it up."

"You certainly did. Cole tells me that a visit to Ny-nes is in the works, to find children with power."

"I really need to have Sherra and Barth in attendance before we have any discussions on that."

"Then invite them to breakfast."

"I think something happened to you while you were recovering," I accused.

"It probably did. Shall I send mindspeak?"

"I'll do it," I held up a hand. "By the way, is this how it's going to be from now on?"

"Probably. We both need an incentive to get back on our feet. I'm happy to assist in that endeavor."

Barth, Sherra, will you join Hunter and me at the garden table for breakfast?

I will be there shortly, Barth replied.

I'll come. Sherra's response was brief, sharp, and I deserved worse.

I sipped tea while watching Hunter lift his cup to drink. Today, his hand only trembled slightly. A night's rest had done him good, it appeared.

"I'm getting better at it," he said after realizing that my gaze was focused on his hand. "I can hold it with one hand instead of two, now."

"Hunt, I," I dropped my gaze. "I'm glad you can move at all, and speak," I mumbled. "I should have told you that two days ago."

"We've both been in a dark place," Hunter replied. "I have no desire to return to it. I hope you feel the same."

"I feel its presence," I admitted. "As if it waits to devour me."

"Move away from it, then. We cannot survive the coming threat without your guidance and experience." I opened my mouth to argue with him, then snapped it shut. "You are the King, and the Commander of Az-ca's army," Hunter reminded me. "You and you alone can wield the power and knowledge you have. The people of Az-ca place their trust in the King. That King is you and no other."

"Sherra," I began.

"Is your Queen and has been carrying both your burdens recently. Take your duties back, Thorn, and allow her the freedom to do what she does best. If we devise a plan to defeat Kaakos, then she will be an integral part of that. Do not place the rule of the country on her shoulders, too."

"I'm not sure you've ever handed my ass to me in such a deft manner," I said as guilt washed through me.

"I hope it won't be necessary a second time."

Barth arrived at the table, interrupting the conversation. He smiled at Hunter before turning to me, the question of why he'd been summoned forming frown wrinkles on his brow.

"We have to devise a plan for the trip to Ny-nes, to find talented children," I told him. "And, as I have no real idea how large Ny-nes is, we'll need information regarding that and how many diviners we must send."

"You'll need protection for your diviners and supplies to feed them and their guards. I hear food is quite scarce, there," Barth countered.

"True," I agreed.

Sherra arrived, then, pulling a chair out to sit beside Hunter. I tried to hide my frown, but wasn't successful. Why should I feel slighted if she wouldn't sit beside me, when I'd refused her company in my suite?

"Are you feeling better today?" Sherra's first words were spoken to Hunter.

"I feel stronger today," he acknowledged. "The exercises help, and merely getting out of bed does wonders."

"Have you tried to make fire?" She was now smiling at him.

"Let's see." Holding out a mostly-steady right hand, he concentrated. Eventually, a small flame bloomed in his palm.

"Yes," Sherra whispered. "Thank the first warrior-rose. You'll be forming shields and such in no time."

"I'm pleased you think so. I feel very weak at the moment."

"That will change," Barth said. "When the strength returns to your body, the same will be true of your talent."

"How do you feel?" Sherra turned to me, then. "Do you feel weak? If that's the case, I swear I'll find North and punch him again."

"I am physically sound," I said. "He only draws away my talent."

"I still may punch him again."

"Tell me why," Hunter said, sounding like a patient parent.

"Because I want to. If I figure out a way to stop the drain on Kerok, he'd better watch his back where I'm concerned."

"I can't argue with your reasoning," Barth told her. "As for me, I'd like to put my hands on him, to see what he's been up to all these years. I want to know whether he's holding back anything else of importance."

"I'd like to know that, too," I agreed. "He and Kyri have been far too secretive, and we've all paid the price for it."

A breakfast tray was set on the table; plates of fluffy, fresh-baked bread, eggs and ham were laid down for Sherra and Barth. Fresh, hot tea was served all around, along with small glasses of fruit juice.

"Barth, Hunter and I were discussing the children in Ny-nes, and how to go about testing them for power," I told Sherra. Not once had her eyes met mine. Perhaps she didn't want me to see the pain I'd placed there. Still, I felt remorse for it.

"I'll have to work with Kyri and North," her shoulders sagged as if she were weary. "I sat up last night, thinking about it. They know more about Ny-nes—at least North does—than anyone else I know. The swine." She frowned as she cut her ham into bite-size chunks and stabbed a piece with her fork.

"Do you suppose the maps Kyri offered will depict Ny-nes?" Barth asked. I'd forgotten about those and was grateful he'd remembered.

"I don't know, and she said those maps were from long ago, before the End-War," Sherra pointed out. "It could have changed greatly since then. I may be able to search mentally for talent," she added. "I'm working on that idea now."

"Like searching for Kaakos' gold?" Hunter turned toward her.

"Yes. Something like that. I just haven't worked out how to focus on what I want to find."

"It would be a tremendous help if we didn't have to touch every child in Ny-nes," Barth admitted.

"Perhaps you should allow your dreamwalker to solve that riddle," Hunter suggested.

Sherra turned sharply toward him and blinked, her eyes wide. After a few moments, she dipped her head in a half-nod. "I'll send for a marching draught," she sighed. "With as little sleep as I've gotten lately, she hasn't appeared. Perhaps it's time to rectify that."

"Whom do you wish to guard your body, if your dreamwalker arrives?" I asked, lowering my eyes to my plate. Before, I'd have zealously guarded her unconscious, physical body while her dreamwalker worked to solve the puzzle of remaining talent in Ny-nes.

I no longer had the power to fight off anyone who approached her.

"Caral or Misten," she said.

"I'll ask for both," I decided.

"I'll send mindspeak," Barth said. A marching draught was delivered to the table a few minutes later, Sherra stirred the powder into her tea, finished it and her breakfast and then slumped in her chair.

"We'll take her to her suite," Caral, Misten and Cole arrived. Cole lifted my Queen in his arms as if she weighed little, and all three *stepped* away.

I should have carried her myself, and the idea had only now occurred to me.

Arresh

I stood at Kaakos' barrier surrounding Ny-nes. Most of it had been removed when he'd killed his warrior-priests. The blood spell he'd employed to form the barrier had died with them, except for the parts he'd constructed with his own power.

That barrier was so subtly-formed it was nearly undetectable. Whomever crossed it, either in or out, would be known to Kaakos. He couldn't detect those who *stepped* in and out; only those who physically crossed.

Perhaps he was waiting for the citizens of Ny-nes to leave, and he'd capture them in secret, to turn them into his slaves again.

I doubted Kyri or North were aware of this trap; they hadn't mentioned it the day before. We would have much to discuss when we met again. Kaakos' barrier was giving me an idea, however, on the problem I was asked to solve.

It merely had to be considered carefully before being implemented. Of more concern were the living conditions within Ny-nes, and the lawlessness that could occur, once all its citizens learned they were no longer ruled by the evil that was Kaakos.

North would be forced to assert his power and institute new laws, or Ny-nes would drown in its own blood.

I considered destroying Kaakos' barrier, before deciding against it. Instead, I placed my own, just outside his. He wouldn't know mine was there, as they didn't touch. Like him, I'd know if anyone crossed it. If he came to take hapless citizens, I hoped I could be there to stop him.

There were other things to attend to before I returned to Az-ca. Reaching out with power, I allowed my senses to travel far, then *stepped*.

～

Armon

"Caral and Misten went to protect Sherra, while her dreamwalker is roaming free," I told Levi. "At Thorn's command."

"Is that why we're falling behind on training today?" Levi asked the rhetorical question, knowing I wouldn't have to answer.

"Sherra only asked for one of them. Thorn decided to take both."

"He's been through a lot, and you can't expect him to behave rationally all the time," Levi defended our Commander and King.

"I know."

"We need to set a date to select the *King's Eagles*," Levi changed subjects.

"I know that, too. Now that they have the incentive, you have no idea how many older warriors and escorts have suddenly become interested in the new fighting methods."

"I hope you're treating them appropriately—with healthy skepticism," Levi snorted.

"I am, and I've pointed that out to them—that they've balked at the new training in the past, and that they'll certainly have a tough battle to face before I'm convinced they're worthy. I've told them numerous times that their battle methods could change in an instant whenever something new is introduced. Many of them have assured me that they've seen the error of their ways and are now amenable to change."

"Hmmph. They were too ready to believe that fool, Merrin. This is where that got them."

"I didn't bring that up. If they haven't realized their blunders yet, they never will."

"Are there any of them who are doing well in their training?" Levi asked. "I don't want them to cry foul if we exclude all of them."

"There may be a few. I'll let Sherra make the final determination on them, though. If she touches them, she'll see their true motivations."

"I hope she makes them sweat."

"As General for Az-ca's army, I'm not supposed to think that sort of thing, but I do," I didn't try to hide my grin. "I dislike it when troops make decisions on new training before they've ever witnessed its effectiveness, or lack thereof."

"Do you think Sherra will be able to convince Thorn to do away with the forced bonding? She really wants that, you know."

"I want it, too," I said. "Troops could be assigned easily to battle pods, rather than single rose-warrior teams. Pods are more effective; we've seen that already."

"Plus, it opens up the possibility of roses and warriors bonding with regular citizens. We could end up with more talented children, that way."

"I hear that," I agreed. "What do you think will happen with the children from Ny-nes, if any of them are found with power?"

"Either teach them or suppress their talent," Levi shrugged. "I know it won't be that simple, but it's a place to start."

"We'll have to find someone to teach them—they must be educated before they begin to learn how to use their talent," I said. "Unless we have many volunteers who wish to face hardship in Ny-nes, we'll be forced to bring them here."

"You've been thinking about this," Levi turned toward me.

"I have. I worry that Kaakos' foul religion will follow them to Az-ca, and we'll have to deal with that, in addition to teaching them how to read and write."

"Not a pleasant prospect," Levi crossed arms over his chest. Az-ca had been at war against that religion so long, that it felt treasonous to allow any believers past its borders.

"But what if they're like Cole and his people?" I argued. "They were happy to get away from that terrible evil."

"Perhaps those are the ones the diviners will search for," Levi let his arms drop with a sigh.

"I'm sure Sherra and Barth will make the final decisions," I patted Levi's shoulder. "They won't place us in danger that way—not after they've seen the damage Kaakos can do."

"And that bastard came from here—as did Ruarke," Levi said.

"That's why we can't turn our backs on those who deserve our help. Will they all be perfect? No. These are children, remember? I wasn't perfect when I was young. I'm not perfect, now. I suggest a series of tests and divinations as they are educated and developing their talents. Those who aren't suitable can be weeded out. We don't need or want another Kaakos developing, because we're convinced we can change the unchangeable."

"I think there may be problems with even that system, but it could be a starting point, I suppose."

"See, I told you I wasn't perfect."

"You're perfect for me."

"Awww. I'll show you perfect, later," I told him.

"I'm looking forward to it."

～

Kerok

"This is the information I have," Barth set a stack of notes on my desk. I'd asked him to bring what he'd gathered on blood spells, so we could begin writing the laws to forbid them.

Hunter insisted on being present to assist, although he couldn't hold a pen very well, yet.

"You think Kaakos took blood from all those who served him—so he could draw away their power whenever he wanted?" I asked.

"I believe that to be true," Hunter said. "Except in those cases where the blood has a connection to yours already, as it is with you and North."

"And in North's case, with Kaakos," Barth added.

"I can't believe I'm related to either of those bastards," I slapped a hand on my desk in frustration.

"Perhaps that was kept from you—by design," Hunter said.

"I imagine it was," I said after thinking about that for a moment. "I was led along like a calf to slaughter, with no idea what waited for me at the end."

"Where shall we start, then?" Barth asked. "With the taking of another's blood for nefarious purposes, or exploiting your blood relations for the same reason?"

"If the blood relations are royalty, then it's treason, first and foremost," Hunter pointed out. "Then the laws against blood spells come next. If guilty of treason, the perpetrator should die for his crimes."

"I'd say that anyone found guilty of creating blood spells should face the same sentence," I said. "Those spells are an abomination."

"Agreed," Barth began writing.

"What are the age cutoffs—between adult and child in these crimes? Will children face the same sentence, if convicted?" Hunter asked.

"Depends on the crime," I said. "If murder is committed intentionally, I don't particularly care how old they are."

"Unless there are mitigating circumstances?" Barth stopped writing for a moment and raised his eyes to mine.

"It depends on the circumstances," I allowed. "Although a child should have no idea how to create a blood spell unless taught."

"How did Kaakos learn?" Barth asked.

"He likely learned from his father," Hunter cleared his throat. "In one way or another."

"Are blood spells covered in his book of divination?" Barth asked.

"I don't recall any," I said.

"I don't think there were any," Hunter's mouth formed a grim line. "That, perhaps, means there was another book—or another way—that Kaakos could get the basics from his father."

"Then we need to ask North more questions, do we not?" Barth frowned. I hadn't forgotten that he wanted to do a divination on the man in question. I doubted North would agree to such a request—or an order.

"Might we send mindspeak to Kyri? Perhaps she knows," Hunter said.

"That's possible, but I prefer to let Doret pose that question, if she doesn't know herself," I said.

"I can ask Doret," Barth went back to writing.

"Then I'll leave that part to you," I told him.

All of us leapt from our seats as Sherra's dreamwalker appeared suddenly, dropping a burned man atop my desk and knocking Barth's papers to the floor. "Kyri's on the way," she shouted. "Call for a physician to help her."

CHAPTER 5

*K*erok

Sherra held a cup of tea while wrapped in a blanket. Still, she shivered after her dreamwalker reconnected with her body. She knew what her dreamwalker encountered, and couldn't bring herself to speak of it, yet.

"Who is that man?" Doret laid a hand on Sherra's shoulder. Several moments passed while the blanket was pulled tighter about her with a free hand. Finally, she answered.

"I found him. He was the only one alive."

"Where?" Barth asked. I could tell he wanted to put his hands on her, but held back at my gesture.

"Far. East and north. Kaakos came. Took what he wanted. Killed the rest."

"Of course he did," Doret snorted. "It's what he always does."

"You found a village?" I prompted.

"City. Large. Many lived there. Not now." Her voice was shaky.

"Who did he take?" Hunter asked.

Sherra raised her head and gazed at him. "Those with power. I felt it in the man he burned and left for dead."

"There are others with power?" Barth breathed.

"Was. There may be other cities or villages Kaakos hasn't reached, yet. We have to find them." Sherra's voice was becoming steadier, her breathing more regular.

In the palace infirmary, Kyri and the palace physician were attempting to save the burned man. I worried he wouldn't live, and I very much wanted to speak with him.

The only thing worse than Kaakos with an armed military is Kaakos with an armed and talented army, Barth sent mindspeak. I'd been thinking the same thing. *He'll place them under a blood spell and they'll do what he wants or die.*

I agree, I replied. *This is the foulest of news.*

"The man Arresh brought back has power," Sherra sipped her tea. "He tried to stop Kaakos. If Kaakos hadn't thought him dead, he wouldn't have survived. I hope Kyri can save him."

"How did you know he had power?" I asked.

"He moaned. Arresh went to him. He has mindspeak. His language is different, but he showed us images. We recognized Kaakos immediately."

"You don't know the name of the country where he was?" Hunter asked.

"I only know the name of the city. L'on-Alberr."

"How many dead?" I asked.

"Too many to count. I had to bring the man away to preserve any hope for his survival."

"Can you take someone back with you?" Kyri walked into my study to join the meeting. "He's resting," she held up a hand to stop Sherra's questions. "We won't know for a day or two what his chances of survival are."

"I know where to set my feet," Sherra said. "I only want those experienced with shields and blasts to go with me, should Kaakos return."

I ground my teeth; she was right, though. I would be a hindrance if Kaakos returned. "Take Kyri, Caral and Levi," I said.

"North wants to come," Kyri said.

"Then by all means," Sherra waved a hand. "He can see firsthand what his interference has cost these people."

North appeared in my study seconds later, looking somewhat subdued. Sherra glared at him anyway. Levi arrived moments later, nodding to Sherra and Caral. He didn't react in any way to Kyri or North's presence.

"Let's go," Sherra stood and handed her empty tea mug to Misten. "We'll be back in a few."

Sherra

I didn't give anyone time to say anything before folding my small company to L'on-Alberr. Bodies still littered the stone streets where they'd been blasted by Kaakos' power. None were spared, including the children.

"These buildings are very old," North commented while placing his hands on the corner of the nearest one—a three-story behemoth constructed of large, heavy stones. The structure leaned slightly from the weight of its years and troubles. "From long before the End-War, I think," North added.

"It was—perhaps centuries before," Kyri agreed. "Some of these buildings could be depicted in the historical accounts in my library."

"What should we do with the dead?" Levi asked.

"Let's make sure there are none who still live before we make that decision," I said. "We can gather the dead and either burn or bury them afterward."

"I've never seen such mountains," Caral pointed to tall peaks in the distance. "Is that snow on the tops?"

"I think it is," Kyri said. "Those mountains are tall enough that snow doesn't melt as it does in most places."

"It's cool, here," Levi said. "Almost cold."

"Higher elevation than Az-ca," North explained. "It is much like the lands north of Cole's village."

"How do you know about Cole's village?" I snapped at him.

"I showed him. They are in no danger from North," Kyri replied.

"Hmmph." I turned away and walked down the narrow street, leaving those two behind. Anyone who knew of North or his whereabouts was in danger from Kaakos. Kyri should know that better than most.

At least we had our shields up when the attack came. A blast bloomed against my shield, accompanied by shouting in a language I didn't understand.

This wasn't Kaakos. I could only assume these attackers were either from this city or somewhere nearby. Three of them walked toward me, where I stood behind my shield, waiting for them.

Another spate of words I failed to understand were spoken.

They're asking about the man, Kyri sent to me. *Will you allow me inside your shield?*

Go ahead, I told her. Barely a blink later, she appeared beside me and began speaking to the three men who now stood at the edge of my shield, staring at me. Kyri knew their language, or something close enough, because they answered her.

"Lower your shield; they only want to talk to us," Kyri told me after several minutes of conversation between them passed.

I'll keep a personal shield up, I sent, and allowed the outer shield to drop. By that time, North, Levi and Caral joined us while Kyri continued to speak to the men.

"They're from a nearby village," she explained. "They are the only ones there with power, and they'd gone hunting in the mountains. When they learned of the attack here on their return, they came to investigate. The man we're treating is a friend. I told them we're trying to save him, but he's badly burned. I also gave them images of Kaakos and told them he is hunting those with power."

"We need to put a shield over their village," I said. "So Kaakos won't attack it so easily. We'll know if he attacks, too."

"I'll explain that to them." She turned toward them and began speaking again in their language.

"They wish to see their friend—in case he doesn't survive," Kyri said after the conversation ended.

"We can come back afterward, and set the shield," Levi said.

"All right," I conceded. "Did you tell them it's far away?"

"I tried to."

"Then tell them we're going."

Kyri spoke; they nodded. I *stepped* them to the infirmary in the King's palace.

Kerok

"Pierre says that Jean gave him the same images we did of the one who attacked L'on-Alberr," Kyri said as we sat in the small dining hall, having tea with three strangers. At least we had a name for the burned man—Jean, although it was pronounced far differently than we'd pronounce it.

"I intend to place a shield over their village, so they'll be safe—or as safe as I can keep them—from Kaakos," Sherra said.

Kyri translated the words for Pierre and his companions, Luc and Enzo. They nodded their agreement, then Pierre asked a question. I was grateful Kyri understood him and the others.

"He wants to know if the shield will keep Kaakos' minions out," she told Sherra.

"Anyone who is infected with Kaakos' blood spells will be held back, unless they are stronger than I am," Sherra replied. "Make sure they know that the shield will only provide protection while they're inside it. They'll have to provide their own shielding if they go hunting again."

Kyri relayed Sherra's words, which brought puzzled expressions to all three faces.

"They don't know how to shield," Kyri informed us.

"I'll teach them," Sherra squared her shoulders. "After we've finished here."

Kyri told the men what Sherra offered. With widened eyes, they nodded their agreement.

"Let's hope they learn fast," North mumbled, speaking for the first time.

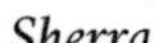

Sherra

I took Pierre's hands first and sent him images—of what I could see in him. He was astounded and spoke excitedly to Kyri. Then, I showed him what I wished for him to do; drawing his power and forming an invisible wall about himself.

"That's right," I nodded as he constructed his first shield. Caral, who offered to help, tossed a small rock at Pierre's shield. It bounced off. He was very happy.

For the next three hours, Caral, Kyri and I taught three strangers how to shield themselves from harm, and advised them to practice it often, making the barriers as strong as their power would allow.

I hoped it would save their lives.

Then, we stepped them back to L'on-Alberr. From there, they *stepped* us to their village.

It was a small version of the larger city, with stone structures and cobbled streets. We arrived near dawn, which was only after midnight in Az-ca. They'd had a long day, just as we had.

They watched as I constructed the shield about their village. "At least Pierre has mindspeak," Kyri sighed as we prepared to leave. "He can stay in touch with me or send images to you. North is removing the dead from L'on-Alberr. If needed, we can use it as a base, if Kaakos' new home is near here."

"I'm more interested in their gardens and such," I said. "I don't want them to be taken or vandalized by Kaakos. I'm sure Pierre's village could benefit from the extra food."

"Do you have a solution?" Kyri asked.

"Not yet. I'll think on it when I'm not so tired."

"I'll put a shield over it," Caral offered.

"That doesn't help the plants, or the rain or bees that need to get inside," Kyri pointed out.

"True. I'm not sure I could keep Kaakos out, either, like Sherra can."

"If I could put the whole thing inside a bubble shield and float it to Pierre's village," I sighed, intending humor.

Kyri stared at me, open-mouthed.

"What did you just say?" Caral gripped my arm.

"Uh, well," I hedged.

"I think those of us here, if we combine our power, can do just that, if Sherra takes point and directs the attempt."

"I'll have to force my shield beneath the soil until the bubble connects below ground," I said. "That will take a lot of power, especially since we don't have a storm brewing or a friendly lightning strike to help me drive it in."

"Let's try. This could mean help for others," Kyri insisted. "Imagine floating planted gardens to Ny-nes, to feed those starving there."

"Or floating game animals or such—most of those things have long since disappeared from Ny-nes as a food source." North had arrived and joined our conversation. "If we move them in such a way that they have a few seasons to breed without a threat from natural predators, then we could let loose herds across Ny-nes."

"I think there is much to consider before taking living creatures to live in a bubble," I huffed.

"Then we will think about it. Let's take the garden, first, so Pierre and his friends can *step* inside the bubble with other villagers, to tend and harvest."

I'm going to sleep for a week after this, Caral sent.

I feel the same way.

Kyri *stepped* us to L'on-Alberr's garden.

Kyri

North hesitated when Sherra reached out to touch his hands. I wondered why that was, but after only a few seconds passed, he allowed it. She nodded when she had the feel of his power, then reached out to connect with all of us.

With gentle precision, she drew away the power needed to

accomplish the task, as we stood at a safe distance from the field where tender plants were beginning to grow. Without upsetting a single butterfly or bumblebee, the shield began to form and then dig deep into the soil outside the garden's perimeter.

I imagined the removal of such a large amount of soil would be deafening. It wasn't. Somehow, Sherra had muted the sound of the shield digging in. She could make the shield permeable to water, too, and still keep Kaakos from getting through. He'd have to kill more slaves—many more—to defeat this structure.

Once the process was complete, we watched as the clear shield lifted from the ground until it floated thirty feet above it.

"I'll let Pierre know we're coming," I said aloud and sent mindspeak to him. His reply was almost garbled, he was so astonished.

Still pulling energy from all of us, Sherra *stepped us* and the massive bubble shield toward Pierre's village.

"Here. This is your focus point for stepping," I told Pierre in his language as we stood inside the massive bubble, which now contained L'on-Alberr's garden.

"We can see this clearly from our village," Pierre argued.

"You won't see it for long," Sherra said. I was forced to explain what she meant—that the shield would become a mirror shield, that would project only the sky across its surface. He needed the focus point inside the bubble to get inside it, once it became invisible to all eyes on the ground.

"I had no idea this was possible," Pierre waved an arm to convey his amazement.

"I will teach you and your friends," I offered. "Just not now—we need rest, as do you."

"The rain will get through?" he asked.

"Yes. Air, too. Sherra is quite talented at building all sorts of shields."

"Then tell me what to say to thank her properly."

I told him. He nodded. Then, with slow deliberation, he spoke the words, "Sherra, thank you," and offered a half-bow.

"Tell him he's welcome," Sherra said. "And get some sleep."

Kerok

"You're telling me they moved a massive garden to another village?" I asked Doret.

"Kyri sent images. It's astounding. Sherra didn't want the food to be wasted or taken by Kaakos."

"I don't want that either. Why didn't we consider this before?" I demanded. Sherra was asleep, as were Caral and Levi. Kyri and North had returned to Ny-nes, presumably to rest as well. I had to ask Doret the questions for which I wanted answers.

"Sherra thought she was joking. The others took her seriously, and here we are, with a floating terrarium hanging over a small village."

"I wish to see if this is something that can be done for our own in Az-ca," Hunter hobbled in, a hand on Marc's arm to steady himself.

"Glad to see you're walking," Doret smiled at Hunter.

"I'm glad it's still possible," he said, although he dropped onto the second chair in my study with a relieved sigh. "Marc was good enough to write up the information for our records," he added. "So I wouldn't tire myself before my walk."

"Here are the papers," Marc gave me the notes Hunter had dictated earlier.

"I suggest having Sherra or Caral look them over for mistakes or additions before adding them to the archives," Hunter said. "Is there a chance that you have water in that pitcher?" He nodded to the tray on my desk.

"It is water," I said, reaching for a clean glass and pouring for him.

"Walking is thirsty work," he said, taking the glass from my outstretched hand. Hunter barely shook as he drank the entire glass and set it on a corner of my desk. Marc took the glass and returned it to the tray.

"Thank you," Hunter nodded to him. "I wasn't sure I could rise enough to place it there myself."

"I agree with Hunter, about providing floating gardens for our own," Doret said. "But our problem will be the lack of rain here in Az-ca."

"Why can't we send water in other bubble shields?" Marc asked.

I locked eyes with Hunter, as he considered it for a moment before nodding. "Ask Sherra about a spell to remove salt from sea water, after pulling it directly from the ocean. That would perhaps be a swifter process than putting a strain on the pipes and desalination pumps in the King's City," Doret suggested.

"Perhaps you'd present that idea to her? She's not on the best speaking terms with me at the moment."

"Hmmph." Doret turned her head. I'd hit on a touchy subject with her, that was plain to see.

"Go ahead and speak your mind," I told her.

"Whose fault is it that you're not on the best speaking terms with your rose?"

"Mine," I said, rolling my shoulders. "All mine," I added.

"Hmmph," Doret repeated, and that was the end of our conversation on the subject. Wisely, Hunter and Marc remained silent, although Hunter was clearly not on my side in this.

~

Jubal

At least I was given a larger cell in the lockup after I'd been sucked dry by the King's Chief Diviner and that witch of a Queen. She'd said I might prove useful now and then. They hadn't told me everything they'd seen in me, either.

I'd seen all the images the witch showed me when I was injured. Somehow, she tried to make it look like my fault.

It wasn't.

Once they'd seen the filth who'd kidnapped me and hauled me to Ny-nes, they'd kept their hands on me still—for much longer than I wanted. They never said why, either, and that made me think they'd seen other things.

Surely the witch wasn't talented enough to see others through me.

Even if she did, I wished her luck with the evil filth who'd enslaved me. He'd won in Ny-nes; she hadn't.

Probably *her* fault.

"Food," the guard knocked his stick against the bars of my cage. "You're eating better than plenty of others, so eat fast or I'll take it back and give it to someone who'll appreciate it."

He always said that. He never did anything about it. I'd been served poor rations in Ny-nes; I had no loss of appetite as a result. Food always arrived lukewarm at best, so I didn't take more time than necessary to consume it.

"He's disabled, too, you just can't see it from the outside. He was once in the army, just as you were. He doesn't blame others for what happened to him."

She was there, suddenly, inside my cage.

Alone.

I wasn't foolish enough to attempt an attack; I'd heard she could fire blasts just as well as most warriors. Instead, I spat at her. My spittle hit the shield she held around herself and slid, slick-like, down the side until she employed power to burn it off.

"You've never been a pleasant one, have you? Take after your father, don't you?"

"You don't know a damn thing about me."

"I saw too much of you the last time I was here. I saw your childhood, Jubal. How your father beat your mother, until she only knew how to serve him—and you—and nothing else. Until she died. You blamed her for dying, just as you blamed your escort for what happened to you in your first battle. After your mother's death, when your father forced you to cook and clean, you developed a hatred for all women.

"When you were taken by the army, you were told you had to work with a woman; that you'd be forced to do so. You did this to yourself, Jubal. Hatred disabled you. Hatred got you involved with Ny-nes and the enemy. Hatred almost killed you a second time. If Kaakos hadn't found a use for you, you'd be nothing more than ash in Ny-nes."

"I'd never harm myself intentionally," I snapped at her.

"No, but you wanted to harm your escort. Your first battle was also the first time you weren't under scrutiny from your peers and instructors. Whether you consciously made the decision, it ended in her death because she protected you until the end.

"Just as your mother protected you until the end. Your father began beating you after her death, didn't he?"

"Hmmph." I turned my back on her. Lifted my plate and sniffed my food. It was cold. *Her* fault, for showing up at mealtime.

"You want your food warmed?" I whirled back to stare at her. How did she know these things?

"Because I am not Sherra. I am Arresh, and I always know. Become more of a liability, Jubal, and I will see to your death myself. Your food will go to someone more deserving."

Her eyes turned red, then, and the plate became so warm in my hands I nearly dropped it. When I looked again at the place she'd stood, she was gone.

Eating my food before it became cold a second time, I attempted to tell myself that I was safe enough where I was.

Except it was a lie. Somehow, the filth who'd taken me to Ny-nes and forced me to serve him had sent a tiny bit of power into my mind. For now, it was easy to block. I hoped it would remain so.

~

Sherra

"It ruins your natural rhythm," Pottles told me as I drank tea after rising. It was late afternoon; I'd gone to bed only a few hours before sunrise.

"Arresh threatened Jubal," I said, in between sips of strong tea.

"Hmmph. I'd do it, too, if I wanted to visit the lockup. Which I don't. There's not much use for him, and no chance of redemption. Garkus on the other hand—he still has a chance."

"At least Garkus accepts his wrongdoing as his own decision, and doesn't blame anyone except himself," I snorted.

"Deep down, I don't think he's realized yet how many people died because of those rash decisions," Pottles said.

"His place is in Ny-nes, now. He can keep working to guard Kyri. That's why Arresh sent him in the first place."

"Then I suggest he make regular reports to someone here. It doesn't have to be the King; he can report to you or to Hunter, but someone needs a record of what's going on—with North, Kyri and the people of Ny-nes. He used to send training reports to Thorn; he can send other reports if he puts his mind to it."

"We still have to check the children in Ny-nes." I rolled my shoulders, attempting to make my brain and body function together. "Maybe I should have asked for another marching draught."

"You wouldn't sleep tonight, and you'd be in the same circumstances, come tomorrow," Pottles informed me. "Better to get through the rest of this day, have a normal sleep period and wake again tomorrow morning at the normal time."

"You're right," I grudgingly admitted. "I just don't feel like I'm awake or that my limbs are connected to my brain."

"Forming a giant terrarium, even with help, after you'd already spent a tiring day? That had to drain you."

"It did. I was afraid to pull more power than I already had from the others to do it—it could have brought harm."

"You'd be the one to know and understand how much they could give."

"I know." I set my empty teacup down and reached for the pot of tea to refill it.

"Just sit still for a while and drink your tea," Pottles patted my free hand. "You'll be connected again, although it may take an hour or two before that happens."

She *stepped* away, leaving me sitting at the small table by the window in my suite. I could send mindspeak to Kerok, asking what he was doing. In the past, I'd have done exactly that.

He'd shut me out; we had nothing to discuss.

Kerok

"Will you look these over?" I handed papers to Cole. "We're drafting the laws regarding blood spells. Hunter and Marc have done what they can, and I need another set of eyes before Sherra and I read through them."

"I'd be honored to have that task," Cole accepted the papers.

"Feel free to discuss them with Hunter, if you have questions. We need these hammered out quickly, so I can sign them into law."

"I'll have them on your desk tomorrow morning."

"Thank you. Cole?" I said as he turned to leave.

"Yes?" He turned back to me.

"Will you let me know when Sherra is awake? I wish to speak with her."

"Doret had tea with her only a short while ago. I'll ask the Queen to come to your study, unless you wish to meet elsewhere."

"Ask her to join me in the garden."

"I will."

He left, then. I rose to stretch before walking downstairs on my way to the garden table.

~

Sherra

What did Kerok want? Why didn't he ask me himself to come? Those thoughts chased one another as I looked in the mirror, making sure I was presentable enough to be seen outdoors.

This time, I walked through the palace before reaching the door leading into the garden. I knew why I dawdled, rather than breaking the rule and *stepping* to the outdoor table.

Kerok was setting other barriers between us, and not just the initial insult of separate suites. Would he continue to ask someone else to contact me, rather than speaking to me directly? He had mindspeak again, yet he refused to use it.

With me.

Was he refusing to speak directly to others? I intended to find out.

By the time I arrived at the table, Kerok was there and a tea tray had been set before him. Was he waiting for me to pour tea, or just waiting?

"I've asked Briar to search the kitchen for pears," Kerok said as I pulled out a chair opposite his. "She says there should be one or two left from the last delivery."

He knew I loved pears. Nothing like getting mixed signals from one's mate, I suppose.

"Why did you send for me?" I asked, keeping my voice steady while reaching for the teapot. I poured his cup first, then poured mine and added honey.

"I want to discuss plans to test the children of Ny-nes, and to talk about the floating garden you created. That spell can be used for Az-ca's people, I think. Do you have a way to filter salt from sea water?"

"I've never thought about it, but I suppose there's a way."

"Hunter thinks creating floating gardens will place too much of a demand on our boilers, pumps and filters. If we could bring water directly from the sea to keep floating gardens moist enough to grow, that would eliminate the problem."

"But first, the salt must be removed. And the fish, too, I suppose."

"The fish could be given to the villages, to supplement their hunting."

"That would be well-received, as would plenty of fresh vegetables."

"Some of the salt could be given to them, too, to preserve game meats and add to their cooking."

"I read in some of Kyri's books that kelp, or seaweed, can be eaten or added to other dishes," I said. "It could be harvested, along with water and fish."

"Why didn't we think of this before?" He frowned at me.

"We were busy fighting a war, remember? Still are, last I checked."

"I suppose things will always look different, from a permanent seat in the palace," he sighed. The scar on his face looked pale in the shade of a nearby tree.

"I don't intend for it to be a permanent seat," I muttered. "If you're referring to being without your power."

"I know you want to help," he said, "But what if there isn't a way?"

"If there is one, I will never stop trying to find it."

"Let's talk about water, salt and kelp for now," he said. "How big do the fish get in the ocean?"

"Bigger than any of us," Hunter appeared. He'd *stepped* to us. That, in itself, was cause for celebration. Marc appeared right behind him, making sure Hunter was all right.

"We really haven't thought about this before," Kerok rumbled, shaking his head. "Sit, both of you," he told Hunter and Marc. "We'll have tea, talk about water, salt, kelp and fish, and how those things can help feed Az-ca."

"And the children of Ny-nes," I added. "If they come to us for schooling and training, we'll have to feed them somehow."

"Yes, we will," Kerok nodded. "Yes, we will."

CHAPTER 6

*S*herra

"Tomorrow, Kyri and North will bring maps and information," I told Armon. He, Levi, Caral and Misten had joined us for dinner; Kerok had invited them.

Using mindspeak.

"We'll outline plans to search for Kaakos, and hope he doesn't kidnap and destroy anyone or anything while we make those plans," Kerok pointed his fork in Armon's direction. "We are also in the preliminary stages of planning how to test Ny-nes' children for power, without sending someone to every village or hut."

"I've been thinking about that," I said. "About reaching out to search for power in our own villages." I didn't tell him what I'd found. I needed to have a discussion with Arresh, however.

How does one have a discussion with one's self? Perhaps I'd know when I fell asleep next time.

"Did you find anything?"

"I may have found a few things." I didn't volunteer more information than that.

"I want to know more about floating gardens," Armon said. "Where will the soil come from?"

"Kyri's maps may have answers," I said, glad they'd steered away from what I'd found in the villages. I now had an answer to why there'd been no children found by the diviners—none who held power, anyway.

That was a conversation for later, between Hunter and me. We'd decide whether Kerok and Barth should know, too.

"There should be plenty of abandoned ground suitable for growing vegetables," Kerok shrugged. "Perhaps poultry and other animals, too. As long as we can provide adequate water and such, there shouldn't be a problem."

"It may take a few years of breeding herds before we can supply all that is needed," Pottles observed.

"They've done without so far," Kerok said. "A few more years may not matter, as long as there are fresh vegetables and fish coming sooner than that."

"Kelp can be used as fertilizer, too," Pottles said. "I learned that from an old book in Kyri's library."

"Part of the hanging gardens can be left open for fresh air and rain whenever it comes," I said. "People will be inside, tending the plants. They'll need a breeze to cool off."

"Those gardens could be an excellent place to grow wheat," Barth said. "Imagine an entire wheat field floating in the sky."

"I'm imagining several," Kerok countered. "Enough to provide flour to the villagers."

"The threshers are here, in the King's City," Barth said. "The large ones, anyway. There are a few, simpler and smaller methods in the villages. I say send wheatberries to them and let them do the grinding when flour is needed."

"Flour can spoil," Pottles agreed with Barth. "Grind what's needed when it's needed. That's what I always heard."

"You can pay the gardeners with produce and a little gold," Armon suggested. "Sell the rest to the villagers at a reasonable price."

"We may be getting ahead of ourselves," Kerok said. "Let's try two or three floating farms, then decide whether they're worth the trouble. Same thing with the livestock and game."

"Determine what you'll plant and breed first," Pottles said. "We can go from there."

I wanted fresh tomatoes—as often as I could get them. *Tomatoes*, I sent to Kerok.

We'll plant those first, he replied.

Kerok

Guilt ate at me as I watched Sherra walk out of the dining room between Caral and Armon. They were discussing how large to make the bubble shields to grow floating gardens.

I should have called her back. I should have asked her to my suite. Kissed her to see where it led. I didn't. Shoving the recollection that I could still reach her with mindspeak aside, I watched her disappear to the right with her companions.

They were heading toward her study, rather than her suite. Should I be involved in their discussion?

Did I want to be?

Armon would let me know if anything important was discussed.

Sherra

Grandfather, how tired are you? I sent to him. Now wasn't the time to call him Hunter—I needed the advice of another who understood a dreamwalker's abilities.

Not too tired for you, he replied.

Armon will come for you, if you can't bring yourself to my study, I told him.

I can bring myself; someone may have to take me back.

Moments later, he appeared in my study. Armon and Caral got him seated quickly. I opened a bottle of wine and gestured to my three guests. All of them nodded their acceptance.

"What's this about?" The voice was Hunter's—the words were

Adahi's. I handed him a glass of wine and poured for the rest of us before I spoke.

"It's about Arresh—my dreamwalker," I admitted. "I think she's been active longer than I realized."

"How long?" Armon asked, his eyes searching my face for an answer.

"Before I was taken to Northcamp," I replied. "Several years before, actually."

"How do you know this?" Adahi asked.

"Because Arresh has muted the power in all the youngest children in Az-ca. Only she knows which ones are talented, and perhaps she knows which ones to train, once the time comes. None of them are marked, and none will be marked—unless they successfully complete their training. Not if I have anything to say about it. I think Arresh recognized that a tattooed rose separates a child from her family at two, and that's wrong."

Caral's eyes widened as she stared at me. "That happened to you—and I know it was the same for others. If it weren't for my sister, I'd have felt the same. Wasn't Arresh afraid that this would bring trouble for you if it were discovered?"

"Arresh wanted to remove their suffering," Adahi snorted, then sipped his wine. "She wanted to spare them the neglect she realized they'd receive, not just from parents, but from their village as a whole. Well done, Sherra." He held up his glass to me.

"It also kept them from becoming targets—of Ruarke, Merrin and ah, others," Armon dipped his head in agreement. "Perhaps that wasn't part of the original intention, but it served as their protection later."

"Will you tell the King?" Caral asked.

"I'll tell him, I just—wanted to talk to my friends, first, and hear your thoughts and ideas before I approached him. He may wish to blame this on me, but I swear I had no idea Arresh was a part of me back then, when this was done."

"And she didn't wish to share that information," Adahi noted.

No, I sent to him. *Did your dreamwalker ever do such?*

Perhaps a time or two.

Maybe you'll tell me about that, sometime.

Perhaps.

"I think you may have saved lives," Armon said. "Of our youngest, talented Az-cans. Surely Thorn will see this as a blessing, rather than a curse."

"There's something else," I admitted.

"What's that?"

"Arresh," I shifted uncomfortably, "Arresh burned the power out of some of them."

"Did she see them as dangerous?"

"I don't know what she saw. That's why I want to have a talk with her—if that's even possible."

"It may be that your dreamwalker will wait until she desires you to know," Adahi said.

"No pressure," I sighed and drank from my wineglass.

"Does this mean you felt the residual power in those children, when you looked for them?" Caral asked.

"Yes. I felt it, and I figured out how it was done, and by whom. I think I can teach you and a few others to do the same in Ny-nes. It may take a few days, but I now believe it can be done."

"Do we practice here, or go straight to Ny-nes?" Armon asked.

"I'm not sure they can feel the talents here as well as they might in Ny-nes. Those talents haven't been muted, as they have, here."

"When do you suppose Arresh will awaken those talents?" Adahi spoke next.

"When they are old enough to start training, I think."

"Twelve, sixteen or eighteen?" Caral asked me.

"Somewhere around that is my guess. Old enough to know reading basics, because they will have to continue their studies, as well as learn how to use their talent. It may also depend on what kind of talent they have, and the strength of it."

"And they will remain with their parents until the proper time, without the stigma of being marked," Adahi said. "I like that idea."

"As do I," I told him.

"When will you tell the King?" Armon asked.

"Tonight or tomorrow," I shrugged. "Whenever he wishes to hear what we've discussed."

"Breakfast?" Adahi said.

"I'll send mindspeak," Armon offered. "Barth and Doret will want to hear this, too, I believe."

"Then send mindspeak," I sighed. Perhaps I wouldn't worry about the impending meeting and get some sleep tonight.

Perhaps swine would grow wings and fly, too.

Kerok

"What is this meeting about?" Doret asked as she joined me at the outdoor table, where I'd suggested we have our breakfast meeting.

"Armon didn't say, only that it was important news," I replied. "Barth and a few others will come—and Sherra, of course."

"Good morning," Barth arrived and took a chair next to Doret's. They exchanged mindspeak; I pretended I didn't notice. Whatever was said brought a smile to Doret's lips, however.

Armon, Levi and their escorts arrived next, followed by Cole, Hunter and Sherra. Food and tea were set in front of us, still hot from the kitchen. Briar set an over-filled dish of butter near Sherra before nodding and taking her tray away.

Sherra buttered a roll first thing, while Armon sipped tea before clearing his throat. "Sherra had interesting news last night," he began. "News that even she didn't know until she began searching through Az-ca's children, for hints of talents before turning her attention to the children of Ny-nes."

"What news might that be?" Doret turned toward Sherra.

"News that Arresh has been active longer than I realized," Sherra confessed.

"How long?" Doret's focus was now solely on Sherra.

"Years, I think," Sherra bit into her buttered bread and chewed while I and the others considered her words.

"What did she do—that I should be aware of?" I asked, gripping my mug of tea harder than I intended.

"She, ah, muted the power and talents in the youngest children, going back roughly four or five years," Sherra said. "I didn't discover it until I went searching for remnants of talent among our own people. I found the evidence and understood after a while what had happened."

Fuck me, Barth's mindspeak came. *No wonder the diviners couldn't find anything.*

"Why would she do this?" I inquired, forcing myself to remain calm.

"So the children could live a normal life until they were old enough for training," Doret snapped. "You didn't see how unhappy Sherra was growing up—I did. Every time someone in the village ignored her, or treated her as less or dead, even, a piece of her soul grieved. You don't know what it's like, Thorn, to see a child suffer like that."

"A dreamwalker isn't something you can control, Thorn," Hunter spoke, his voice even. "If they see injustice, they will work on a solution."

Briefly I wondered where he'd gotten that insight, before moving past it. He and Sherra must have talked more than I realized.

"Do you have names and locations?" Barth pointed his question at Sherra.

"Arresh does. I believe she'll inform us when the time is right. I can teach Caral, Misten and a few others to locate the children in Ny-nes who possess talent. If the teaching bears fruit, we can send diviners to specific locations, rather than hunting the entire country."

"When?" I asked, my voice sharp.

"Whenever you want us to go," she replied.

"How many?" I demanded. "How many children with talent did you hide from the Crown?"

"Not enough to fill the gaps in Az-ca's army when they are grown," Sherra replied, a slight quiver in her voice. "Not nearly enough."

Stop badgering the Queen, Hunter warned. *She is doing her best in a difficult situation.*

Stay out of this, Hunt, I growled back.

"Don't forget that Kyri and North are bringing maps and information to our midday meeting," Barth interrupted the silent conversation with my heir. I reminded myself that Hunter was now capable of resuming his duties, forcing Sherra into third place for the throne of Az-ca.

Was that truth or cruelty? I asked myself before ignoring the thought.

~

Sherra

I didn't want to meet with Kyri and North. Not after the accusations Kerok shoved at me. I had no control over Arresh's decisions; surely he knew that. He hadn't been happy that Arresh had hidden those children from Ruarke and Merrin. He'd only seen that they'd been hidden from his diviners.

Was this the remains of his anger and depression following the removal of his power? Regardless, his words had scraped their claws across my nerves and soul. Still, I was determined to return his power; I had no care what happened to North afterward. If he'd chosen to fight his own battles, rather than stealing from someone else to enhance what he already had, that may have been otherwise.

He knew, as did many others, that Kaakos owed his continued freedom to North's interference.

"Sherra, are you coming?" Caral stood in the doorway to my suite as I slipped my uniform jacket on and buttoned it.

"I'm coming, although I'd rather be almost anywhere else."

"Armon said you were upset. That you left breakfast before he could talk to you."

"I'm not upset with Armon."

"I know."

"Sherra?" Now Pottles stood behind Caral.

"I'm coming," I said with a sigh. May as well get this over with. I had things to do, such as attempting to remove salt from seawater, and separating kelp from it, too.

If I could do it, I'd sequester brine from fresh water, much as the pumps and filters did for the King's City, then allow someone to process the brine into useable salt for the villages. Ny-nes could be supplied as well, unless they already had a system in place.

"She's working out a problem," Pottles said, interrupting my thoughts. "She gets like this now and then, whenever something needs doing that nobody has done before."

"Let's go," I said, stretching arms in the air to remind myself that my brain and body were still connected. "If I don't come now, I'll still be thinking about salt and seawater hours from now."

I followed Pottles and Caral as they led me toward the end of the hallway and down the steps, which led to the side door into the garden. We were the last to arrive, and rather than allowing Caral or Pottles to take the blame, I said, "It's my fault. I was trying to work out how to devise a shield that would separate salt from seawater."

Kerok's frown didn't change. Hunter and Barth waved off my excuse. Kyri wore an interested expression, while North appeared downright morose. He and Kerok could have been bookends on any of Kyri's library shelves, but I kept that thought to myself.

"I've pinpointed several places where survivors of the End-War could still be living," Kyri set a stack of maps on the table beside her. "None of the great cities survived; they became targets. Some could have fled toward higher, open ground, or to smaller places where they could hide. Most cities were abandoned, according to the records, but some could have returned afterward, once the fallout from the bombs had cleared away well enough."

"Are any of those same records in the King's Library?" Kerok asked.

"They could very well be, except few can read them now. The ways of writing have changed greatly, to conserve paper."

"Do you know of such, Hunter?" Kerok turned toward him.

"There is an old records section, certainly. I don't believe anyone has attempted to read anything from it in at least two centuries."

"A lot can be forgotten in two centuries," Barth observed.

"A lot can be forgotten in a decade," Pottles sniffed. "Unless people have something constantly shoved in their face, it's ignored and eventually lost."

"Until someone stumbles across it and determines how it could prove useful to destroy one's enemies, such as Kaakos and the airplanes." North wasn't just morose, he was at an angry simmer. I wondered what had caused it; I knew what caused Kerok's anger.

Me.

What tied his tail in a knot? I sent tentative mindspeak to Kyri.

I don't know. He was fine this morning, and then he wasn't. Snapped at all of us around an hour or so after breakfast. I haven't figured this out, yet.

Do you suppose he's pulling more away from Kerok than his power? Can Kerok's anger be siphoned away, too, and leave them both in a foul mood?

I don't know; I've never seen a spell like this one before—not a successful one, anyway. Generally, the unsuspecting half of this type of blood spell dies, giving the taker a temporary boost in power. Kaakos employed it when he drained power from his warrior-priests, his army and his servants.

What if he figures out how to do this, so he won't kill his army next time?

I hope nothing like that happens. He likes killing, so let's hope he doesn't see any benefit in keeping his army alive.

One more thing to worry about, I said, allowing my shoulders to droop. How much stronger might Kaakos be, if he drew power away from those who held power, rather than from untalented humans?

I'd held Kaakos back the last time, until North bungled everything. Who would be strong enough to hold him back next time, if Kaakos built a talented army?

Granddaughter, you look troubled, Adahi sent.

Because I am. We'll talk later, I returned.

Very well.

~

Kerok

"Sherra will go to Ny-nes tomorrow, teach others how to look for children with power, then go with Kyri and North to search the marked places on these maps." I handed the last map back to Kyri, after she'd pointed out two likely places on it where people could have survived.

"On the same day?" Armon asked.

"If possible."

"There are more than sixty places to visit," Kyri pointed out. "What if we find another city like L'on-Alberr? That took nearly a day to sort out, and we still don't have a clue where Kaakos took his prisoners."

You're being unreasonable, Hunter pointed out. *This will take time. Besides, what if they find Kaakos hiding in one of these places? They could be in a fight for their lives quickly. How would you know that, if they were attacked and killed before they could send mindspeak?*

Stop being so damned logical, I snapped back.

"Once you have the operation going in Ny-nes, to search for talented children," I amended, "Choose hand-picked troops to approach each of these locations from within a mirrored bubble shield. Do not give your presence away unless you are sure Kaakos isn't there."

Better, Hunter said.

"There's a very good chance people in these places won't speak the same language, and Kyri doesn't know them all," Doret said. "We may not be able to communicate the danger, and if we do, why should they believe us?"

"Doret is correct," Kyri said. "I don't speak all the old languages— only a few, and some of those not well. The people of L'on-Alberr were killed or taken already, and that meant it was easier to make the survivors believe us."

"It didn't hurt that we brought one of their own here to heal," Barth said. "He's coming along, by the way."

"If he didn't have such strong talent, his wounds would have killed him," Kyri sniffed. "He's more than fortunate that Arresh found him when she did."

"That takes us back to the initial problem," Hunter spoke up. "We can't wait for all these places to be attacked."

"Why can't we send out a call, specifically to these regions?" Sherra asked, pointed to the stack of maps. "You've done this before,

Kyri. How did you manage to leave Kaakos out of your communications?"

"Why would we send out a call?" I growled at Sherra. It made no sense to me.

"Kaakos is only interested in those who have power, if L'on-Alberr is any indication," Doret snapped at me. "We send a call to those with power, because they're the only ones who can hear it. So far, Sherra's the only one thinking ahead on this. If Kaakos finds nobody with power in any of these places, perhaps there's a decent chance he'll leave them be. Right now, any existing cities or villages may be better off if their talented residents leave for a while."

"There may be ways of making this work—especially if Sherra has found a way to search remotely for talent," Kyri appeared thoughtful.

"I've found a way," Sherra said, refusing to look at me. We were back to the reason for our earlier conflict. Arresh had discovered the way, and Sherra had finally realized it. A part of me felt ashamed for being such an ass. Another part was still angry.

"Then I suggest that Sherra, Kyri, Doret and I meet this afternoon and work out how far this talent reaches. That will tell us how close we should get to any of these villages before sending messages of any kind," North said.

"I want Armon and Caral in that meeting," I slapped a hand on the table, not bothering to hide my anger.

"I'd like Hunter to attend, and Cole," Sherra's voice was low and steadying in the ensuing, sharp silence. "Barth, too, if he is willing."

"Hunter and I will prepare a report and notes on the meeting," Barth said. "Those observations will form a proposal, which will be presented for your approval."

"And if I don't approve?"

"Then we meet again and offer another proposal."

"Very well." I still felt angry, though. Turning toward North, who'd made the initial suggestion, I saw something in his eyes—the fire of his own anger, which he'd hidden from the rest of us behind courteous words.

Wise of him not to display such at *my* table, in *my* city. Sherra was right when she told him he'd never be king again in Az-ca. She'd seen it in him on his first visit, just as easily as I did now.

He wanted to be in charge of this meeting. That would never happen, as long as I lived.

And if I didn't live?

North wouldn't, either, and he had nobody to blame except himself.

Sherra

I watched as cracks formed in my wineglass. Kyri's wineglass shattered on the table in front of her. Anger had suddenly engulfed the table, and it was bouncing from Kerok to North and growing stronger every time it did so. Both were so deep in their anger, they hadn't noticed that another glass had shattered in front of Armon, causing Caral to gasp.

You need to leave, I sent to North. *Now.*

Sherra? Barth sent to me. *What is happening?*

They're too close, and the anger is bouncing from one to the other, I replied, standing up. *North, you are feeding the King's anger, and he is feeding yours. You must leave now.*

North jerked his head toward me, then blinked several times as if to clear his mind. "I must go," he said aloud, bowing slightly to Kerok before *stepping* away.

"Give me a few moments and I will come to the secondary meeting," Kyri stood and also bowed to Kerok. She *stepped* away, probably to follow North.

"Would you like to have a glass of wine while we wait for Kyri's return?" Barth suggested to Kerok.

"I think I would," he said. I watched carefully; the anger was already disappearing from his eyes and his posture. Hunter's hand landed on my shoulder, but it was Adahi's voice that sounded in my mind.

Granddaughter, perhaps we shouldn't put them too close together from now on.

≈

North

"This isn't the first time you've fucked up a spell," Kyri reminded me. I'd gone back to my old bunker, where I'd lived so many years unnoticed in Ny-nes. I sat on the damp floor in a corner, my head in my hands and my fingers tugging at my hair in frustration.

I didn't need Kyri's reminder; I'd already told myself the same thing at least a dozen times. I kept Thorn's power for myself, but the emotions—especially anger—looped back to him and then back to me until it formed a vortex that sucked at our sanity if we were close together.

If Sherra hadn't interrupted and brought me back from that dark, whirling fury, I had no idea what would have happened.

Self-destruction—for both of you, whispered in my mind.

I thought back to the first time I'd met with Sherra and Thorn. She'd castigated me. I was humbled.

Thorn was also humbled. Humility, however, was never as dangerous as anger. If Sherra hadn't interrupted, how long would it have taken to explode between Thorn and me?

"I never considered that I'd be drawing away his emotions, and then feeding them back to him and making them worse," I lowered my hands to my lap before looking up at Kyri.

"You'd never done the spell before and should never have considered it. You need to find out how to correct or destroy it, North, or it will kill both of you. One way or another."

I understood that. *Now.* "Adahi was correct; I was too full of myself. Still am, most likely."

Kyri's snort told me she agreed. "I have to go back," she said. "Try not to do anything foolish while I'm gone."

≈

Kerok

Adrenalin made my hand shake as I accepted the glass of wine Barth poured for me. "You're saying North and I can't be close to one another?" I asked him.

"Not when the result is this," Barth frowned at me, then gestured to the glass I held. "Drink. I hope it helps."

"I thought he was only taking my power."

"It appears that your emotions follow it, and those are returned to you, with his added in. It creates an ever-increasing circle of anger. There at the last, not only were glasses exploding, everyone at the table could feel the anger coming off you in waves."

"Do you think he knew this would happen—when he devised the spell?"

"I doubt he saw anything of the sort," Barth huffed. "I believe he was just as surprised as you were when Sherra broke up the meeting."

"She asked him to leave?"

"In mindspeak, yes."

"Why didn't you invite her to have a glass of wine with us, so she could tell us what she saw happening?"

"I believe it's because, as Doret would say, *you two are at odds with each other right now.*"

"So I was already angry, and North was angry, and it ah, escalated."

"Yes, it did."

"How are we going to survive this mess?" I shook my head at Barth. "North has my power, and we can no longer be in the same room together. Possibly the same city, even. One of us dies, the other one dies. How can Sherra ever break the spell, if she can't put both of us together to do it? This is madness, Barth."

"I know."

CHAPTER 7

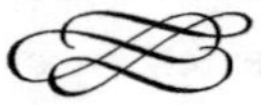

*S**herra***

"See it in your mind," I instructed Armon. "The light —there."

Our eyes were closed as I taught Armon how to find those with power within Az-ca. Although Arresh had muted their power, it could be found this way, rather than direct divination.

"It's like touching them—from far away, isn't it?" He opened his eyes as I blinked at him.

"Yes."

Caral stood nearby; she'd already learned how to search for those with power. So far, I hadn't been able to see anyone in Ny-nes, which meant I had to get closer to sense them. That meant I couldn't search for anyone with talent even farther away; the ability couldn't stretch that far.

We'd had our afternoon meeting; Kerok had attended with Barth. Now that North was no longer present and a distraction, the meeting went smoothly and a plan was emerging.

We'd decided, after kicking around the idea, that Kyri sending out a call to those who were talented could be a mistake; if Kaakos heard even a whisper of it, he could be on Kyri's doorstep in no time.

84

Therefore, we were back where we started on those ideas, so we'd decided on alternatives, instead.

Before dinner, I'd decided to teach Caral and Armon how to search for those with talent. Once I showed them, it was easy.

"I can teach this to others at Secondary Camp," Caral said.

"Choose wisely; we don't need this ability in everybody's hands," I cautioned.

"You're right about that," Armon said. "Only teach the *King's Eagles*, and not all of those. Misuse of this information could bring harm to those children and should involve a punishment of some kind. I'll talk to the King about it."

I was glad Armon offered to discuss it with the King. Kerok and I hadn't spoken about anything other than business at hand, and frankly, I was still angry with him.

He should be here, learning how to do this with Caral and Armon. His mindspeak was still active; perhaps this talent would be too, except that it could then pass to North, and I wanted nothing else of Kerok's to go to that one.

He'd stolen far too much from Kerok—from both of us, to ever deserve forgiveness. Perhaps it was wise of Kerok to bar me from his suite. That might also make its way to North, and he, more than anyone, should never intrude on that intimacy.

"You're frowning," Caral interrupted my thoughts.

"Because North has stolen far more than Kerok's power," I said and *stepped* away.

"I received mindspeak; the palace is searching for you," Cole sat beside me on the sandy beach outside his village.

"I told Caral where I was."

"When?"

"Just now."

"Ah. You've come to the realization that North has taken far too much from Az-ca's King—and her Queen."

"Yes."

"I'm sure he didn't understand fully what would happen when he formed that spell many years ago, or that it would affect more than one man when it was triggered."

"Hmmph. It has affected everybody walking on this planet," I snapped.

"That could very well be true. My concern is this; does he see the error of his ways, now, or is he the same arrogant man he was when he formed the spell in the beginning?"

"I can't answer that question," I said. "Would it matter if he was sorry? For now, we still can't change the outcome."

"Have you given it some thought?"

"Too many nights when I couldn't sleep. Several things come to mind, but any one of them could backfire and we could have two painful deaths from an untried, poorly constructed solution."

"I see you've already worked this out far better than North probably did before proceeding."

"As much good as it does us."

"It could do us a great deal of good. Let us not only consider possible solutions, but trial runs of those solutions—on other things, perhaps."

"And when we figure out what those things are, we can get right on that."

"Exactly."

"I was being sarcastic."

"I know." A half-smile lit his features.

"You know what bothers me most about all this?" I asked.

"What's that?"

"That North doesn't appear to be looking for a solution. Why do you think that is?"

"I haven't thought about that before."

"I have. He wanted to take the throne of Az-ca again. He may still be hoping for that."

"I think the entire country would rise up to stop him."

"You'd think so. I certainly won't let it happen while I'm alive."

"Perhaps he thought you'd all be helpless and leaderless, after he stole Thorn's power."

"I'm not sure what he was thinking, but you were right when you called him arrogant. I felt some of that in him when I touched him to connect with his power."

"Did you feel Thorn's power in there, too?"

"I wasn't really looking for it; I was exhausted and not thinking at the time."

"Then I suggest you do so if you ever touch him again. If Thorn's power can be separated from North's, maybe it can be pulled away and returned to its rightful owner. Then, that filthy ring can be melted down."

"Maybe it's as simple as containing the spell, once the power is returned."

"Perhaps. Once we find the proper things to test that theory on, we may know for sure."

"Right. Well, I should go back before someone comes looking for me." I rose from the sand and brushed off as much as I could. Cole did the same. "Thanks for talking with me," I told him. "Civil conversations are in short supply, lately."

"Any time."

I *stepped* away before I could do something stupid, like giving him a hug.

"What were you thinking?" Kerok demanded when I *stepped* inside my study. He, Barth and Hunter were waiting there.

"I was thinking about ways to either get around that stupid spell or destroy it," I pointed at the ring he wore. "Cole and I discussed a few ideas, but I'm not about to do anything before we know it works. That means we have to experiment on something else."

Hunter, who'd been staring at the floor, jerked his head up to lock eyes with mine. "You mean something—or someone—affected by a blood spell?"

"I suppose so—yes," I admitted.

"We have that," he said.

"What? Who?" Kerok demanded.

"Jubal," Hunter said.

My knees almost buckled; I had to grab the edge of my desk to stay upright. We did have Jubal, who still bore Kaakos' blood spell. Where had my mind been, that I hadn't considered that?

Kerok

"I believe Arresh knew; that's why Sherra asked to keep Jubal alive," Hunter said. Barth, holding a glass of whiskey in his hand, nodded his agreement. "She may not have realized the full potential of keeping that treasonous bastard alive, but he can still serve a purpose."

We three had gone to my study after Sherra claimed a headache and went to her suite. Barth had poured whiskey for us before we began our speculation regarding Jubal's continued usefulness.

"There is another thing to consider in all this," Barth said.

"What's that?" I asked.

"North, and whether he will cooperate, should Sherra finds a way to destroy a blood spell."

"I have considered the same thing; likely Sherra has, too."

"You think he won't consent, even if the method is proven to be effective?"

"I'm not sure what North is thinking, other than succeeding where he failed last time," Barth emptied his glass. "I haven't ordered a divination on him. He may refuse if I do."

"Shall we proceed, then?"

"I believe we must be subtler," Hunter suggested. "We already know that we can't have both of you close together when either of you is angry."

"This sounds like we're fighting not only Kaakos, but North as well," I said.

"I believe that may be true," Hunter agreed. "It fits his personality in a strange way. He has your power, and he has always refused to willingly give up something of that nature. It's why he wrote a book, and then spelled it so it couldn't be used by anyone not of royal blood."

"And then he pretended to be dead for a very long time, until the proper descendant came along," I growled.

"Correct," Hunter said. "Evidently, he lived in Ny-nes all that time and made no move against Kaakos until you defeated the enemy army and the planes he sent against you. North began to show himself to the population, then, by healing them and gaining their trust.

"Then, when you went to Ny-nes to attack Kaakos directly, he made his final move to take down his bastard son, after stealing your power. Too bad he didn't understand that he'd fail in what he considered his master stroke of genius."

"Sherra accused him of wanting to rule Az-ca again," I pointed out. "Do we know for sure that isn't true?"

"What did Sherra say to him about that? Exactly?" Hunter demanded.

"She said she'd die before she'd let that happen," I told him.

"Armon would never bow to that cretin, either," Barth poured another glass of whiskey for himself. "North would have to destroy many before he could ever control Az-ca again."

"I will certainly stand against him," Hunter sipped his whiskey. "He has used his abilities to create a blood spell once, and that is one time too many. Should you find yourself in the position to judge him, Thorn, then have the power burned out of him at the very least. He has misused it too many times to keep it."

I blinked at Hunter in surprise. He'd never been quite this blunt before, but then he'd not been himself for a long while, too. I was beginning to believe he had no sympathy for anyone who'd stoop to Kaakos' filthy spell tactics, no matter their intentions.

"North may have had good intentions when he devised that spell, but we can't say that for certain, can we?" I spoke my thoughts aloud. "If Adahi were still alive, I'd ask him why he thought North faked his death. Was it just to fool Kaakos into leaving Az-ca alone? I seriously doubt that, because there was never a lull in the attacks, according to the military history I read as a boy."

"He was a master of divination—according to him and the title of his book," Barth said. "Did he see that he wouldn't have the power to overcome Kaakos? Did he leave his brother, the named heir, to deal with the attacks until the proper one came along, from whom he could steal sufficient power?"

"That's my guess," Hunter said. "He lied to his friends and family by doing what he did and pretending to be dead."

"Adahi certainly believed that was his corpse in the catacombs," I said. Hunter snorted in reply, before emptying his glass.

"If he did plan to retake Az-ca's throne, how would he accomplish that, without every citizen knowing he'd committed treason to get it?" Barth asked.

"He once changed the likeness of a corpse to resemble himself— exactly," Hunter downed his second shot of whiskey and thumped the glass on my desk.

"Fuck," Barth breathed. Barth never cursed, but it was warranted. I'd been thinking the same thing.

"He'd still have to keep me alive, not only to draw away my power but to keep himself alive," I said.

"True, but whether you're locked away in a cell wearing a criminal's face, or living in a hovel in Ny-nes, it wouldn't matter, would it?" Hunter's eyes hardened. "Doret said he insisted that he wished to share the rule with you—according to Kyri. That could also be a lie, and Sherra was a most formidable hurdle to overcome on his path to the Kingship."

"Why wouldn't he know about her?" It didn't make sense that he hadn't seen her in all this, if he were such a master at divination.

"Because Sherra is an unseeable," Hunter said. Barth cleared his throat and nodded his agreement. "In all his early divinations, North never saw anything about her. Yes, he'd gotten some rumor that you had another rose recently, but you've had several."

"How do you know all this?" I frowned at Hunter.

"Doret talked a lot while she thought I was unconscious."

"You did tell me that," I recalled. "I just didn't tie it all together."

"I've been putting those things on paper, but my hand cramps easily, still, so it will be a slow process," Hunter admitted.

"I'd like to see those notes when you're finished," I told him.

"That was my plan when I began writing them. I'm afraid my handwriting has suffered, but they're still readable."

"I'll take whatever you can give me, Hunt."

Kyri

They're beginning to see North as an enemy, just as Kaakos is an enemy, Doret informed me.

I couldn't disagree with their logic. If North's life wasn't tied to Thorn's, Sherra would be hunting him, just as she was hunting Kaakos. *He can't blame anyone except himself for that,* I admitted. *I'm sure this latest development has pushed them toward that conclusion.*

It has. Did he stop to think about all the consequences before he put this in motion? Doret demanded.

You know he's never gone too far down the road of discovery, once he has an idea in his mind.

That has become painfully obvious. Sherra has been banned from Thorn's suite, and after this latest incident, that may not be a bad thing.

You mean that sort of—thing—might make its way to North?

I imagine so, Doret's mental sending sounded dry.

Just when you think things can't get any worse, I said.

Oh, they can always get worse, she said. *Don't tempt fate, Kyri. I don't know how much more we can handle.*

Do you know if Sherra is willing to help us put floating gardens together for Ny-nes? We have the river here for water, but it will still have to be filtered somehow; Kaakos dumped too many chemicals and garbage into it.

I'll ask; I believe we're coming your way tomorrow, to search for children with power.

Too many things need to be done at the same time, I said.

And it will take Sherra's involvement in most of it.

I know.

I think North should stay out of her way when she's there.

But we may need his power to help form the floating gardens.

Then try to keep him from saying anything stupid. Or doing anything stupid.

He's a man. When has that ever worked?

Good point. I'll make sure they take food with them tomorrow, Doret said. *Enough to feed them and you.*

Thank you.

Sherra

I think the royal jeweler was surprised to see me so late in the evening. "Queen Sherra," he dipped his head to me when he opened the door to his suite.

"Lofflin, I need a few things," I told him. "They don't even have to be made with precious metal, and they can be quite plain, but I need at least a dozen rings."

"Men's or women's?" He didn't ask what they were for, and I was grateful.

"Half each? To begin with? They're for experiments," I said. "Plus, you may be asked soon to design a ring for the *King's Eagles*."

"The *King's Eagles*?" he was immediately intrigued.

"Yes. Those who serve the King in flying attack bubbles."

"Ah. I heard about those. An excellent idea, too." Lofflin patted his shirt, until he located a pen and paper to make notes. "I can have the plain rings for you in three days. I'll have some designs for the *Eagle* rings to bring to the King shortly after that."

"That sounds wonderful. Thank you, Lofflin."

"Shall I deliver the plain ones to your study?"

"If that's convenient."

"Of course." He smiled, making it obvious that he hadn't felt useful in a while. If I could convince Kerok and Armon about the rings, it would make the *Eagles* even more of a special unit, and something for the entire army to aspire to. It would also make Lofflin happy, as he'd have a commission from the King to keep him busy.

Armon, we'll have designs for rings for the King's Eagles *in a few days,* I sent.

Rings? That actually sounds like a good idea. Has Thorn approved it?

Not yet. I think Lofflin's designs will convince him, especially if you think it's a good idea.

I'll talk it up, he replied. *Go to bed, Sherra. We have to be in Ny-nes early tomorrow.*

I know. Good-night, Armon.

Good-night, my Queen.

~

Affa-Gannis

Kaakos

Paper was a rarity here, although my small but growing army was willing to do or find anything they could to please me.

They had to, or I'd kill them. At times the language barrier was a real problem, but they were learning quickly.

A small stack of maps lay on my desk; I'd taken those, the desk and several other useful items from a city named L'on-Alberr, according to its former citizens. The maps were part of that haul, but then the regular population of L'on-Alberr no longer had any use for those things.

Perhaps I should go back to see whether anything else could be found to make my life easier. Better food or vegetables came to mind.

I'd been busy marking the maps I had wherever I'd sensed power of any type, although I had to get closer to the places in question to do my searches. By trial and error, I learned that three hundred miles was the farthest I could be without losing the contact.

I already had blood from everyone in my new army. They had no idea why I'd demanded a cut from each of them, but they were too terrified to refuse.

After the first three refused, anyway.

It was a pleasure to kill them, and more of a pleasure to see the fear in the eyes of those left alive, whenever I turned my attention on them for any reason.

Too bad I'd killed all the children and the few adults in Ny-nes who held power; I could have tapped that source for my new army. All that would be left were those far too young to be anything other than extra mouths to feed.

Az-ca had plenty of talented adults, but they were the enemy and they'd die for attacking me—for taking Ny-nes from me and forcing me to kill my army and warrior-priests to survive.

Yes, they would pay, when I drew all the power from those in my new army and slammed it against Az-ca at the same moment. Let the bitch queen and my father attempt to hold *that* back.

"Oy," I shouted at the closest former citizen from L'on-Alberr. "Food," I mimicked eating. "L'on-Alberr," I pushed out my hands, indicating he should go there to scrounge.

He dipped his head to me before calling others to him. They were too afraid not to obey, and far too afraid not to return. Six men disappeared, while two others babbled and bowed.

❧

Arresh

I felt their presence the moment they landed near L'on-Alberr.

Not Kaakos, but tainted by Kaakos.

I landed not far away, keeping myself invisible to them. After several moments, while they attempted to get past the shield around L'on-Alberr, they spoke among themselves before one pointed toward the community garden—or where it had previously been located. They disappeared; I followed.

They were terrified of the empty, bowl-like expanse where the garden had been before we'd removed it. They couldn't get food here; Kaakos had sent them for food. Would they attempt to attack Pierre's village next?

That's exactly what happened. They disappeared and I followed.

When they found themselves shut out of that village, too, their terror was palpable.

He'd kill them if they returned empty-handed, and there could be other villages that they knew of to attack; villages we hadn't shielded.

I had a choice—kill them where they stood, or capture them and take them back to Az-ca.

~

Kerok

I wasn't sleeping when the guard pounded on my door, but I was dressed for bed. Flinging the door open shortly after my feet hit the floor, I stared at the guard, who struggled to tell me the news.

"Queen Sherra is at the lockup, with six prisoners," he breathed. "None of them speak our language."

"Has anyone called Kyri?" I demanded, turning to find pants and boots.

"Kyri has arrived," Barth shouldered past the guard standing in the doorway. "I'll *step* you to the lockup. I believe the prisoners have been blood-spelled by Kaakos."

"Fucking hell," I hissed, pulling on my boots. "Let's go," I waved a hand at Barth, who transported us to the lockup.

It wasn't Sherra who waited there for us; it was Arresh. I didn't miss the angry glare she leveled at me when Barth and I arrived.

"They've been heavily shielded," Doret appeared beside Arresh. "He won't know they're here, just as he doesn't know Jubal is here."

"Where are they from?" I snapped.

"From L'on-Alberr. Kaakos took them and made them his," Arresh snapped back. "We need subjects for spell-removal attempts. Now we have more than one."

"I'll leave that out when I speak with them," Kyri said as she landed next to Doret.

"Tell them this is for their own safety, then," I growled.

Kyri spoke; the men listened. Their eyes widened as she explained their situation, where they were and why.

"They all agree the bad man is dangerous," Kyri turned toward me. "They understand he killed all the untalented in L'on-Alberr, many of them friends and family. They say they cannot disobey his wishes, and are afraid he will kill them, even here."

"Tell them if Kaakos could kill them here, he'd already have done it," Arresh said. "I must go; Sherra is waking. Mute their power."

I watched as she disappeared.

"Damn," I whispered. Kyri translated Arresh's words for the prisoners, and Barth prepared to assist her in muting power in all six of them.

~

Sherra

I knew what happened the moment I woke; Arresh hadn't hidden any of it from me. We had six prisoners in the lockup that we'd stolen from Kaakos.

I hear you've caused a commotion, Granddaughter, Adahi sent.

When do I not cause a commotion? I responded tartly.

I'll have tea sent to your suite, he said. *Get dressed, and I'll go with you to the lockup, if you want.*

All right.

~

Kerok frowned deeply the moment Adahi and I arrived at the lockup. Earlier, he'd been face-to-face with Arresh, so I wasn't surprised by his anger and frustration.

Kyri, on the other hand, was doing her best to reassure the men that I—*Arresh*—had brought them back from L'on-Alberr. I hoped she was explaining that they'd be forced to stay in the lockup, although it was a far better place to be than anywhere near Kaakos.

At least they wouldn't be hunting for their food during their stay.

"I've told them that Jean is here, recovering from the wounds that Kaakos gave him," Kyri turned toward me. "I also explained that they'll have to stay here as long as Kaakos has a connection to them—through the wounds he gave them to take their blood. They're terrified by the truth of it."

"As I would be," Hunter grumbled.

"Did you explain that they're heavily shielded?" I asked.

"I tried, but like Pierre, they are unfamiliar with shielding."

"Wonderful," I shook my head at Kyri. "Do your best to convince them that we'll protect them as well as we can."

"What do you intend to do with them?" Kyri asked.

"Make the attempt at destroying the blood spell and their connection with Kaakos. It will give me practice and insight on breaking the bond between North and Kerok."

"We'll be using Jubal for the first experiment," Kerok growled.

"Yes, we will, because he's a traitor and expendable," Hunter agreed. "These men haven't committed crimes against Az-ca, so I'd like to keep them alive for the information they may hold. If they know where Kaakos took them, we desperately need that information."

Kyri turned back to the six men to ask more questions. After several moments of rapid-fire questions and answers, I understood by the set of her shoulders that they didn't know much.

"They only know they were in mountains, where it was quite bare and rocky, with many caves and very little ground to grow food. Kaakos never mentioned a place name."

"Of course he didn't," I sighed.

"It may help us narrow the search, if those map descriptions are still relevant," Hunter observed.

"Then let's hope they're still relevant." Kerok turned on his heel and walked out of the lockup.

"Damn," Barth muttered, before following Kerok.

"We have work to do in Ny-nes today," Kyri told me. "Let me know when you're on the way." She *stepped* away from the lockup, leaving Hunter, Pottles and me staring at six men, split between two cells.

"Get them something to eat," Pottles told a guard before I *stepped* us to my study in the palace. I found Cole waiting there for us. "I called for him," Hunter said. "I'd feel better if he went with you to Ny-nes."

"Thank you," I said to Cole. "Caral and the others should be here shortly. We need breakfast and more tea if we're to function today."

"I'll arrange for that, and for extra food to take with you," Pottles said and left my study.

"Every day, I feel as if we're teetering on the verge of disaster," I admitted and dropped onto the chair behind my desk. "Sit down. Breakfast should be here soon."

~

Kerok

"I'm sure she does what she does to keep all of us as safe as she can," Barth attempted to calm my anger.

He meant Arresh. Probably Sherra, too. A part of my mind recognized the sense in what Barth was saying. Another part couldn't hold back the fury that was growing.

Barth's eyes unfocused for a moment, telling me he was sending mindspeak. Seconds later, his vision cleared and he gazed at me. "I just spoke with North. He is angry that Kyri left without telling him where she went, and ah, I believe you are feeling that effect as well."

"Then tell him to calm the fuck down," I smashed my fist against my desk, making several things rattle atop it.

"He said he would try."

"Trying isn't fucking good enough. Is he in Ny-nes? Has it traveled that far?" I demanded.

"He, ah, has been in the King's garden for the past half hour or so, waiting for mindspeak from Kyri. He has now returned to Ny-nes."

"He is no longer welcome in Az-ca, unless I give permission," I hissed.

"I will send the message, my King."

CHAPTER 8

N y-nes
Sherra

"We can use this room as our base," Kyri led us into a large room with rows of marble pillars supporting a high ceiling. An intricate, mosaic path led to a glass coffin at the back, which contained a rotting corpse. It was one of the few places inside the palace that had minimal damage.

It's supposed to be the Prophet's body, Kyri sent. *It's Adahi, set there by Kaakos so he could keep an eye on the body and gloat.*

That's sick, I replied.

It is. North and I have shields around it, so the body won't be disturbed. This is why Adahi could never return to Ny-nes after his physical death; the pull of his body would be too strong and all of him would die. As it turns out, that happened anyway. Kaakos killed my friend twice.

I considered telling her it wasn't true—she appeared genuinely saddened by Adahi's deaths. Instead, I kept the information to myself and nodded to acknowledge her sending and her grief.

"I can turn the shield opaque, if that will help," she said.

"Please. It's—disturbing."

Kyri performed that small bit of a spell while Caral, Cole, Armon

99

and I found chairs to arrange in a half-circle. We'd do our initial search here, pinpoint our findings by connecting to North and Kyri, and those findings would be transferred to a large, paper map of Ny-nes that North was setting on the floor nearby.

Pottles told me in mindspeak that Kerok's earlier anger was due to North's presence in the King's garden, where he had no right to be. North's fury at Kyri's unexplained absence resulted in his unplanned visit to Az-ca. Once there, Kerok's disapproval was fanned into a growing anger by North's nearness, before Barth discovered the problem. Afterward, Barth had passed the information to Pottles, and she'd told me.

Pottles and Barth—they were growing close. I wondered what their relationship would eventually become, or if I were misreading the signs.

Pushing those thoughts away, I settled on a chair beside Caral, before closing my eyes and beginning my search.

~

"It's a place to start." Kyri stared down at the map after we'd finished our search three hours later. She'd drawn points on the large map, which all of us now studied.

"At least we only found fifty-one sources," Armon rolled his shoulders. He wasn't used to sitting in one place for so long and his muscles had stiffened.

I silently agreed with Armon; there could have been so many more, but then Kaakos and Ruarke, with their warrior-priests, hadn't been gone that long from Ny-nes. They'd been looking for and murdering talented children until the end, no doubt.

"I suggest we suppress the talent in any child younger than seven," North said. "Leave them with their parents. I can say they are healed of any affliction and are normal. Those seven and older, we will decide on a case-by-case basis."

"I doubt we'll find any older than two or three," I said. "Kaakos was thorough in his extermination, I think."

"Will we keep records of those whose talent has been suppressed?" Kyri lifted an eyebrow at North.

"Of course. Then, when they are older and better able to decide for themselves, we can offer them the option of training or the destruction of their talent."

"After a divination, to ensure they won't misuse their power," I said.

"So you'd interfere with their free choice in the matter?"

"I doubt any child who has grown up torturing and killing animals is ever a good choice," I shouted at him. "Yet you asked Kyri to train him. To change him. Do you see where I'm going with this?"

"How do you know this?" Kyri whispered.

"When I touched your necklace—the one you handed me long ago, when I was searching for a way through Kaakos' barrier. I saw you—and him. He'd killed some hens. He lied and told you it was an accident. I knew then it was no accident. It was through that vision that I learned how to get past his barrier—and get you past it as well." I snorted at the idiocy of it all.

"Then, when I saw him through Jubal, I found even more," I said. "He killed his mother, before you ever started training him. Plenty of small animals died around him from the time he could crawl. Need I go on?"

"You saw that he killed his mother." North's voice was flat.

"When I looked at him through Jubal, yes. He left her body outside the village for the scavengers to take—after he burned her to death."

North cursed and turned his back to me. "Your son was a homicidal sociopath from birth. I have no desire to create another in his likeness," I flung at him.

"I thought he could change—with the proper teaching," Kyri sighed. "I knew his mother had filled his ears with poison against Thorn—North. I didn't know how twisted and cunning his mind was until it was far too late."

"I left him with Kyri, thinking it was only a matter of time before he came around. When I learned better, it was too late, as you say," North confessed. "I was desperate to find him—to combat this menace, except that I discovered he was stronger than I, and willing to do any evil deed to have his way."

"You simulated your death, then waited until you could link your power with someone else, to have enough to take Kaakos down," I accused.

"Yes."

"I think he's tearing a page out of your book, now, and pulling talent to him, to finally destroy all of us."

"I know." I'd never seen North look haunted before. His face had turned pale as white ash and his eyes were downcast. "You're right. Someone with compassion that leans toward justice should do the divinations on these children, before any of them are trained."

Armon

Sherra stood on one side of the map of Ny-nes; Kyri and North stood on the other. She refused to back down from either of them, and the image of her, tall, straight, and angry, will remain with me always.

I doubted Az-ca had ever seen a Queen of her caliber. Some of us were hearing things about Kaakos—and about North's past, that we hadn't been privy to before. Even Kyri was astonished by the depth of Sherra's divination talents. I thought I'd understood that she could see others while divining an individual, but I imagined she needed Barth to accomplish that feat.

Instead, she could see those things in a person or even a simple object, without help.

"I suggest we eat, before we begin with the children," I cleared my throat to reduce the tension in a now-silent standoff.

"Yes, that sounds fine," Kyri agreed, moving as if she'd just wakened from a dream.

"I'll send for Garkus and Soobi." North strode out of the massive room, leaving the rest of us behind.

I don't think North likes being told how wrong he is, Caral sent to Sherra and me.

He'll have to live with it, because the rest of us have suffered for his bad judgment, I said.

Kyri's too, Sherra added. *Although she really thought there was something salvageable in him early on. She wasn't the one to take another's power, either. That crime is North's alone.*

"Sherra," Kyri approached the Queen. "I'd like to speak with you in private."

"All right," Sherra's nod was curt and I watched them disappear.

Let me know if you need help, I sent to her.

I'll let you know.

Sherra

"I should have told you everything from the beginning," Kyri paced inside an empty, broken room of Kaakos' former palace. Half of it was now a pile of rubble.

"It doesn't matter now, does it?" I asked as gently as I could. "I've learned it on my own, but if I'd known what North was planning," I didn't finish.

"You'd have killed him," Kyri wrapped arms tightly about herself.

"Removed his power, at the very least," I said. "Kerok was tied to him from the moment he placed that cursed ring on his finger. Instead, North could have come to Kerok at any time and offered his help, and together we could have destroyed Kaakos. Like you, he thought to do it all himself, and that was the first flaw in his plan. I doubt anyone can achieve this on their own, now more than ever."

"I know." Kyri bowed her head. "I learned that during the attack on this palace. If I could change the past, I would," she lifted her eyes to me, begging me silently to understand.

"As would I," I agreed. "Had I known more at the time, I would have kept hammering at Kaakos, rather than stopping to help Kerok."

Her eyes widened and she blinked at me in shock. "North wouldn't have drained Kerok," I explained. "His life was on the line just as much as the King's. I didn't understand that at the time—I thought Kerok was dying."

"I would have thought the same," she agreed. "Neither of us knew better; that complicated the issue and allowed Kaakos to escape."

"Yes, it did."

"Anything you want to know from now on, just ask. I will be honest and as forthcoming as possible," Kyri told me.

"Thank you. I wonder if North feels the same?"

"If he doesn't, he should."

"Let's go back; I'm hungry," I said. Kyri snorted a laugh.

I should have known the people we approached would bow to North. They saw him as not only a healer, but their liberator, now. Armon's mouth tightened whenever a family crowded about North as he touched this child or that, before allowing me to do the same.

He'd set the stage for this, I realized. It wasn't a bad way to convince the citizens of Ny-nes to flock to his cause; it was his final method of achieving their liberation that I had an argument against.

Living conditions hadn't improved much in Kaakos' absence, but there was a tension in the people that had evaporated with the deaths of his warrior-priests.

We really need to get those floating gardens up and running, Caral told me as we came to the next hovel, where a young boy stood outside a crooked doorway, as if he were expecting us.

His skin is darker than his mother's, Armon pointed out as North approached him. Instead, the boy slipped past North and came straight to me.

Stick thin, with thick, black hair that pointed in every direction, he gazed at me with dark eyes. "You," he pointed at me. "Take," he pointed to himself.

"May I hold your hands?" I asked, offering mine.

"Take." He laid his hands, which looked small and fragile, inside mine. I gripped his fingers and nodded to him, before closing my eyes and searching for his power.

Drawing in a ragged breath at what I saw, I reached out to him. *Do you see?* I asked him. *This is wonderful, and it is you.*

See, his mindspeak was uncertain and filled with awe.

He was nine years old, and he'd hidden himself so well that nobody knew he had power.

He was waiting for me to arrive. He'd seen me in a dream, and that had given him hope and the will to stay alive.

One day, if he completed his training, he would be a royal diviner.

"Take," he said again as I opened my eyes and smiled at him.

"Ask his mother," I said. "He really wants this and deserves to come with us."

North nodded and spoke to the woman who'd come out of the hovel, holding a baby.

"What's your name?" I asked the boy.

"Klete," he replied.

"Do you suppose one of his ancestors was dark-skinned?" Armon asked, reaching out to tousle the boy's hair.

"It could be," I said. "But surely not too far back. He doesn't know his father; he died not long after the boy was born. The baby's father was the second husband."

"This is in an area far south of the capital city," Kyri came to stand beside me. "Kaakos and his warrior-priests avoided it as much as they could, because the swamp is not far away, and most of it surrounds this place."

"That would explain a few things," Armon agreed.

"She wants Klete to go with us; she worries that he'll die of fever, like his father."

"What about her and the baby?" I asked.

North shrugged.

"I can put them in my city," Kyri offered. "This way, Klete won't lose his family while he learns."

"Want," Klete nodded enthusiastically.

"I think you just got your wish," I grinned at him. His smile was broad and illuminating.

~

"We made it to all of them," I said. "fifty-one in all. One was a baby, only twelve days old. All except one were too young to take. We muted their power and recorded names and parents' names. I suggest returning every year or two, to update our records."

Armon, Caral and I sat in Kerok's study, answering the King's questions. At least Kerok had enough sense to have fruit juice and water waiting for us when we returned to Az-ca, to give him a report on the day's events.

"Excellent work. Give the information you have to Hunter." Kerok focused solely on me, then. "Where is the young one you brought back?" he leaned forward in his chair.

"He is in Kyri's City at the moment, with his mother and younger sister, getting food and baths," I said. "Pottles will arrange for his education to begin, and a few lessons in divination, too. He'll be a strong diviner, Kerok—I felt it in him."

"How old?"

"Nine. He already knows enough to hide what he does from anyone in Ny-nes. He was waiting for me when we got to him."

"How did he see you—if you're an unseeable?" Kerok moved a pen on his desk.

Armon turned to stare at me. Biting my lip, I considered that for a moment. "He said he had a dream about me. Is that the same as divining?" I turned back to Kerok to ask.

"I don't know, but Barth may."

"I'll ask him, then," I said.

"He's on his way," Kerok informed me. He sounded strange—detached, almost.

Moments later, Barth walked through Kerok's open door. "You have questions, my King?"

"Sherra does," he pointed toward me.

"What do you need?" he asked.

"The boy we brought back from Ny-nes says he saw me in a dream. Is it possible that he can see an unseeable?"

"He saw you in a dream?" Barth sounded surprised. "I haven't heard of a dream diviner in years. The last one saw Thorn. All he said was that he'd be strong. As you can imagine, they have to word their dream-visions carefully."

"So a dream diviner can see unseeables," Kerok said flatly.

"It's not that easy, Thorn," Barth said. "They can't command their dreams, like a diviner can command visions to come to them when they touch someone. The dreams come or they don't; the diviner has no control over that. I imagine that he saw you," Barth turned back to me, "because it affected his own life."

"He walked right past North, too, when none of the others did," Armon explained. "As if he knew that North wasn't everything the others believed him to be."

Kerok frowned at Armon. "What do the others believe North to be?" he asked.

"Their savior—and a healer," Caral snorted. "I can't argue with the healer part, because he apparently did that, but the other is pure fiction."

"Damn right it is," Kerok sat back and appeared thoughtful. "His name? The boy?" he asked after several moments passed.

"Klete," I replied.

"See that Klete has competent teachers."

"Doret is already doing that," Barth said. "I received mindspeak only a few minutes ago. She believes the boy will learn quickly, because of the talent he possesses. I asked her to bring Klete to me tomorrow afternoon. With your permission, Thorn, I'd like to be the one to introduce him to divination."

"I would prefer that you teach him in that respect," Kerok agreed. "There. That's settled. Armon, will you and Caral join us for dinner?"

"Of course, my King."

～

Kerok

I'd begun a mental list of everything North had cost me. I'd hesitated long enough to understand that he was draining my ability to love, and that was costing me my Queen.

Sherra sat before me during our meeting, with an uncomfortable expression on her face. She didn't want to be there; I blamed myself—and I blamed North. Her answers to my questions were defensive, as if I were accusing her of wrongdoing.

As I'd done when I heard of Arresh's suppression of power in Az-ca's youngest. Now, after thinking about her actions for a full day, I realized it was for the best, but my initial anger had been hot and immediate. That I blamed partially on North.

I'd already asked Armon for a complete, written report of the day's events in Ny-nes and told him in mindspeak not to leave anything out. He promised to have it on my desk in two days.

Hunter would get the report after I read it, to add to the archives.

More and more, I was beginning to question whether my actions and emotions were my own, or those dictated by North. Sherra, Hunter and Armon needed to know this now, because I was afraid it would eventually consume me, and only North would be left behind—inhabiting two bodies rather than one.

Conversation was sparse at the dinner table as we ate; I understood that Sherra, Armon and Caral were exhausted and only wanted to eat and rest. Hunter and Barth watched them, and when they thought I didn't notice, they watched me, too.

Had they come to the same conclusion I did—that North could be taking over Az-ca in a different way? By overtaking *me,* first?

"I want all of you to listen carefully to what I'm about to say," I began. Suddenly, all eyes were on me and utensils were set down beside plates.

"You know North's emotions and such are having an impact on me," I said. "This worries me a great deal."

"It worries all of us, Thorn," Hunter said quietly.

"I know. What concerns me now is whether my reactions to any news, good or bad, are now North's reactions, rather than mine. I fear that given enough time, he will take me over completely, and have the rule of Az-ca in a way we've not imagined before."

Sherra's hands curled into fists before dropping into her lap to hide her reaction to my words.

"I refuse to let that happen. I refuse to believe it," Barth said.

"But what if it does?" I locked eyes with my Chief Diviner.

"What would you have us do, Commander?" Armon asked.

"Kill North," I said. "He and I will both die, but the true culprit will be ultimately responsible for both our deaths. I'm telling you now that if he inhabits my mind and body, I do not wish to live."

"I will not let that happen," Sherra hissed, her eyes on her lap and clenched fists. "I will not let that happen."

She *stepped* away before I could call her back.

Armon

"Say nothing about this—to anyone," I warned Caral when we returned to Secondary Camp. "Not even Misten. If you have questions, discuss them in mindspeak and only with me, unless Sherra wishes to speak of it."

"I understand, and I won't," Caral promised. "This—it sounds insane, doesn't it?"

"It does, and that statement will go no further."

"Yes, General."

Caral *stepped* to the cabin she shared with Misten; she'd been granted permission to leave the palace by the King—to rest for two days.

I stood alone outside my cabin, hoping that Levi was asleep already. *Sherra*, I sent, *are you all right?*

I'm fine. She sounded beyond weary. *I just have some thinking to do before I go to bed.*

As do I. Let me know if you need anything, even a willing ear.

I will. Thank you, Armon.

I wished her good-night, then *stepped* to the bedroom, where Levi lay awake, waiting for me.

"Long day?" he asked, sitting up and folding back the covers on my side of the bed.

"Longest day ever."

~

Sherra

Was North driving Kerok to insanity, or was the worry of it taking him there instead? I cursed North without sending him mindspeak; if he were indeed influencing Kerok's thoughts and emotions, I wanted no part of making things worse.

We should be searching for Kaakos and putting all our effort into destroying him before he became strong enough to destroy all of us. Instead, we were fighting internal battles, and all of those revolved around North.

And, by their connection, Kerok.

You're too tired to think right now, a small voice reminded me. *You can't devise a way to separate those two if your mind and body are exhausted.*

I stood on the shore of the lake outside North Camp, the water lapping at my feet as I gazed across its dark surface, the ripples catching bits of light from a half moon overhead.

Yes, I'd go back to the palace and sleep. Then, I would consider approaching North and asking him how, specifically, he'd devised the blood spell to ensnare Kerok.

~

Kyri's City
Anari

"You must be Klete," I smiled at him as he walked into Kyri's library. I'd come early to return two books and look for others I hadn't read.

"You?" He pointed at me.

"Anari," I said. "These are books," I held up one I'd found to take with me. Doret had told me about Klete, and that he, his mother and little sister were staying at Kyri's house at the moment. I hadn't expected anyone to be awake so early.

"What—for?" His dark eyes studied the book in my hand.

"They are filled with words, and those words make stories," I explained. "I love to read the stories."

"How—read?"

"They'll teach you," I said. "It'll be the most wonderful thing, ever. Next time, I'll bring Kyal and Laren with me. I know they'd like to meet you."

"Anari, are you raiding my library again?" Kyri appeared in the doorway. I opened my mouth to explain, but she smiled and held up a hand to stop me. "Don't worry, as long as you bring them back, you can read as many as you like."

"I read?" Klete asked Kyri.

"Yes. I think you'll be reading quickly," she replied. "I imagine that Anari, Kyal and Laren can help, once you master the basics."

"I'd love to help," I said. "But I have training to get to. I have to go now, or I'll be late. I'm so glad you're here, Klete," I reached out to squeeze his hand. He blinked at me in surprise. I waved and *stepped* to Secondary Camp.

Kyri

Klete was surprised—and pleased—that Anari had touched him. "We'll begin your lessons today," I told him. "This afternoon, you'll meet Barth, who wishes to speak with you."

"Barth?"

"He is the King's Chief Diviner in Az-ca. You'll like him, I think."

"Meet Barth," his eyes lost focus for a moment before they cleared and he nodded. "Meet Barth," he repeated.

"All right. Come with me; breakfast is ready, and your mother and sister are already eating."

A smile lit his face and he followed me out of the library.

~

Sherra

"Caral has two days off to recuperate," I told Cole when he arrived in my study. A tray, empty cups and a pot of tea were on the corner of my desk; I merely hadn't poured for myself, yet.

"You should do the same," he chided, setting out two cups and pouring tea for us.

"Cole, I really have to find a way to separate North and Kerok," I sighed. "No days off—a few minutes could make a huge difference in this."

"Drink," he set a cup of tea in front of me. "Enjoy the taste of the tea. For a moment, concentrate only on that—the warmth, the taste, the familiar comfort of it, and the beautiful morning outside your window."

"But," I began.

"No. Focus on the now. Right now. The taste of tea, the comfort of the warm cup in your hands, and the morning outside your window. I hear the birds; don't you?"

I turned in my chair until I could look out my window; birds were calling in the trees of the King's garden. Lifting my cup, I sipped the tea. "Enjoy it," Cole coaxed. "The taste of it, and the birdsong outside."

Ease the muscles, Cole told me in mindspeak. *Let them relax. Breathe in, hold it, and breathe out.*

I have no idea how long it lasted, but when I came back from that small, gentle journey, I felt better. I found Cole standing beside my chair, his cup in his right hand, as he gazed out my window. Turning toward me, he smiled and saluted me with his cup.

"I need to do this every morning," I breathed.

"Yes," Cole agreed. "It truly is a beautiful morning."

Kerok

"Thorn, there's been a bit of mischief in one of the villages," Hunter entered my study as I stared morosely out my window.

"What mischief is that?" I asked without turning.

"A broken engagement, and the demands of the groom's family after the bride refused to marry her intended."

"They want the dowry, don't they? Why was the wedding called off?"

"I believe the groom gave his fiancée a black eye."

"Bring them before the King," I snapped, turning around to face Hunter. "I'll let them know how things should be. Then, I want to examine all the laws concerning marriages—customs, too. We'll put a stop to this nonsense."

"I'll have them brought in this afternoon."

"Do it. I want Barth there with me, to perform divination. We'll get to the bottom of this."

"Barth is expecting Klete this afternoon," Hunter reminded me.

"Bring him, too. If he's to be a diviner, may as well show him the bad as well as the good, eh?"

"I'll see to it," Hunter dipped his head and walked out of my study. I went back to my consideration of the King's garden outside. It had turned bleak; many flowers were in bloom, and I couldn't recall a single scent of them.

Sherra

"Look who's here to help," Cole said as Anari, Kyal and Laren entered my study before lunch. They wore broad smiles; I hadn't seen them in days. I wondered who'd sent them? Someone who knew they'd lift my spirits, perhaps?

"Just in time for lunch, too," I smiled back at our young ones.

"Maybe you can help Cole and me figure out how to filter drinking water from sea water afterward," I told them.

"I'd love to do that," Kyal breathed, as he studied the rough drawings Cole and I had made. They represented floating gardens, and nearby, floating bubbles containing clean water, but none with a way to create the clean water.

"A different perspective," Cole chuckled as Kyal lifted the top drawing to study it.

"That's exactly what we need," I said. "But first, I think we should go to the garden and have our lunch there."

"Goody," Anari grinned. "I was hoping you'd say that."

"Look who else is here," Pottles walked in, Klete beside her. His eyes were wide as he took in my study.

"Klete," Anari clapped her hands. "This is Kyal, and this is Laren," she introduced her companions. "And that's Cole," she pointed toward Cole, who nodded to Klete. "Can he have lunch with us?" Anari turned back to me, her eyes pleading with me to say yes.

"Of course," I said. "We'll just ask for extra plates."

"I thought it would be easier to meet Barth over lunch," Pottles lifted an eyebrow.

Good idea, I sent to her. *Let Klete get used to all of us, so he'll be comfortable.*

I thought so, too.

And you don't mind having lunch with Barth, now do you?

Is it becoming obvious?

Maybe.

For now, we're just willing to see where it goes. There's no plan; we'll let it unfold naturally, she told me.

Good for you. And Barth.

I certainly hope so.

"Well," I said, rising from my chair, "Shall we go to the garden, and see what they have for lunch?"

CHAPTER 9

*S*herra

Klete was quite careful as he ate; already, he was copying manners and the way others held their forks and knives. I wasn't sure I'd ever seen such an observant child before.

Barth set a second roll on Klete's plate when he'd finished the first one, with plenty of butter.

"He could be your child," Pottles sniffed as he carefully buttered this second roll.

I doubt he's ever had butter before, Barth said.

I think you're right, I agreed. *Or had such good bread.*

True. Barth smiled at his protégé with a budding affection. A day's passing had brought a world of change to Klete. Here, he was clean, dressed in nice clothing instead of dirty rags, and wore a smile as he enjoyed food he'd never tasted before.

Back in Kyri's City, the same was true for his mother and younger sister. I hoped their good fortune continued—Kaakos could still ruin everything.

For all of us.

"The King requests your attendance at a judgment this afternoon," Barth told me aloud as dessert was served later. "It seems a wedding

115

was called off after the groom hit the bride, and now the groom is demanding the promised dowry, after the bride refused to marry him."

"I'd punch him back," Anari said, dipping into her peach cobbler. "Then tell him the wedding was off."

I ducked my head, attempting to stifle a snicker.

When I lifted my eyes, I found Kyal and Laren, sitting on either side of Anari, bumping her shoulders with theirs and trying not to laugh.

"Klete will be going with me, by the King's command," Barth went on. He didn't sound pleased about that.

"Go," Klete nodded, dipping his spoon into his dessert. "Mmmm," he sighed and closed his eyes at the heavenly taste of the food.

"I suppose that's settled, then," I locked eyes with Barth. Was Klete already seeing things about this judgment?

We'd find out soon enough.

Kerok

"You should eat," Hunter pointed at my plate. He and I were having lunch in my study, while we discussed the current laws and customs regarding marriages in Az-ca. Past decisions in this type of case were murky at best and depended upon the monarch passing judgment.

Those loose interpretations of right and wrong were about to be subjected to fresh scrutiny and new laws, but first, we had to write the damn things.

Regardless, I would hear the case today, rather than a town magistrate, who'd then carry what he'd heard to the King or the King's representative. I wondered how many of these my brother had fucked up while he was in charge of the Council.

Sherra is coming, Barth answered my previous request. *The boy actually wants to come. Sherra thinks he may have seen something already.*

That sounds unlikely, I replied.

We'll see, Barth countered.

Yes, we will.

"I think Sherra, Caral and a few other women should help in writing these new laws," Hunter said. "We need that perspective before we put anything to paper."

"You're right, of course. Hunt, you must continue to be my conscience. If anyone can keep me on track so I'll remain myself, it will be you."

"I'll do my best," Hunter dipped his head. "Now, eat. I'm keeping it warm for you."

"Thank you."

Sherra

Word on this judgment traveled fast, which was unusual; the entire Council had come to hear the testimony and decision.

Most of these were relatively new members, and they should attend, as this was likely going to be an indication of how similar cases in the future would be handled. Barth already said that Hunter and Kerok were studying the old laws, and preparing to write new ones, so this judgment would hold much significance.

Doret brought Anari and the boys, but they'd be in the audience, in seats reserved for special guests. When I walked into the Council chamber with Barth and Klete, the bride, groom and both families were already sitting in the witness boxes.

Less than half the Council rose when I arrived; the rest stood when Kerok, Marc and Hunter walked in. At least some of them had stood for me. I noticed neither the bride nor groom had risen for my entrance.

Caral would be more offended than I at the slight. For now, it didn't matter.

"Be seated," Hunter told the gathered crowd, once Kerok settled on his chair. Everyone sat with a collective sigh. Klete reached out and took my hand as we sat beside Barth.

"Bring forth the petitioner in this case," Hunter called out. The groom stood. "Your name for the record?" Hunter demanded.

"Salik," the man replied. Marc, who'd come to take notes for Hunter, wrote down the name.

"Very well. State your petition before the King," Hunter went on.

"My intended wife ended our engagement. I demand that she pay the promised dowry, since she is the one who ended the relationship."

"Why did she end the relationship?" Kerok asked as Marc continued to write.

"For no reason," the groom said. Whispers went around the chamber, until they were silenced by Hunter's admonition.

"For no reason?" Kerok continued. "Did you hit her before or after she broke the engagement?"

"She was promised to me—to do for me as other wives do for their husbands. It is my right to do as I please with her."

"Is it, now?" Kerok was frowning, and I knew his anger was growing. "Answer my initial question; did you hit her before or after she broke the engagement? I will have your answer checked for honesty by my Chief Diviner."

Salik's eyes widened and became fearful. "Uh," he swallowed nervously, "uh, before."

"Before the engagement ended, and obviously before you were married, yes?"

"Yes." He didn't want to answer that, but he didn't want Barth to touch him, that was easy to see.

"So. She was not your wife when you hit her. As she wasn't your wife, whom you claim you could treat as pleased you, you hit a woman not your wife. Is that so?" Kerok's voice was a near-growl.

Salik turned frightened eyes on Barth before answering. "Yes, that is so."

"What is the current punishment for assault?" Kerok turned toward Hunter.

"First offense is three months in lockup," Hunter replied.

"Is this the first offense?" Kerok asked Salik. My head turned toward the bride, who gasped aloud.

What else had he done to her?

Kerok was thinking the same. "Barth," he jerked his head toward Salik, who suddenly appeared petrified.

Barth rose from his seat in the dignified manner he always had and strode toward the waiting Salik.

"No," Klete cried out. "He," he pointed at Salk. "Kill," he pointed from Salik to Barth. "Knife," Klete made a stabbing motion.

Salik launched himself toward Barth, but the distance was too great, and I'd slapped a bubble shield around him before he could take two steps. Chaos erupted within the groom's family, as six of the ten who'd come with him rushed Kerok, knives drawn. While shouts sounded dimly from within the chamber, I corralled them in a second bubble shield.

I have the others trapped inside a shield, Adahi informed me.

Was this a planned attack against the King? Barth, too? I felt a fiery rage as I stepped off the dais, leaving my chair behind. Klete, for some reason, refused to release my hand and came with me.

Kerok, who, like the Council members in attendance, was now standing and furious at this turn of events. Salik and six of his relatives had just attempted to kill the King and his Chief advisor.

Trick, Klete's voice sounded in my head. *Them*, he sent the image of those who'd sat during my entrance. *Them*, he sent the image of Salik and his family.

Klete didn't have many words, but the word trick wasn't misused. I understood through him that this was a plan that the participants had hatched to prove that the King was incapacitated. What they planned to do with that information afterward was anyone's guess.

We had many divinations in our future, because I intended to get to the bottom of it.

Good, Klete told me. *Help.*

You've been a tremendous help already, I squeezed his fingers. *Now we just have to prove that the King is still the King.*

Kerok, I sent to him, *we need swift justice against these would-be murderers.*

I'll send for my Assassin.

No, it has to be you.

You know I, he said.

We will do this. Pass your judgment now. Hunter and I will do the rest.

I will deflect the blast, Hunter told both of us. *Sherra will send it behind a mirror shield. These seven will die, and we will determine the fate of the other four, after Barth examines them in the lockup. We shall do the same with the bride's family, too.*

Let's do this, Kerok said.

"You seven have committed treason by attempting to assassinate the King," Hunter announced. "The King will deliver justice himself in this."

Slowly, Kerok lifted his arms, as if he were preparing a blast. None of those within the shields cowered. They thought they knew. Well, somehow, they did.

And they would die for it.

The mirror shield hid my blast perfectly as I fired it; Adahi provided a deflection shield, pointing the blast at the seven who waited.

They died before they realized it was even possible.

"Nobody in the army has discussed this with anyone, I swear it," Armon paced before Kerok's desk. "The few who know are sworn to secrecy."

"Then where did this information come from?" Kerok demanded. "We've checked the palace servants; they haven't told anyone or had contact with anyone in the Council. Nobody else from Az-ca knew."

"Except Kyri, North, Garkus," Pottles ticked names off on her fingers.

"And Jubal," I said.

Kerok stilled, his mouth forming a grim slash. "Jubal," he hissed. "Shall we take a journey to the lockup, Barth?"

"I believe that would be a good place to start. After Jubal, we'll examine all the guards and the physician."

"Let's go. I want this dealt with quickly," Kerok said.

Jubal had talked. And talked more—to the lockup physician. The physician, then, had approached a few Council members, who'd contacted others, and soon enough, half the Council knew that Kerok had returned to Az-ca without his power. While it was unclear how it happened, somehow, they imagined it was Kaakos, rather than North, who'd stripped the King of his talents.

It was common knowledge that the enemy escaped, but none understood exactly how that happened. We were done with those in the lockup, now Kerok was focused on those in the Council, and what might be done about them.

"If we call it a conspiracy against the King, we can justify the divination of the Council," Hunter advised. "Everyone at the judgment saw the King blast seven men at once. If we begin to question any of them without a clear motive, they'll suspect something isn't right about all this."

"I agree," Barth sighed. "The physician has been charged with conspiring against the King already. Let them sweat when they hear of his treason and judgment. If we're lucky, some of them will come forward and confess, rather than waiting to be found out."

"Sherra?" Kerok turned to me. "What do you think?"

"I think the experiment with Jubal just moved to the fore. I no longer care if he dies during the attempt."

"Neither do I," Kerok dipped his chin in agreement. "Is tomorrow too soon?"

"I was thinking the same," I said.

"What are your plans?" Cole asked when I reached my study after dinner.

"Well, I don't want to follow the spell back to Kaakos, so I'm going to put my hands on Jubal to see if I can disconnect it on this end," I said. "If he dies, he dies."

"Good. I remember the last time you were connected to Kaakos through someone else."

"As do I. I won't give him that opportunity again—not if I can help it."

"I would prefer to be there with you, in case things go wrong."

"Several others have said the same thing, so be prepared for a crowd."

"Will it bother you—that so many are there?" Cole was concerned about that.

"I don't think so. Once I connect with Jubal, everything else gets shut out."

"When will the divination of the Council begin?" He changed the subject.

"In two days. Barth says let them sweat long enough that some will turn themselves in rather than let him examine them. We're watching all exits from the domes, in case any think to flee."

"Probably a good idea. What about the four remaining family members of the groom?"

"All of them knew, so all of them are in the lockup, awaiting the King's justice. I figure he'll let his assassin take care of them."

"What about the bride's family?"

"Oblivious, although Salik had hit her before; we found that out when Barth put his hands on her. She's well rid of Salik; I believe Kerok will award her all of his belongings as restitution, and Hunter is beginning to rewrite the laws."

"Long overdue, I'm sure," Cole agreed before changing the subject. "Kyal had a suggestion for the floating gardens," he unfolded a drawing and handed it to me.

"What's this?" I asked, studying two floating bubble shields, one larger than the other, and both connected at the top by a thin, tube shield.

"He suggests we put seawater here," Cole tapped the larger sphere, "And then heat it until it boils. The steam will escape through the tube at the top and condense in the other bubble as clean water. Boiling the water will remove impurities, and when you have a salt sludge left, you spread it flat to let it dry. Afterward, you have salt for your table."

"How did he come up with this?" I breathed. "This is genius."

"He says he found it in a book in Kyri's library, so he wasn't the original inventor. He just adapted it to bubble shields, rather than glass or metal containers."

"We'll have to find the cleanest source of seawater, or we'll still have to separate kelp and other things from it before boiling," I said, setting the drawing on my desk. "I wish we could work on this tomorrow, rather than dealing with Jubal."

"Having second thoughts?"

"No, but at least this would be a fun thing to do," I said.

"Then consider it a reward after we deal with Jubal."

"Good idea."

L'on-Alberr

Kaakos

I thought the fools were dead. I should have known better. There was a shield around the city, and it had her stink all over it. None of us could get through; I'd already ordered the remaining former residents of the city to try.

As for the garden outside the city—it looked as if giant hands had scooped it from the ground and taken it elsewhere.

Elsewhere in this case was no doubt Az-ca. That filthy sorceress had taken what should be mine and had probably destroyed six of my men as an afterthought. Then, she'd put a shield around the city, so nobody else could get in.

My father was still on my *kill first* list, but the bitch was a close second. Both were making my life miserable, by simply existing. My small army needed food before we began to hunt for others with talent. I should have taken the food when I took the city, but I wanted to perform the blood spells first.

I wouldn't make that mistake again.

~

Sherra

I didn't want to deal with Jubal in the lockup; too many eyes and ears in that place had already caused trouble. Kerok suggested Secondary Camp, and I agreed.

"Haven't been here in a while, have you?" Armon asked Jubal, who limped along in chains toward an empty cabin.

Around me, I listened to the wind blowing through the evergreens that dotted this portion of the camp, breathed in the scent of resin from the trees, and listened to the birds calling to one another. I hadn't forgotten Cole's lesson, and already it was making me calmer before I dealt with Jubal.

Barth, Kerok and Hunter had come, with Marc, Wend and Cole. Pottles stayed at the palace with Klete, Anari and the boys. Today, they'd be helping with Klete's lessons.

Armon, Levi and Caral met us outside the empty cabin, where we settled with our prisoner. If Jubal didn't understand yet that his hours might be limited, he'd get that idea soon.

I let Armon and Levi escort Jubal inside the cabin. "What's your plan?" Hunter asked. I knew Adahi wanted to know, because he'd been with me the last time I'd connected with Kaakos, after trying to get him to turn loose of Hunter.

"I'll try to disconnect the spell on Jubal's end. If it doesn't work," I shrugged.

"No real loss," Kerok grumbled.

"It's worth the effort. If nothing comes of it, then we try again with someone else," Barth agreed.

"Pull away if things begin to go wrong," Cole advised.

"I will. I'm ready," I drew in a final, evergreen-scented breath before striding toward the cabin.

~

Kerok

I hope you understand how difficult this is for her, Hunter sent as Sherra walked into the cabin ahead of us.

He'd know—he'd been in Kaakos' grip. If Sherra and Adahi hadn't helped, he'd still be in Kaakos' grip.

Or dead, because of it.

I *should* feel sympathetic. I should feel *something*. Numb was the best description of my current emotions. Was this North's interference, again? Unless I was free of him someday, I might never know.

For now, I was no better than an automaton, as Sherra attempted to solve the puzzle of blood spells.

To free me.

I was numb and couldn't force myself to feel otherwise.

Jubal was already cuffed to a heavy, wooden chair at the center of the room when I arrived with Barth and Hunter. His eyes told me he was beginning to understand his plight. He could see his death, and it was only a short distance in front of him.

"We'll pull you away if necessary," Armon laid a hand on Sherra's shoulder.

"Thank you, Armon." She stepped forward, then knelt next to Jubal. I watched as she reached out to put her hands on him. This would be no normal divination. This was chasing a ghost that lived inside this treasonous bastard.

I worried that it could be as insubstantial and ephemeral as a thin plume of smoke.

Sherra

I had to focus on the divination of a single occurrence—when Kaakos performed the blood spell, locking Jubal to him.

When I found it, I found myself an unseen observer of that act.

Recognizing the room Kaakos chose to perform the act was first; I'd stood in it myself two days before. The original was far different from the half-destroyed, empty expanse I'd seen. A rich carpet covered the stone floor; Kaakos demanded the best, even if he intended to spill blood upon it.

Kaakos held a knife, sharp, deadly and long, as he stared down at Jubal's cowering form. He anticipated the delight of spilling blood to create the bond between himself and his captive mindspeaker.

Jubal had talked too much during his life, physically and mentally. Much of that talk had been complaints. The rest had attracted the attention of all the wrong people, and he'd gone down a dark path.

He hadn't cared, as long as the money was good.

I was shocked when Kaakos drew the knife across his left arm first, collecting blood on the blade, before hauling Jubal up and slicing his arm with the bloody instrument.

"You are mine," Kaakos whispered, twisting his free hand in Jubal's shirt and bringing the terrified man's face close to his. I watched in horror as Kaakos' eyes glowed red. He whispered a phrase, "*tuum est sanguis meus.*" I didn't understand, as I hadn't heard the language before.

Follow the blood!

Arresh was shouting at me from the depths of my soul. In less than a blink, we were atop Jubal's arm, as if we'd shrunken in size to fit there. Shock made my body stiffen; the red glow in Kaakos' eyes shone also in his blood, and, as it mixed with Jubal's, it also began to glow.

Until all of Jubal's blood was affected—or infected—by that of Kaakos.

The only way to cut off the spell at this end was to drain Jubal of all his blood, because all of it was tainted by Kaakos'.

Unless a counter-spell could be devised, and I had no way to do that—that I knew of. *Disengage!* Arresh shouted at me again, before shoving me away from the scene. I didn't understand the significance of her warning, until much later.

~

"His blood is tainted with Kaakos'," I explained later over a cup of tea in the officers' mess. "You'd have to drain every drop of Jubal's blood to get rid of that curse."

Wrapped in a blanket and still shivering, although it was quite warm outside, I stared at Kerok, who sat opposite me. "You don't have the same sort of spell," I told him. "You wear a spelled ring. I should have thought of that before."

"You're certain that Kaakos' blood infected Jubal's?" Hunter was scribbling information on a piece of paper he'd found somewhere.

"I saw it. As if I'd become tiny and stood on Jubal's arm to watch the mingling. Kaakos' blood had a strange glow about it. Once it touched Jubal's, his glowed, too, until all of it was the same."

"What about the spell itself? Did you hear Kaakos say anything?" Barth asked.

"I heard words, but they were in a different language."

"Can you repeat them?" Hunter asked, his pen poised over paper.

"Uh, *too-um est sang-weess may-oos,*" I formed the words as best I could.

"Makes no sense to me," Kerok shook his head. Hunter was still writing. "Do you suppose Kyri will understand these words?" He looked up to find me blinking at him.

"She understood the men from L'on-Alberr," Barth pointed out. "This could be something she'd know about."

"Send mindspeak," Cole spoke for the first time. "Repeat those words to her."

"All right." *Kyri,* I sent, *do you know what these words mean?*

What words?

Too-um est sang-weess may-oos, I replied.

There was silence for so long, I wondered if she'd been interrupted by someone where she was. Instead, a sigh came through with her sending. *Yes, I know what that means. Is that the blood spell Kaakos used?*

On Jubal, yes.

It means your blood to mine. *He infected Jubal's blood, didn't he?*

As near as I can tell.

This isn't good news.

I agree. I don't know of any way to counteract this.

Neither do I.

Jubal will be executed now, won't he?

Probably in the next hour or so. He's having his last meal right now.

Such a waste.

Agreed. He'll probably blame it on his dead rose with his dying breath.

This means we can't help those men from L'on-Alberr, doesn't it?

It doesn't look good for them, as long as Kaakos is alive. I hope all of this dies if he does.

It may be that they'll die when he does—as Thorn will if North is killed.

I wish you wouldn't say that. I'm still determined to find a solution to that problem. North didn't use blood to perform that spell.

Because he already bears a blood kinship, Kyri observed. *As North did, to get past Kaakos' barrier—and his shields.*

But I was able to get past his barrier, I reminded her.

That bears thinking about. Perhaps a way can be found, but it's not with Jubal or those men from L'on-Alberr.

I know.

"What did Kyri say?" Hunter asked when I ended the mindspoken conversation.

"She says the words mean, *your blood to mine.* Kaakos infected Jubal's blood with his."

"My blood isn't infected with North's," Kerok became thoughtful. "Just as you said."

"And that gives me hope," I told him. I didn't tell him what else Kyri said—I didn't want to destroy what little hope this might give Kerok.

"We're back where we started, then," Barth said.

"At least we have more information," I told him.

"Yes. We do have that."

∾

Cole and I *stepped* to the palace after eating lunch at Secondary Camp; we had no desire to witness Jubal's death. The others stayed to watch and record it.

I'd seen enough horror that day and wanted no more of it. At least the shakes had stopped, although I still felt uneasy.

"Shall we turn our thoughts to happier things?" Cole asked, setting Kyal's drawings in front of me. "We can build this, I think, and look for sources of seawater."

"Maybe that's what we need—construction rather than destruction."

"You are correct, my Queen."

Kerok

"I don't want any part of him on Az-ca's soil," I said, after Armon *stepped* us outside the massive crater formed by Kaakos' bomb-carrying planes. Jubal looked terrified—too terrified to speak, and that was unusual for him.

"With your permission, my King, I'd like to take this execution," Hunter told me. I stared at him; he'd never offered to do such in the past, but then he hadn't performed blasts or anything else until Sherra came along and taught him.

"I'm happy to give him to you," I pointed to Jubal, who was now quaking with fear.

"Don't worry, little betrayer, I'll make this quick," Hunter told Jubal. Before Jubal could swallow nervously, he was nothing more than ash, blown apart and discharged into the crater by the force and severity of Hunter's fireblast.

"You would have made a fine addition to the King's army," Armon slapped Hunter on the back. "Well done. Come, I think Levi and I have a bottle of whiskey to share."

Sherra

I hadn't mirrored the massive bubble shields yet, and both, connected by a curved, pipe-like tube, hung in the air outside the domes of the King's City. One was slightly smaller than the other, as it would collect and contain the steam from the first, which would then condense into clean, salt-free water.

"A good, solid first step." Cole, his hands on his hips, declared of our combined handiwork. "Shall we have tea and then look for the source of our saltwater?"

"I think we should," I said.

"Garden or your study?" He grinned at me.

"Oh, the garden. Most certainly the garden."

"After you."

"We'll go together." I linked my arm in his and *stepped*.

CHAPTER 10

*K*erok

When Barth *stepped* Hunter and me back to the garden table, we found all its seats filled. Sherra, Cole and Doret were having tea with the young ones—Anari, Laren, Kyal and Klete.

I hadn't heard such joyful laughter in a long time, and it made my heart yearn for my youth. My brother and I had sat with our parents at this very table, when Mother was still alive, laughing and teasing with one another.

Shaking the memory away, I walked toward them.

"King," Klete was on his feet first, and bowing his head to me. The others were almost as quick to acknowledge my presence.

"Is there any tea left?" I smiled at the young ones.

"Laren may have drank it all," Kyal teased the older boy standing next to him. Klete snickered; Anari giggled and tousled Klete's hair.

"I think we can find tea for the King and his court," Sherra said. "I'll get more chairs."

Briar and a footman brought more tea and cups; Sherra floated chairs from another portion of the garden. Soon, Barth, Hunter and I were sitting at the table, listening to the young ones talk while we drank tea.

I needed to clear my head after two glasses of whiskey shared with Armon and the others. I realized after a moment that Kyal and Sherra were now having a conversation about the method to distill fresh water from seawater.

"The bubble shields are floating outside the domes now," Sherra said. "Cole and I set them up; we only have to find the cleanest source of seawater to begin the process."

"I'd like to search north of my village," Cole suggested. "We can work our way down if we don't find something suitable."

"We can always construct a temporary collection bubble, to transport the water to the boiler bubble," Sherra suggested.

"Good idea," Doret agreed. "That way, it doesn't have to be maintained or moved in both directions."

"If we leave the bubbles where they are, we can clear a space in the desert outside the domes to dry and process the salt," I said. "Another temporary bubble can carry fresh water to the floating gardens."

"You don't mind that the bubbles will be outside the domes?" Sherra asked me.

"You can put more than one set out there, if we need it."

"We have the King's permission," Cole chuckled. "We don't have to move them."

"Where will we put the gardens?" Doret asked. "Have you thought about that?"

"I'd like to place several in different locations, to see if hotter or cooler temperatures work best," Sherra said. "Or, we can choose the locations based on what is grown inside each garden bubble."

"I want watermelon," Kyal spoke up.

"Then our first planting will include watermelon," Sherra laughed.

Frankly, I wanted watermelon, too, and couldn't recall the last time I'd had any. "Definitely watermelon." I smiled at the boy, whose grin was contagious.

~

Sherra

Pottles, Cole and I escorted Klete to Kyri's City, following our afternoon snack. It was time for him to rejoin his mother and sister.

They met us at the front door of Kyri's home, the woman smiling; the baby sitting on her hip.

She's learning, too, Pottles informed me as Klete walked through the door and hugged his mother. *She asked to be taught. Now, she and Klete discuss their lessons over dinner.*

I think that's a very good thing, I said. *So they won't get disconnected in any way.*

Except for the power part. She's more accepting of it than I thought she'd be.

Good. We don't need anyone accusing him of being a demon—or worse. His talent is amazing.

He's learning fast, just as you said he might.

Good. He wants to catch up to Anari and the boys. That's motivation, right there.

"Thank," Klete's mother, Beri, spoke.

"You're welcome," I smiled.

"Tea?" Beri asked.

"I think I'll stay for a while," Pottles said. "Go find seawater." She shooed Cole and me away from the door.

"I guess we're going for seawater," I told Cole.

"I'll take us; I think I know a good spot," he said.

"Kyri calls this an inlet; the rough waves don't reach here unless there's a big storm," Cole explained as we surveyed the sandy expanse before us. "At times, we collect clams and shellfish from here, but not too often—there are still remains of chemicals in the water and it can harm us if we eat too much."

To the west, I could see tall rocks and cliffs, which acted as protection for the inlet, and took the brunt of tall waves, allowing quieter waters to wash into the inlet with the rising and lowering of the tide.

"The water looks so clear," I breathed. "This would be perfect, I think."

"As do I. This is not high tide—you can see ridges of sand in several places," he pointed those out. "The best time for collection would be high tide; there'd be less chance of taking in sand with the water."

"You know a lot about this," I shaded my eyes from the lowering sun in the west.

"I've lived near here most of my life. Some of it was bound to soak in. Come. Take off your shoes and walk the water with me."

Our pants legs were rolled up; we carried our shoes and stepped through the cool, soothing water. "Are those rocks?" I asked as we passed two pieces of semi-clear, green stones.

"Sea glass. It still washes onto the shores from the End-War, or so Kyri says. "I've seen other colors, too."

"There's so much we don't know, isn't there?" I turned to look at him.

"Yes. Don't worry about that for now. Let the peace of this place calm you. Let all the stress of your life go; at least while you are here."

Looking down at my feet, which were ankle-deep in clear water, I saw tiny fish swimming about. I found myself delighted to watch them as they darted around me, completely unafraid. When one of my tears dripped into the water, I realized I was crying.

"Tears of joy," I wiped my cheeks and gave Cole a watery smile. "I'm just—this makes me so happy."

"Then our walk turned out better than I hoped."

"This is one of those memories that you can see clearly, long after the event has passed," I said. "Thank you for this."

"There's another inlet south of here that is nearly the same, but not nearly as scenic as this one. We'll take the water from there," Cole patted my arm. "Your tiny fish friends will be safe."

"Good."

"I must go home," he told me. "I am invited to dinner tonight with several friends. Have a good evening, Sherra."

"Thank you. I'll see you tomorrow." I *stepped* away before he could; I didn't want him to see me cry again.

Kerok

Sherra had showered and changed before arriving at the dinner table. Hunter, Barth and I waited for her and Doret.

"Did you find a source for seawater?" Barth asked her as she took a seat to my left.

"We did. It's quite clear, too. I could see the sand beneath the waves. If we want kelp for fertilizer, we may have to look for it elsewhere, or farther out. This water is in an inlet, or that's what Cole called it."

"Did he go home?" I asked.

"Yes. He said he was invited to dinner with friends in his village," Sherra shrugged.

"We forget that he has another life outside Az-ca," Hunter said.

"He is loyal to the Crown in Az-ca," Sherra pointed out, as if someone had challenged her about Cole's allegiance.

I wanted to tell her that Cole was loyal to the Queen of Az-ca, but those words stayed behind my teeth. If she weren't here, Cole wouldn't be, either, or any of his army. We'd needed their help in Ny-nes, and, to some degree, it irritated me.

We need allies, I reminded myself. Any King or Commander should recognize that basic truth, and I was both those things.

"I'm sorry to be late," Doret arrived, her smile pointed in Barth's direction. "I was too involved with my students and lost track of time."

She probably taught Klete and *his mother to read and write over a cup of tea*, Sherra informed me, humor in her sending.

Her words shocked me; we hadn't exchanged mindspeak in a while, and certainly not anything of a humorous or teasing nature.

Doret stayed to speak with Klete's mother? Does she have a similar vocabulary to the boy's?

Yes, Sherra replied. *One-word sentences, most of the time. They've never been taught, Kerok. Now, they're soaking things up like a sponge. Klete wants to read books like Anari and the boys do. That's his goal, and he won't shy away from the harder lessons because of that.*

Can we trust the boy?

Kerok, he trusts us. Don't do anything to change that.

You trust him, then?

I did my own divination on him. Don't destroy the connection with him— he stood first when you arrived in the garden earlier.

Yes, he did. That means nothing. He's from Ny-nes, Sherra.

And he's the only one I brought back, or have you not noticed?

I didn't intend to pick a fight with you, I said.

Then stop doing it.

"What are your plans for tomorrow," I asked her aloud.

"I'll start on the list of places where Kaakos could strike next; if he hasn't sneaked around to do it already without our noticing."

"Why would he do that?" I nodded to the servant who refilled my wineglass.

"Because he knows by now that we kept him out of L'on-Alberr and took six of his captives away. He'll approach the next target with more stealth. I doubt we'll be as lucky next time as we were with L'on-Alberr."

"I don't think those from L'on-Alberr would consider themselves lucky. He killed most of them," Doret pointed out.

"There are seven survivors. I doubt he'll leave any for us to find next time, and he'll take the food and supplies with him when he goes, instead of coming back later for the spoils." Sherra's hair, which had grown past her shoulders, crackled with energy about her face. I'd made her angry, and Doret had innocently tossed fuel to the fire.

"I can only do so many things at once." Sherra stood, tossed her napkin on her chair and stalked out of the dining room.

"What did you accuse her of this time?" Doret turned narrowed eyes on me.

"I questioned her judgment in bringing Klete to Az-ca."

"Well, I understand her anger, now." Doret rose, tossed her napkin on her chair and followed Sherra's path out the door.

"Does it take a great deal of thought and effort to disrupt meals, or does it come naturally?" Barth asked before scooting his chair back and going after Doret.

"I'll see to Sherra," Hunter rose and walked out the door, leaving me alone at the table. Had I so little sense anymore, that I'd start fights over nothing?

It took several moments to come to the actual reason I'd started the argument; Sherra had spent much of her day with Cole, and she'd returned looking happy.

Then, like the lowest, most jealous lover, I'd spoiled her mood and sent her out the door before food was served. I knew Cole could never be her lover. Not in the physical sense. I'd been useless lately in that capacity, too.

Perhaps it was time I asked Cole how he'd done it. How he'd made Sherra feel happy, and in the mood to tease and amuse.

Before I'd ruined it.

"You're a fool, Thorn Wulfson Kerok Rex," I said aloud. "And don't let anyone tell you otherwise."

Sherra

When Hunter knocked on my door, I answered, ready to tell him I wanted to be alone. Adahi's concern showed in his eyes when I saw his face, and Briar peeked out from behind him, a tray of food in her hands.

"Come in," I waved them inside my suite. Briar set the tray on the small table by the window, before asking if I wanted her to pour wine for us.

"Pour wine, and then take the rest of the night off," I told her. "We can handle the rest."

I watched Briar pour two glasses of red wine, then place the cork in the bottle. "Thank you," she smiled and scurried out the door, closing it softly behind her.

"What do we have to eat?" Hunter lifted a cover off one of the plates. "Looks like pork," he said. "With stuffing."

My stomach rumbled at the mention of the food, so I didn't try to say I wasn't hungry. "Let's eat," I said, taking a seat on the opposite side of the table.

"Where do you plan to go first, tomorrow?" Hunter asked, dropping a napkin on his lap and lifting his knife and fork.

"I was thinking of asking Klete if any of the dots on Kyri's map held his interest or felt urgent to him."

"Then do it. Clearly, the boy has deep talent. Besides, it never hurts to utilize all available resources."

"It can't hurt," I agreed. "I imagine Kaakos is more than furious that we took some of his prisoners and kept him out of L'on-Alberr. He knows that I'm involved in all that. He's probably deciding who his worst enemy is at this point—me or his father."

"I think the same; I didn't want to worry you with the information, so I didn't tell you. You've come to the same conclusion yourself, I see."

"Yes, I've come to it." I allowed my shoulders to sag as I breathed out a sigh. "Cole has managed to reduce my stress the last two days, just by being calm and rational. The moment I get close to Kerok, he says something and ramps it right up again."

"Go ahead and tell me what he says is asinine, because it is," Hunter lifted his roll and bit off the end.

"He has a lot to deal with, and he has to take it out on someone." I stabbed my pork cutlet that had turned cold and ate.

"Just as you have a lot to deal with. I haven't noticed that you've belittled anyone because of it."

"I still have my power. He hates feeling helpless," I defended Kerok.

"The measure of a man is how he deals with adversity," Hunter said softly. "I understand that North may have some influence on Thorn's emotions, but he goes too far, sometimes."

"I refuse to believe that the real Kerok would behave this way," I said, dropping my fork to stare out the window. It was too dark to see much, although Cole's method of bringing me away from my worries was foremost in my mind. Struggling to keep my fears at bay, I went back to my meal.

"I hope you're right." Hunter kept eating.

Kyri

"Thorn now believes you are influencing his emotions and reactions, even when you're far away," I told North.

"I don't see how that's possible." He looked up from the carved wood bowl he'd shaped and was now sanding.

"How connected are those rings you both wear?" I demanded. "Yours obviously allows your anger to transfer when you're close together."

"I have no idea how that happens," he turned the bowl in his hands, looking for rough spots to work on.

"I want to know what you intended when you created those rings —other than stealing another's power."

"That was my only intent," he shook his head. "I didn't consider anything else when I set the spell."

"What, exactly, was the spell you set?"

"Similar to the one Kaakos sets on his subjects, using only my own blood. The second ring would recognize the blood relationship in another wearer."

"And the words of the spell?"

"*Omni vi mea.*"

"All strength is mine? Does that mean all the weaknesses are his?" I accused.

"Do you think that's what happened?" He was actually curious about the effects of his own spell.

"Well, the weaknesses have to go somewhere, don't they?" I pointed an accusing finger at him. "What about the fact that you're tied together now, and neither of you can remove the ring? Was that a separate spell?"

"*Removere non possunt*," he sighed. "I had to hold onto the power, once I took it."

"Cannot be removed. Wonderful." I walked out of the room before I attempted to blast him for pure stupidity.

~

North

I didn't think this through, I chided myself. I should have asked Adahi for help. He could have steered me away from making two grievous mistakes.

Except he'd never have gone along with my plan to sap Thorn II's power. He was the more honorable of us, and the second ring would never have been placed on Thorn's finger if he'd known what it would do.

Adahi, old friend, I sent, knowing he wouldn't hear me, *I should have told you everything from the beginning. I'm sorry for the pain I caused you.*

You should be glad you are where you are, old friend, Adahi's caustic reply shocked me so much I dropped the wood bowl, which broke in half at my feet.

Where are you? I stood, terror causing my heart to stutter.

You will never find me, and you should be glad of that. Your apologies should go to the Queen and King of Az-ca, because you are destroying both their lives. You've learned nothing in your old age, have you, Thorn?

Does anyone else know you still exist? I asked the question while I searched my mind for how it was possible.

Two others know, and they will never tell. Should you think to tell someone, I will kill you myself, regardless of the consequences.

You will kill the King of Az-ca if you kill me, I argued, although there was no lie in Adahi's words.

Do you think you haven't killed him already? I knew him before, remember? This man is nothing like the Thorn I knew, and you are responsible. I know not how you did this, but when I learn of it, I will give the information to the one who may be able to do something about it.

Sherra. My sending was flat. Unemotional. Adahi would make good on this promise; I felt it in my core.

Yes. Although she has to worry about killing your bastard first, doesn't she?

I can help her, I began.

Like you did last time? If I were you, old friend, I'd be searching for a way to remove the ring from Thorn's hand just as diligently as Sherra. Adahi cut off his sending then, leaving me to pick up the pieces of a bowl I'd worked on for two days, because Kyri wanted something to hold wild fruit.

Sherra

At first, I couldn't sleep. Hunter and I had a second glass of wine after dinner, but we'd been lost in thought most of that time. Eventually, he patted my hand and told me to get some sleep before *stepping* out of my suite.

If only getting sleep were that easy, nowadays. Kerok's attitude was becoming worse, and North wasn't anywhere near Az-ca. If I found out he was responsible for this turn of events, I would make his life miserable until I found a way to destroy the spell.

After my discovery with Jubal, and how he'd been infected, I worried that nothing about this would be simple, and it could be beyond anyone to remedy. Would we watch as Kerok descended into true madness, and only see anger in him from now on, rather than the protectiveness that he'd been known for all his life?

Find Kaakos first, the small voice I was coming to recognize as Arresh, reminded me. Yes. Kaakos came first, before he could destroy more lives and increase his strength. Then, I would deal with North and his subjugation of the true King of Az-ca.

North

In the past, I'd have gone to bed, put the whole incident out of my mind and slept deeply. Instead, I kept waking after short, shallow naps, followed by uncomfortable feelings of deep guilt.

Until the last time. That dream was different.

Undeniably different.

I dreamed of her.

Sherra.

As if I loved her.

Kyri was correct—I was siphoning everything away that was considered a strength in Thorn, while giving back my callous anger and indifference. How had it traveled so far?

Because you take his power away from such a distance, too, I reminded myself. Were we each becoming the other? That terrified me. Was I losing myself, because of my own shortsighted stupidity?

More than anything, I wanted to contact Adahi again, present this latest fear to him, and then ask for his advice. He was so angry that he'd probably ignore my request.

Would Kyri offer advice? What if she went to Sherra?

What would Sherra do? My heart twisted in my chest as I thought about her. *I'm not in love with her*, I chastised myself. *You're destroying their lives*, Adahi told me. Destroying *her* life, in addition to that of Az-ca's King.

Kyri, I sent, suddenly feeling desperate. *I'm losing myself.*

Kyri

"What are you saying?" I demanded. North had wakened me in the middle of the night with a strange, desperate message—*I'm losing myself.*

I'd found him sitting on the side of his bed, half-dressed and his head in both hands. "These things don't happen to me," he moaned without moving his hands.

"What things?"

"Guilt. Love. Worry."

"That's certainly true, you've never worried about much of anything, except how it affects you in the long term," I folded arms across my chest as I watched him. He still hadn't looked up at me.

"I think it's the spell. I'm taking Thorn away from himself and sending myself back to him. I'm losing my identity," he dropped his hands and looked up at me. His eyes held an empty, deep loss; one he hadn't considered possible before now.

As much as he'd wounded Thorn II, he'd wounded himself just as badly.

"This is your fault, and you know it," I snapped at him.

"I know. I understand that, now. Don't you see, Kyri? Before, I'd never have felt this guilt."

"Or admitted it," I agreed. "What do you expect me to do about it? I don't have a solution against this stupid spell you created. If Sherra can't find a way out of it, then I have no idea what to say or do."

"I feel as if I've been punched in the gut—and the heart."

My breath stopped at his words. Hesitating before putting this new fear into words, I studied him. He looked pale—and afraid.

"Are you saying you've stripped away Thorn's love for ah, others?"

"I think that's happening, yes."

"I want to call you the worst King in Az-ca's history right now, but I may have to go to Az-ca and say those words to the one you've stolen from to get the proper message across," I said.

"It feels that bad," he rose from the bed, dressed only in sleep pants. "I've created the worst conundrum ever, and it's because of greed and ego. Truly, I believe I couldn't bear it that my bastard son was not only stronger than I, but I'd unleashed his evil on all of us. I thought I was the only solution to the problem. How was I so blind?"

"Now, I'm beginning to worry," I said softly. "The man I knew would never have taken the time to sort through all that and accept the blame for it."

"Kyri, neither of us are who we were," he pleaded. "Please contact Sherra. Please. Warn her that things are turning upside down."

"I'll send a message to Doret. She'll tell Barth, and they can decide how to approach Sherra and the King."

"Thank you."

~

Sherra

Pottles? I was only half awake when she sent mindspeak a second time. I'd been dreaming—at first about Kerok, who'd spoken soft words to me—words of love and hope. I'd reveled in those feelings until they were torn away and another dream took its place. That one was of fear and uncertainty, and I didn't understand it at all.

Meet us in your study, Sherra, Pottles said, her mental voice sounding sharp and worried.

I'll be right there. Pushing back bedcovers, I set my feet on the floor while struggling to clear the dreams from my mind. I shoved arms into the sleeves of my robe and *stepped* to my study as Pottles directed.

Barth, Pottles, Hunter and Kerok were waiting there for me.

"What's wrong?" I asked, still feeling confused.

"Everything," Kerok snapped. "How in the name of the nine levels did I get here? I was in Ny-nes ten minutes ago."

"There's been an ah, unfortunate side effect of North's spell," Barth said, while Pottles nodded at his words.

"I disagree. The spell was sound enough," Kerok glared in anger at Barth. "It should have worked better than this. I have no idea why this is happening."

"You haven't merely traded locations with Thorn," Hunter pointed a finger at Kerok. "You've traded his spirit for yours. While you now resemble Thorn II, you are North at your core."

"I *am* North. Why are you saying I no longer look like myself?"

"This can't be happening," I moaned as I looked from Kerok to Hunter and back again.

"It is happening," Kyri appeared, North right behind her. "He woke me not long ago, telling me he was losing himself. Now he sounds more like King Thorn with every passing moment." She pointed toward North, who stood at her shoulder.

"Sherra, I am so sorry," North apologized. "I have no idea how this happened, but I've been pulled into—this." He gestured toward himself.

"I was sound asleep," Kerok whined. "This could have waited."

"I believe that's not everything that's happened," Kyri admitted. "The spell North performed sent all strengths to this one," she tilted her head toward North, "and all weaknesses to him," she nodded toward Kerok.

"Are you feeling his anger, now?" Pottles directed her question to North, or the one whose outward appearance was North's.

"No, just some confusion and regret, but I believe that's all mine."

"I'm angry," Kerok snapped. "This is untenable. I never intended the spell to do this."

"And yet here we are," Hunter's words were dry.

What are we going to do? Pottles sent to me.

I think we're going to have to deal with two Kings in Az-ca for the moment, until this gets straightened out.

How about changing their outward appearances in the meantime?

There's that, I suppose, but it can only be temporary. Too many things can go horribly wrong, and everybody will be miserable the whole time.

That's the truth of it, Pottles confirmed.

"I'll change your appearances, to reflect your ah, current situations," I addressed North and Kerok. "Everyone will be less confused that way."

"Good," both said, although only one sounded angry—the one who currently held North's spirit and his not-so-redeeming qualities.

Drawing on my power, I set the spell on each, until their faces reflected their character. "There, that's done," I sighed. "Kyri, he has to stay here," I pointed to the new Kerok. "The other one, too. Will that cause hardship in Ny-nes?"

"I doubt it," Kyri frowned at the new North. "He brought this on himself, and he'll look for someone else to blame before the day's over."

In other words, she didn't want to be responsible for the nasty one and intended to leave him here for us to deal with.

"I'll send him to the lockup myself if he fails to behave

appropriately," Hunter glared at North.

"I agree with Hunter," Kerok said.

"Hear that?" I turned to North. "One wrong step and you're in jail," I told him. "Show him to an empty suite," I instructed. "He can catch up on his sleep there."

"Will you be all right? Do you know where to go?" Barth asked Kerok.

"My memories are intact," Kerok sighed. "Although I have no idea how all this is possible."

"I believe we'd all like the answer to that question," Barth said. "Doret, will you come with me? We'll show North to his new suite."

"Of course."

I watched as Barth pulled North toward the door, and those three walked out of my study together, leaving Kyri, Hunter, Kerok and me behind.

"Now what?" I made a desperate gesture with my hands.

"None can know of this, or Az-ca will be in more turmoil than it already is," Kerok pointed out.

"You speak the truth of it," Hunter agreed. "This knowledge goes nowhere else. I'll ensure that North keeps it to himself."

"Thank you. He's the deepest worry I have in all this."

"I feel the same," Kerok looked grim. "Too many things can go wrong, and the results could be disastrous."

"Do you want tea for thinking, or wine for sleeping?" Hunter asked him.

"Tea. Have it sent to my suite. I have plenty of thinking to do. Sherra, I wish I could ask you to come with me, and I hope you understand why I can't."

I understood perfectly. Beneath the disguise I'd given him was North's body, although it was no longer North's mind. I thought nothing could be worse than Kerok's dismissal of me after his power was removed.

I was wrong.

"Enjoy your tea," I nodded to him and *stepped* to my suite, leaving him and Hunter to sort things out.

CHAPTER 11

*S*herra

"Armon, you need to know this—you, Caral and Levi," I told him. I'd invited him to breakfast the following morning, after spending the rest of the night in restless contemplation.

"Who do we attempt to save, then, if it comes down to it?" Armon asked.

"As far as I know, they're still connected and if one dies, so does the other. The answer is both," I shrugged.

"This is confusing as hell," Armon rumbled.

"Agreed. It was hard enough when I thought I only had to stop power from flowing from one to the other. Now it's everything that can be perceived as a strength that has gone to one, leaving a whiny adult behind in the other."

"In other words, we have Thorn's brother, Drenn, to deal with again."

"I never met him, but from what I've heard, you're right."

"Doret actually threatened to put him in the lockup?"

"She did, if he failed to mind his manners. He looks like North, now, so there won't be any confusion for the guards."

"But underneath the disguise is Thorn's body?"

"Yes. His mind, on the other hand, is definitely with the other body."

"How in the name of the first warrior can anyone screw up a spell like that?"

"Kyri seems to think it was the words he used, which could be interpreted in more than one way. Except for the removal of the ring—he apparently got that part right."

"So you still can't be together because of the ah," Armon didn't finish.

"Yes. We had a very brief conversation about that last night. Separate suites it will be, unless and until we get this reversed."

"What will you do if it never happens?"

"I don't know. For now, I refuse to contemplate it."

"I'd go crazy if Levi and I," he shrugged.

"I know."

"What about Misten? She'll know Caral is keeping things from her."

"Then tell her, and make sure she understands that to reveal this secret will be considered treason."

"As it will be," Armon nodded. "We don't need more rebellion from the Council, who think to test their theories before the King himself, while the Queen is standing there with him. If they'd ever stood on a battlefield, they'd have known better than to challenge anyone capable of firing blasts at the enemy."

"Perhaps it's time to conscript a few from each village, to work with the army," I said. "They can see for themselves, understand that we're not monsters, and learn that we do wield a great deal of power in their defense."

"We could use them as guards, medics, lookouts and ground troops," Armon agreed. "If they step out of line, they can be set to filling in blast holes."

"Some of those could take ten years to repair," I smiled at Armon.

"Exactly," he grinned. "That would be the incentive not to step out of line."

"Shall we present this to the King, then, and ask his opinion?"

"If he's truly reasonable, now, then certainly."

Kerok? I sent.

My rose? I drew in a ragged breath at his response. Memories clouded my mind, as the words settled on my soul like welcome rain on a dry garden.

Armon and I would like to meet with you, if that's possible.

Come now; Hunter, Barth and I are at the garden table, having breakfast.

All right. We should have their input anyway.

"They're at the garden table. Bring your tea and we'll talk," I told Armon.

He rose and *stepped* us to the table where the King held court.

Kerok

Sherra had already explained the situation to Armon, who appeared skeptical at first as I invited him to sit at the table.

"I hear you have an idea?" I asked him.

"Sherra and I think that conscripting ground troops from the villages might be a good idea," Armon said. "We've discussed the fact that the recent ah, rebellion in the Council might not have taken place had they been fully aware of what someone capable of firing blasts could do to them."

"You think they're ignorant of such? I can see that's possible," Hunter appeared thoughtful. "They especially should have known not to attack the King when the Queen and several others were present who were capable of retaliating."

"I doubt they were prepared to lose their lives over it, even to prove a point," I said dryly. The memory of the event was clear, but it still felt as if I were—and weren't—present at the time.

I hoped the double-vision effect would leave me eventually; until it did, I was resigned to feeling uncomfortable about it.

I also had memories of things that had occurred in Ny-nes before the attack on Kaakos' palace, but I didn't want to worry those seated at the table with me—especially Sherra. She had enough worries.

"I believe they were prepared to prove their point, and point their fingers at the same time," Sherra quipped. "What they intended to do if their point was proven is anyone's guess."

"Should we find out?" Barth asked. "We still have a few in the lockup to question. I can do divinations, to see whether that information was given to any of them."

Briar approached our table, carrying a tray with a fresh pot of tea. I waved her forward. Sherra smiled and thanked the woman as she poured for the Queen, first.

"Do you still intend to search those places on Kyri's map today?" I asked Sherra as Briar continued filling cups.

"Yes. I want to see Klete before I go. He may have some insight as to where to go first." She was testing me in this. I'd started a fight with her the day before, after questioning the loyalties of a nine-year-old who'd never lived anywhere except a swamp in southern Ny-nes.

That was another double-vision recollection for me. In my mind, I'd been in both places, to see the boy and Sherra's divination of him, and again at this very table when I'd questioned the boy's right to be here.

Do you think the boy will know what happened when he sees me again? I asked Sherra.

I don't know, but if he does, I think he'll recognize the importance of staying silent on the issue.

I hope you're right, but in the meantime, perhaps we should stay apart, Klete and I.

I can't fault your logic. I'll let Pottles know. I think he can be taught in Kyri's City for now. Anari and the boys can help; they've stayed at Kyri's house before. They know their way around.

Good. That's settled. Let me know whether the boy knows anything about those dots on Kyri's map.

I will.

Who will go with you, besides Kyri and Cole?

I'll take Caral and Levi.

They would be my choices, too. If you need me, I began.

I know you're willing. With North here, though, someone with a clear head should also be here to make official decisions.

You're worried he'll do something stupid?

Yes. We don't need guards or other prisoners carrying stories, either. You know we can't pass judgment on that particular prisoner, even if he commits the most heinous of crimes.

I ah, see your meaning.

He'll be better off where he is, and under close supervision. Put Marc and Wend on that. Tell them to contact you immediately if North gets out of line.

"My King, Lofflin has asked to see you," Briar was back.

"Lofflin?" I had no idea why the royal jeweler would ask to see me.

"Oh," Sherra gasped. "I forgot all about that."

"Forgot what?" I frowned at her.

"I ah, asked him to make some designs for rings—for the *King's Eagles*. I meant to tell you, but other things happened," she said.

"Oh. That sounds like an excellent idea," I said, smiling at Briar. "Send him to the table. Can we get a fresh cup of tea for him?"

"Of course," Briar poured a cup of tea from the tray and set it before an empty chair. Lofflin, carrying a wooden box, approached the table.

"You have something for me to see?" I asked him.

"I have three designs, and I would be delighted to make any of them for members of your elite force," Lofflin smiled at me as he set the box on the table at my elbow.

"Take a seat; we've poured tea for you," I offered the empty chair.

"Thank you, my King." Lofflin walked to the chair and seated himself while I opened the lid of the box.

Inside were three rings, each with a different eagle on the crest, and made of gold to give the weight, feel and look of the final product.

"Ah. This I like," I pulled out the ring that drew my eye immediately. The crest bore an eagle in flight, prepared to strike. Its wings were spread, the beak wide in a silent battle cry, and the claws extended to grasp the enemy in its talons.

"What do you think?" I leaned forward to give the ring to Armon, who took it from my hand.

"This is exquisite," Armon breathed, setting the ring on his finger and forming a fist with his hand to ensure he could still flex easily.

"The other two are quite nice," I handed those to Armon as well, "but the one you're wearing is my favorite."

"Mine too," Armon examined the other rings before setting them down. Sherra pulled Armon's right hand to her to see the ring for herself.

"Lofflin, this is beautiful," Sherra smiled at the jeweler.

"I was hoping you'd choose that one. It will be a pleasure to make those for the *King's Eagles*."

"How many?" I asked Armon.

"We'll need thirty, plus one for the King and Queen," Armon took the ring off his finger and passed it back to me.

"How many men's and women's?" Lofflin asked.

"Half each," Armon replied. "Make a few extra, in case we train new troops."

"Of course," Lofflin sounded pleased. "I will have these ready in three months."

"Finish your tea, Lofflin," I smiled at him. "You've earned that and much more with these designs."

"Thank you, my King. Queen Sherra, those plain rings you ordered are in a box on your desk," Lofflin turned to Sherra.

"Plain rings?" I asked her.

"For experimentation only," she said.

"Ah." She was still looking for ways to reverse the spell. As she'd said before, I couldn't fault the logic. "I'll release the additional gold from the treasury for your work, Lofflin, and issue a bonus for such fine craftmanship."

"You are kind, my King." He dipped his head to me.

Today, I was kind. I couldn't say that about many, many days before this day, however. I sighed and sipped my tea, finding it had grown cold. Without thinking, I employed power to heat it again, and it answered my call like a well-trained pup.

Tension I hadn't realized I carried drained out of me. Sherra didn't have to protect me from the Council from now on; I could do it myself.

I'll come with you to the lockup for your divination, I told Barth. *I'd like to get to the bottom of this conspiracy, and deal with it head-on.*

It's good to have you back, Thorn, Barth said.

It's good to be back, I countered.

Sherra

I'm not sure how to feel about it. He sounds whole, reasonable and pretty much like I'd expect Kerok to sound, I told Pottles after my arrival at Kyri's home.

Cole was already there, having a cup of tea with Beri at Kyri's kitchen table.

"The young ones are in the garden; I believe they're shaping shields into letters of the alphabet," Pottles said aloud.

"That's genius," I said. "It teaches two things at once."

"Anari thought of it," Pottles said. "They're getting pretty good at shaping all sorts of shields."

"Are they set for a break anytime soon? I want to ask Klete about the map."

"In a few minutes," Pottles said. "You can ask while they're having a snack."

"How Klete," Beri began, searching for words to shape her question. "Power?" She still wasn't sure of the word she'd used.

"How does he have his power?" I asked her.

"Yes," she nodded enthusiastically, happy that she'd gotten it right.

"We don't know," I said. "Neither of my parents had power. It's the same with most others—some are just born with it. It's not wrong or bad, it just is."

"You're probably wondering why the former Supreme Leader of Ny-nes said the children born with power were bad," Pottles turned her teacup in her hands.

Beri considered Pottles' words for a moment. "Yes," she replied after several seconds passed.

"He had power, too, and he didn't want anyone to threaten his rule," Pottles said. "So he killed all the children who could grow up and oppose him."

Beri thought that through, then her eyes widened and she stared in shock at Pottles. "He—evil? Leader?"

"He is no longer the leader of Ny-nes, and yes, he is still as evil as he ever was. Perhaps more so, now that he's been forced out of his country. He was a child murderer, and a liar," Pottles huffed, her long-held anger evident in her voice.

"Babies—die for—nothing?" Beri sounded sad.

"They died for nothing," I told her. Reaching out, I took her hand and squeezed it. "We hope that never happens again in Ny-nes."

"We're looking for him," Pottles explained. "Sherra and others are trying to find him and destroy him, so he can't kill anyone else."

"Help?" Beri now sounded hopeful.

"Klete may be able to help," I smiled at her.

"Thank," Beri sighed. "Hope."

"Me, too," I gave her hand one more squeeze and let go.

I'd asked the others to go to the garden for their snack; even the baby was crawling on a blanket Pottles set out for her.

That left Klete and me in Kyri's kitchen, where I unrolled the map on the table.

Klete's eyes darted from one mark to the next until he'd looked at all of them. "This one—gone," he pointed out a mark near the center of the map. "This one, gone." He pointed at the nearest mark to the first. "This one. This one." He pointed at two more.

"Kaakos has already been there?" I asked Klete as gently as I could, although I feared the worst.

"He take some. Kill others."

"Can you see images of these places?" I asked.

Dark eyes gazed into mine. *See,* he sent images to me, while pointing at a new mark. Visions crowded my mind of a lake, high in the mountains, with houses short and tall built around it. *Go there soon,* Klete added.

Kyri, Cole, I sent, *we have our first target on the map.*

Where is it? Kyri asked.

Swee'n? I said after reading the name on the map.

I'll be right there, Cole said.

Caral? Levi? I sent. *We have a target. I'll come for you when Cole arrives.*

We're ready, Levi answered.

"Take," Klete pulled on the sleeve of my uniform.

"Honey, I don't want to place you in danger," I told him.

"You," he pointed at me. "Need," he pointed at himself.

"Are you sure?"

"Sure."

"We have to tell your mother and Pottles."

"Take Anari, Kyal and Laren. Too."

"They need to come?"

"Yes. Take."

"If you're sure," I repeated.

"Sure," he nodded.

"All right. We'll have to explain this to two people who may be more skeptical than I am about this."

"Sure," Klete smiled.

"He's sure," I explained for the fifth time. Kyri, like all the others, had questioned the necessity of Klete, Anari and the boys joining us on this mission. Kyal and Laren were happy to be included, while Anari kept a hand on Klete's shoulder most of the time. Already, he was fast friends with her and the boys, and had no desire to be separated from any of them.

"Do you have a *stepping* point?" Kyri asked.

"Klete gave me images. I think we can make it all right," I said.

"Then take us." Kyri still sounded skeptical, but we'd come this far. *May as well see how good Klete's information is.* I *stepped* us to Swee'n.

Kerok

"I know you," I told the man behind the bars of his current home. "I thought we were rid of you after Drenn died."

"Except my village sent me back," he sneered at me.

"I'm sure they were ignorant of your previous misdeeds, or they wouldn't have," I flung at Buck.

"They knew and they still sent me back. I'm the voice of the people, don't you know? Drenn always said so, and it's true."

"Then I hold those people just as suspect as I hold you," I countered.

"I see you've brought your Chief Diviner this time. Think you'll find something the others didn't find last time?" he taunted Barth. Buck's hands were on the bars at either side; his face was pressed to the two closest ones.

"Perhaps. If I can't find what you're hiding, I'll ask Sherra to help. If there's anything to find, we'll know it before we're done," Barth said, his voice even and unthreatening.

"I pity you if the Queen finds anything," I told the prisoner.

"Hmmph," he muttered, although worry now clouded his gaze. "I'm still trying to figure out how she managed to do what she did for you in the council chamber."

"You think she did that, do you?" I gripped the two bars he'd pressed his face against and sent heat into them. Buck leapt back with a yelp of pain. Two red stripes now marked his face. I could have done worse than that—much worse. My father should have sentenced this one rather than letting him return to his village unscathed.

"He's from the same village that produced Merrin," Hunter stepped in beside me, surveying my handiwork with a critical eye.

"No surprise," I shook my head. "Shall I have the entire village divined for conspiracy?" I asked Buck.

"I need a physician," he snapped at me, touching the burns on his face and wincing at the pain.

"Send for a physician," I barked at the guard standing nearby. The man took off at a run. Turning back to Buck, I said, "After the physician has covered your face in sticky salve, Barth will do a preliminary divination. Pray that he won't have to ask the Queen for help."

"If you kill me, thousands will rise against you in my place," Buck threatened.

"Is that treason I hear?" Hunter, whose arms were folded across his chest, turned to ask me.

"It certainly sounds like treason," I agreed. "Were you the one who planned the attack in the council chamber?"

"Ask your diviner."

"You asked for me?" A young man—much younger than the former lockup physician, arrived carrying a bag.

"You're not in league with that one," Hunter pointed toward Buck, "or the previous lockup physician, are you?"

"No, Prince Hunter."

"Barth?" Hunter jerked his head toward the new lockup physician. Barth moved forward and placed his hands on the man.

"You have faint power," Barth pulled away and blinked at the physician.

"They said that when I was a child, but there wasn't enough to do anything with," the man shrugged. "I trained as a physician instead."

"What's your name?" I asked him.

"Collin," he replied.

"Well, Collin," I pointed at Buck. "Slap some salve on that one in there, before Barth does his divination. We don't want him in pain while we examine him."

"Of course not," Collin agreed. The guard stepped forward to unlock the cell; Barth, Hunter and I followed Collin inside. I wanted no harm to come to the physician, who was only trying to help.

I'd ask Sherra to check on Collin after she returned; he'd sounded disappointed that his power hadn't been sufficient for the army's needs. If anyone could draw another's ability to the surface, Sherra could.

Buck didn't like that we'd come in with the physician; we learned why after Collin finished and Barth placed his hands on Buck.

Hunter was the one who grasped Buck's right hand before he could reach his pocket; Buck dropped the knife he held after Hunter placed a burn on the man's wrist. Collin, who stood by, watching, gasped at the brazenness.

"Well, we'll be checking in with a few guards after this," Barth breathed after he let Buck go. "I'll ask Sherra to help me later. This one has deep information, I think, and Sherra will see his conspirators, unless I'm very mistaken."

Fear filled Buck's eyes after Barth spoke; he had no idea that Sherra could do anything of the sort. A new worry of my own arrived; this could place the Queen in more danger than she was already in.

"Keep him isolated from all others," I snapped. "Hunter, I need trusted guards from the army; the more powerful the better. I want him shielded against sound while he's our guest."

"I'll ask Armon to send four right away," Hunter said.

∼

Swee'n

Sherra

I wasn't sure what to expect, but empty houses weren't on my list of possibilities.

"They," Klete swept out a hand. "Know. Like I," he pointed to himself.

"They knew we were coming?" I asked the boy.

"Some," he pointed toward Kyri and the others.

"I see." They hadn't seen me, but they'd known the others were coming. That meant they'd either fled on foot or someone had *stepped* them away.

"How?" I asked Klete, mimicking running with my fingers.

"Not," he shook his head. "*Step*."

"Then they certainly have a source of power among them," Kyri said. "Someone who can *step* many others, or so it seems."

"Alloo," someone appeared nearby, wrapped in a heavy, transparent shield. Someone who could obviously *step*.

Kyri began to speak different languages to the man, until they arrived at some sort of communication.

"He says he wouldn't have returned, except we have children with us," Kyri turned toward me and translated. "He's heavily shielded and wants to know what we want."

"To warn him," I said. "Can you give him images of Kaakos? Tell him that Kaakos has already destroyed several villages and cities, searching for those with talent to conscript."

"I'll explain it to him," Kyri nodded and went back to speaking with the man. While Kyri talked, I turned toward the lake, which was breathtaking in its beauty. The water reflected the blue of the sky and resembled smooth, rippled glass. How amazing would it be to wake and see it every day?

"It's so pretty here," Anari echoed my thoughts.

"It is," I agreed.

"If Kaakos comes, will he ruin it?" Her voice sounded small.

"Can we put a shield over it?" Kyal asked. "That he can't get past?"

"I think so, but we can't be sure," I said. "He's already gathered power to him, and if he draws on that, he may be able to break through. I'd hate to tell these people they're safe behind a shield, when they may not be."

"That sucks," Laren said.

"Kaakos sucks," Kyal agreed.

"What are you saying?" I asked. I'd never heard that term before, when it apparently meant something was awful, rather than the proper meaning.

"We read it in an old book," Anari said. "People used to say weird things like that."

"We like it," Kyal announced.

"Then be prepared to explain yourselves whenever you use it," I told him.

"Cool," Kyal held up his hand, palm outward. Laren slapped Kyal's palm with his, then both bumped clenched fists together.

"Unbelievable," I said.

"Lusern is asking where his people should go to avoid Kaakos," Kyri said, drawing my attention away from the boys.

"Klete?" I asked him.

"Come," he took my hand and approached Lusern. Lusern dropped his shield, although he remained wary.

"Will you tell him we only want to touch?" I asked Kyri. She conveyed our message; he nodded his agreement. Klete and I came close. Klete was the one to place his hands on Lusern.

Visions streamed through my mind so fast they were a blur, until we arrived at a future point. Klete showed Lusern and me an abandoned village high in the mountains, and then showed Lusern placing shields, followed by me placing shields. My shields were comprised of power drawn from everyone I'd brought with me.

Lusern nodded when Klete pulled his hands away. He knew where the abandoned village was. He spoke to Kyri.

"He says he'll meet us there with his people in roughly an hour," Kyri translated. "They have to gather food and such—Klete thinks six weeks will be enough time for them to escape Kaakos."

"I still want to put a shield around this place," I told Kyri. "Maybe it will make Kaakos think we've taken the residents before he could."

"Good idea," Kyri said. "Make it the same as the one around L'on-Alberr."

"I will. I'll need to draw from all of you to add to Lusern's shield in the high village, though. Klete thinks it's necessary."

"Then we'll do it."

"Tell him to gather his people. We'll meet him there after I create this shield."

～

Kerok

Buck wasn't happy as he sat glowering on his bunk. I'd built the first shield around him; Armon's hand-picked troops—two warriors and two roses—set their own shields outside mine. If Buck said anything that could be heard past that, he was more talented than anyone I knew.

"Shall we begin working our way through the guards?" Barth asked.

"I say yes."

"I'm with you," Hunter said.

"We'll go to the lockup commander first, then," I strode away from Buck's cell.

~

He's whining that he's hungry, Wend informed me in mindspeak as I studied the lockup commander. She meant North.

Have a tray delivered to his room. I don't want him wandering about while I'm away from the palace.

I'll tell him. What do you want me to do if he tries to leave the suite?

Place a bubble shield around him and let him chase his own tail inside it, I instructed.

I'll do that.

I'll look forward to your report later, Lieutenant Wend.

It will be my pleasure, King Thorn.

~

Swee'n

Sherra

I had no idea how close Kaakos was, but it turned out that he was quite close. If Klete hadn't tugged on my sleeve before sending me images, I might have taken longer to set the shield around Lusern's village.

Gasping at the vision Klete showed me, I poured power into

forming the shield, making sure the giant bubble connected below ground before tying it off and gathering the others to *step* away.

Kyri's eyes were huge when we landed abruptly in the high village, stumbling on the uneven trail just outside.

"He's coming, isn't he?" she breathed.

"He is. We have to hurry."

Lusern arrived; Kyri began speaking rapidly to him. He set the first shield while I pulled power from the others to build the second.

"Hurry," Klete spoke aloud, shoving power in my direction.

"No," I told him. "I won't allow you to empty yourself." Forcing some of his power back, I gauged the others, took as much as I felt I should and built the best shield I could with that considerable energy.

Cole nodded to me the moment I pulled away from the invisible structure.

"We go," Klete said.

Nodding to the boy, Kyri, Cole and I pooled the last of our reserves to *step* all of us to the King's City.

CHAPTER 12

*K*erok "Klete was right; we did have to go to that village first," Sherra said. She lay with her back against the thick pillows on her bed, a cool, damp cloth across her forehead. I'd brought Collin in to tend her; she'd nearly collapsed following her arrival.

"How close did he come?" I asked, meaning Kaakos.

"Too close. We almost didn't finish in time. I hope he doesn't go looking for those people; he'll do everything in his power to break through our shield. Are the others all right?"

"The others are having a meal in the kitchen and getting whatever they want to eat from the cooks," I said. "Cole wanted to come with me to make sure you were well, but I told him to stay and eat."

"He's not a threat to you," Sherra pulled the cloth away from her eyes and blinked at me.

"I know, but it's my job to see to you. It's time I did right by my Queen."

"Please don't go there. I don't think my heart can take another beating," she pleaded, setting the cloth over her eyes again.

"Are you hungry?" I asked, rather than engage in the quagmire of emotion that she'd just referred to.

"I am, but I don't want to go to the kitchen."

"I'll have something brought; just tell me what you want."

"What's ready?"

"Fowl with little dumplings, some roasted beef, that sort of thing."

"I want the fowl, with lots of little dumplings," she sighed. "How did the questioning go at the lockup?"

"Good and bad," I replied. "Barth and I want you to do a divination on a council member named Buck."

The cloth came down again. "I recognize that name," she said. "Your father should have put him out of our misery."

"I agree. Before I do what should have been done before, I want you to take a look. I fear there may be a growing conspiracy, and he may be at the center of it."

"Then I'll do that tomorrow, before Klete and I look at the map again."

"I think you should rest tomorrow—after you do a divination of Buck."

"What if I can't? Kaakos will be angry enough that we thwarted him today. Another village could be in just as much danger tomorrow because of that."

"Then consult with Klete, but if it's something that can wait, then we wait."

"Then we're agreed."

"Yes, we are. I'll leave Collin here with you and go fetch your food myself."

"Collin?" The cloth came off a third time.

"There in the corner—our new Royal Physician," I grinned at her. "Collin, if she gets out of bed, I expect you to let me know. There's one more thing," I told her as she frowned at me.

"What's that?"

"Barth felt a bit of talent in Collin when he did a divination. I'd like you to check him, too, and see if there's something there we can work with."

"I can do that now," she grumped. "That doesn't take any power at all. Come here, Royal Physician Collin, and I'll see what you have."

Collin couldn't decide if he were in a dream or a nightmare as he approached Sherra. "You shouldn't be afraid, I don't bite," she told him.

"You really don't have to," Collin stuttered.

"Here." She reached out to take Collin's hand before he could draw away.

~

Sherra

"What is it?" Kerok demanded when I drew in a sharp breath.

Collin has healing talent, I informed Kerok. "I'm sure the diviners didn't see it as useful to the army, because they were looking for fire instead of the opposite," I said aloud.

"Then I suppose it's a good thing he studied to be a physician, isn't it?" Kerok grinned at our new Royal Physician. "Tell me, do your patients have a tendency to get better faster than other physicians' patients?"

"They dislike me for it," Collin hung his head. "It's why I was assigned to the lockup after the other physician there became one of its ah, inmates."

"Jealousy is always the bane of the truly gifted," Kerok slapped Collin on the back.

"Kyri can show him how to use that talent," I said as Kerok headed toward the door.

My rose, he informed me as he opened the door of my suite and walked through it, *I can show him how to use it.*

Kerok had North's abilities as well as his own. I should have realized that already.

"Collin, I see a long and illustrious medical career ahead of you," I told him. He blushed and laughed at my assessment.

~

Kerok

Sherra's party were still eating and talking when I walked into the kitchen. I'd forgotten that Klete would also be there.

His curious gaze lighted on me the moment I entered the boisterous kitchen, which turned silent quickly as servants stopped whatever they were doing and bowed to me.

"King," Klete slid off his stool and bowed with them.

"Klete, finish your food, young one," I pointed him back to his place at the counter. "I'm here to take something to Sherra."

"What does the Queen want?" Briar was at my elbow quickly.

"The fowl with dumplings," I said. "She said lots of dumplings, actually."

"I'll put a tray together." Briar bustled away.

"I hear you had an adventure today," I approached the counter where Anari, Kyal and Laren were lined up next to Klete. Kyri nodded but allowed the children to tell the story.

"We missed Kaakos by this much," Kyal held a thumb and forefinger roughly an inch apart.

"Klete knew he was coming, so Sherra had to hurry," Anari said. "If he hadn't warned us, we may have had to fight him and whoever he brought with him."

"Did you see others with Kaakos?" I asked Klete.

"Yes." He began tapping the fingers of one hand with the forefinger of the other, until he'd tapped all five fingers six times.

"He had thirty?" Cole was also watching Klete carefully.

"Yes," Klete said. "All—sick. Like—Kaakos."

"Then he's already placed them under a blood spell," Kyri huffed. "The filth."

"How many of ours will we need next time, to defeat a spell created with the power of that many?" Cole's eyes locked with mine.

"I have no idea, but when Sherra feels better, I think we should discuss it."

"I wish to be included in that discussion," Kyri said. "Also, may I see North before I leave?"

"You may, but word is he's not happy inside the bubble shield we've been forced to put around him."

"He'll survive," Kyri said, her words dry. "He did this to himself, whether he admits it or not."

I didn't say what had recently occurred to me about that; if we kept North imprisoned, and he held both our faults and none of our strengths, there was nothing to stop him from killing both of us if he tired of being a prisoner.

"I'll take the tray up," Briar was back, bearing her burden of food and drink.

"I'll take both of us," I said and *stepped* us to Sherra's suite.

Swee'n

Kaakos

This was *her* work. Again. Was she taking certain ones away from me because they held more power? Could she even determine their levels of power, or was it a different game she played against me?

Cursing under my breath, I turned away from the shield she'd placed around the large lake village I'd targeted. How many had she stolen this time? My anger mounting, I considered my next move, and whether I should attempt to set a trap. Somehow, I had the feeling that she'd barely eluded me this time.

Should that happen again, I was determined she not get away. For now, the witch was neck and neck with my demon father for the most wanted on my enemy list. Only time would tell which of them might rise to the top.

Sherra

Whatever Collin had done after I ate allowed me to sleep through the night. Arresh hadn't put in an appearance, or, if she did, I wasn't aware of it. Staring at the ceiling above my bed, I focused on my schedule for the day.

"Feel better?" Kerok appeared unexpectedly at the foot of my bed.

A sleeve of his black uniform was lit by a shaft of light intruding between the curtains of my window. I focused on that for a moment to adjust to his sudden—and unannounced—arrival.

"I feel much better," I admitted, then stretched on the bed like a cat to get the kinks out of my muscles.

"Good. Let's have breakfast, then visit Buck in the lockup."

"Let me get dressed, first," I mumbled, scooting off the bed.

"You are so beautiful, my rose," he blurted as I tossed my hair back to get it out of my face.

"What?" My cheeks heated at his words as I turned to gape at him. Yes, he looked like Kerok, but beneath that disguise was another man's body.

"I'm sorry, I know this is confusing to you," he lowered his gaze, now feeling as uncomfortable as I did.

"Thank you for the compliment. I'll get dressed and we'll go to breakfast and the lockup," I said in the silence that followed his apology. Then, I loped toward the bathroom, his eyes on me the whole time.

～

Kerok

More than anything, I wanted to make up for lost time with Sherra, now that I felt whole again—or mostly so. *Take things slowly,* I warned myself. *She doesn't know who you are any longer.*

Honestly, I barely knew myself any longer, but the love I felt for her was now threatening to overwhelm me. There wasn't anyone with whom to share my dilemma, who'd give me honest advice on the matter.

Yes there was; I'd merely forgotten it with the recent changes.

Adahi? I sent, my mindspeak tentative and apologetic. *Things have taken a rather unusual turn,* I told him.

I am aware. His sending was gruff but not as angry as I expected. *I hear you're more Thorn II rather than Thorn I at the moment.*

I—believe that's true. There's a part of me that's North, because I recall how to heal people, I admitted. *And a few other things. The rest is all, well, the current King of Az-ca.*

Better for you, or I'd make good on my promise to kill you.

I understand that, and I mostly agree with it.

Then we are in agreement, he replied. *Is there anything else?*

Sherra, I admitted. *I don't want to frighten her, and she knows that beneath this disguise, I wear North's skin.*

And you desire to be with her now.

Yes.

You will have to win her again. I cannot help you in this.

Will you help keep an eye on North? I asked. *I worry that the qualities he holds will bring mischief to all around him.*

My concerns are the same. I will watch him as often as I can.

Thank you.

Your thanks will be better spent on Sherra. I'm sure you know how—lacking—you have been with her recently.

I do. You can't make me feel guiltier than I already do about that.

At least you can feel guilt. North had a notable deficiency of that emotion.

You'd know that better than anyone.

Yes.

I have many of those old memories, I told him. *Aligning them with the King's will be an interesting process.*

I am still attempting to work out how this happened, Adahi grumbled. *Not that I'm angry that it did, because it appears to be better for Sherra and all of Az-ca. We need a united front and a focused King, rather than a fractured effort to defeat the enemy.*

We may be dealing with an enemy in Az-ca—again, I told him. *And not only Kaakos.*

I know this. I do get around, after all. His words bore a shade of humor that my memory now recognized from the past. Refusing to point it out, I merely grunted my agreement.

I have to go; Sherra's dressed and ready for breakfast, I sent.

Then treat her gently.

I will. Thank you for speaking with me.

Ah, politeness. What a blessing, coming from someone who lacked that courtesy for centuries.

A part of me has always had it, I argued, although I wanted to laugh.

The part that is less than a century old, or do you not recall that?

I'm working on putting things together. Stop trying to trip me up.

I believe I'm entitled to trip you now and then.

Yes, I suppose you are.

Sherra

"He said that?" I asked.

"Buck sounds convinced that if he dies, thousands of others will take up his cause," Barth explained at breakfast.

Cole, Armon and Caral had come from Secondary Camp to join us; Kerok had invited them. I learned that two warrior-rose pairs had guarded Buck inside a bubble shield through the night, too.

There may be a deeper conspiracy going on than what we witnessed in the council chamber, Hunter sent.

This concerns me, I replied, *because Arresh has been noticeably absent lately. Do you think she may be working on this and keeping it from me?*

It's possible, although her reasons may be more altruistic than before. Hunter gave no indication that we were having a silent conversation. The others around us continued to talk about Buck and what his words could mean to us and to Az-ca.

Altruistic? In what way?

By keeping you focused on the enemy outside, while she deals with the one inside. It may preserve your sanity, considering everything else you've been dealing with.

I'll hope for that, then, rather than suspecting her of keeping secrets that I should know about.

We'll both hope for that.

"What do you think we'll find with Buck?" I asked aloud.

"I hope we'll see the others involved in the conspiracy, if there truly is one," Barth said.

"I hope we find it's Buck's delusion, and that his conspiracy died with those in the Council chamber," Armon interjected.

"There's that," Kerok agreed. "Sherra, do you need more butter?" He tapped the dish with a finger while winking at me.

"Maybe," I said. He pushed the butter dish in my direction.

Lifting my knife, I was just about to dip it into the golden goodness that was butter when the missing Arresh screamed *fire* into my mind. Reflexively, I *stepped* everyone at the table to the lockup, which was now engulfed by a blazing inferno.

Kerok

"I'm certain they intended Buck to die in this," I said, watching as smoke rose from the smoldering remains of the lockup. Sherra had smothered the fire with a tight shield, and the only ones to walk out of that mess were the warriors, roses and the bubble shields they'd built containing Buck and the six from L'on-Alberr.

Everyone else inside had perished.

"We knew to place ourselves inside bubbles containing as much fresh air as we could gather," Armon's Lieutenant approached us after his rose released their bubble shield.

"My King," Lieutenant Samm dipped his head to me.

"Good work, Samm," I told him.

"I'm sorry we didn't have time to save any of the others," Samm's rose, Glindi, apologized. "It happened so fast."

"There's no evidence of fireblasts causing this," Sherra studied the ruined building. "But something was used to accelerate the blaze."

"Kerosene, most likely," Armon growled. "I think that's what I smell, anyway."

"Then someone brought it in last night," Hunter said. "We'll question the night guards when we're done with Buck."

We turned to the man trapped inside the bubble. Buck was sweating, and not all of it was due to the heat of the fire.

"Did you think they'd get you out?" I walked toward his bubble shield. He shook his head violently.

"You expected to die, then?"

Another shake of the head.

"You had no idea this was planned?"

Buck's chin dipped in a nod.

"Someone else is running the show. We have to find out whether that's only true now, or has been true all along," Hunter folded arms over his chest.

"Shall we take him to my study? We can do the divination there," I suggested. "Hunter, alert the guards around the palace. If anyone has come or gone that we don't recognize as trustworthy, I want to know. I dislike the idea of the palace burning down around us."

"I'll have a report for you shortly." Hunter *stepped* away.

"I say we take him to Secondary Camp for questioning and divination," Sherra turned to me.

"That's a better idea," I agreed. "Samm, will you coordinate with Hunter to protect the palace while we're gone?" I turned to the Lieutenant.

"With pleasure." Samm dipped his head to me a second time.

"Good. Shall we?" I asked Armon.

"Of course."

This time, I *stepped* everyone to our next destination.

Sherra

I felt a watchfulness surround us as we landed at Secondary Camp. Kerok took us to the officer's mess, where we were served tea before turning our attention to Buck.

Somebody here told Buck that you were without your power; I can feel it, I sent to Kerok.

Is that what's making my spine tingle? he responded. *I dislike that feeling.*

Me, too.

Only a few officers were present in the building as we occupied a long table. Buck sat with us, surrounded by a smaller, pliable shield so he could have limited movement. I passed a cup of tea with honey inside the shield I'd built around him. The worm didn't have the decency to appear grateful.

He knows his minutes are numbered; he won't waste effort on gratitude, Kerok informed me.

That explains it, then. I sighed and lifted my cup of tea to drink.

Do you suppose his allies here will attempt to attack us? Kerok asked.

Not if they know what's good for them. I'm running short on patience.

As am I. If we find the culprits, whether through Buck or by divining everyone here, then they may burn beside Buck.

What if this cancer runs deep into Az-ca? I asked.

That's worth investigating. I'd like to find the root of this new threat. So far, we've seen no taint from Kaakos, but I suppose he could be behind it in some way.

I worry that he isn't connected. What if this is deeply-rooted in the Council and goes back to Drenn and his jealousy of his younger brother? If none of these have power, they could have created an us-against-them conflict, when there shouldn't be one.

Father should have sentenced all of them to death, Kerok fumed. *Those who followed Merrin caused us trouble; now those who remain and were unseated have found a new way to destroy Az-ca from within. Who needs Kaakos? The enemy lives next door.*

We don't know that for sure, yet, I cautioned, although my worry was the same. For years, Kerok and the army had protected Az-ca from Kaakos' invasions, which would have destroyed the entire country and everyone in it.

Instead of working alongside us, Az-ca's untalented citizens were searching for ways to tear the country apart.

Those idiots probably still think I'm responsible for Drenn's death, Kerok drained his mug of tea and thumped it on the table.

"Time to find out what you know," he growled at Buck, who quivered inside his shield. "Armon, gather my *Eagles*. I don't want an unexpected attack while we're looking into Buck's involvement."

~

"Are you ready?" Barth asked me.

"I'm ready," I nodded.

"I wish to be connected, too," Kerok announced.

"Are you sure this is wise?" Armon held up a hand to warn Kerok.

"Barth didn't see anything dangerous before," Kerok said. "I want to see what Sherra sees—unless she doesn't want it." He turned dark, pleading eyes in my direction.

"If you want," I shrugged. Arresh hadn't sent a warning or offered advice, so I didn't see the harm in it.

"Good. I'll touch Buck, Sherra will see through me," Barth told Kerok. "You touch Sherra."

"Of course," Kerok agreed.

Buck was now backed up against the wall of the perimeter shield the *Eagles* formed about us, and those same *Eagles* now watched as we approached Buck.

Barth went first, just as he'd said. I connected with Barth, then Kerok placed his hands on my shoulders. Buck whined as Barth began; images began blurring past until we reached the place where Barth's divination ended.

Kerok and I, together, sailed right past that point, slowing until we could see the faces of Buck's contacts.

Many of them we recognized as former Council members. Others we needed to study. Some were village leaders. Others were those dissatisfied with the way things were for them.

Buck hadn't seen all of his supporters, however. Each face branched into a dozen others, in dozens upon dozens of villages. Even young men and women were being recruited to the cause, as that was what it had become.

They called themselves the *Republic of Az-ca*, and each new member had been sworn to secrecy.

The whole thing made me ill. At least a third of the population had turned against the King and his army, with more being added to the cause every day. Once the information had been slipped to them that the King was without his power, they'd become bolder. Buck's strategy of revealing that fact before the Council had backfired, but it hadn't deterred the Republic of Az-ca.

I only saw a few faces who hadn't joined the movement willingly; those were wives, sons, daughters and husbands of members who refused to let them be.

Half of Kaakos' work had been done for him, and he hadn't lifted a finger to accomplish any of it.

I've seen enough, Kerok sent.

We haven't seen the culprits from Secondary Camp yet, I told him.

Then hurry.

All right.

Faces blurred again as I raced through them, searching for someone more familiar. I found three. Kerok gasped audibly when he saw them.

As did I.

CHAPTER 13

*K*erok

Buck was now in the camp lockup, waiting to be sentenced. I sat in Armon's office, staring down the three before his desk. Sherra, Barth and Armon flanked me on both sides as I considered which questions to ask first.

"All of you decided against having your power restored," I said, curbing my temper. Two kitchen drudges, both friends of Caral's sister, and an older male washout who was assigned to Secondary Camp to make repairs to buildings and fixtures, gazed back at me, defiance in their eyes. All of them received a salary, housing and food from the Crown. "How long have you been Buck's eyes and ears here at camp?" I demanded.

"Not telling," Jem snapped at me. The two women beside him remained silent.

"You may as well," I snapped back. "If you don't volunteer the information, I'll have my diviner pull it out of you."

"That's why we don't like you filth," one of the women spat. "We have no rights. It's always you first, and everybody else last."

"Hush, Meka," Jem hissed.

"Why do you think you have no rights?"

"We were forced into this life. Tell me it isn't so," Jem said. "Forced to leave our village for training. Forced to quit because we weren't good enough. Forced to serve the army after that, whether we wanted it or not."

"We're working to change those laws," Sherra said quietly. "These things take time. Why didn't you bring your concerns to your Commander?"

"Think they'd listen to the likes of us?" Dree, the second woman, huffed. "They tell us to keep quiet and get back to work."

"That has certainly not been true since Armon took over," Sherra denied. "He will not refuse to listen to anyone, and your concerns would have been brought to the palace."

"We're not as important as the warriors and roses," Meka huffed. "That's always how it's been."

"Then why did you refuse to have your power reactivated?" I asked as calmly as I could.

"Too late, far as I'm concerned," Jem spat on the floor. Armon moved slightly, but it was Sherra who, with the precision of the finest marksman, cleared the spit off the floor with a small, well-aimed blast.

"Dishonor the King again and you'll be next," she warned.

"Hmmph. Think we don't know already what our fate will be?" Jem accused.

"Then why do this?" I asked, keeping my voice even.

"Things are finally changing," Meka said. "People are starting to wake up."

"To what?" Armon asked.

"That the enemy you've been fighting all this time is gone," Jem said. "They haven't been back for several seasons, now. The army is no longer protecting the people of Az-ca—they're leeching off them instead."

"You really believe that?" Sherra demanded.

"It's true. Don't try to deny it," Jem shouted.

"I think it's time you saw what the enemy is up to, then." Sherra *stepped* to Jem's side.

"Keep your hands off me, you filthy witch," Jem yelled as she grabbed his arm.

His words were lost in the *stepping*; we landed in a city far away from Az-ca, where bodies littered the streets and the stench of rotting cadavers was all around us. Kaakos had come here, and he'd killed everybody except those he'd kidnapped.

Meka promptly fainted; if doing so made the smell better, I'd have attempted the same. Pulling the collar of my uniform up to cover my nose, I looked about us.

The village had been a prosperous one; beneath rotting, scavenged corpses, the cobbled streets were in good repair, as were the buildings around us. Kaakos had leveled the population throughout, that was more than evident.

"Fucking hells," Jem shouted, before he began to retch. Dree was crying and attempting to cover her nose at the same time.

"There are four other cities just like this one," Sherra shouted at Jem, while Armon pulled a shaking Mika to her feet. "Would you like to see them, too?"

Jem stepped backward to get away from my Queen; he had no desire to see anything else like this today.

Like Jem, I wasn't willing to go anywhere except to Secondary Camp.

Take us back, I told her. *I think they've received the message.*

Levi brought Buck to the southeast corner of Secondary Camp, where we'd taken the other three traitors.

"What's wrong with you?" Buck snapped at Jem. "You look like you've seen a ghost."

"He saw a few thousand of them," I growled at Buck. "I'm sorry I didn't take you with us; you could have seen what the enemy is up to now, as Jem did."

"The enemy is destroyed," Buck declared.

Meka strode toward Buck; Sherra held up a hand to keep anyone from stopping the woman. Meka slapped Buck across the face—hard.

"Will that happen to Az-ca?" Dree, her voice shaking, spoke for the first time since we'd returned to Secondary Camp. She was still pale and trembling after witnessing the mass death of an entire village.

"It could. Our enemy's name is Kaakos, and he's determined to kill us all," I told her. "Without Sherra, Armon and Az-ca's army fighting that evil, we'd already be dead."

"Then I am sorry," Dree hunched her shoulders and stared at her feet. "I had no idea. When Buck told us you didn't have your power and the enemy was destroyed, we joined his followers," she admitted. "I'm sorry I ever listened to the bastard."

"Any more last words?" I glanced at the other three prisoners.

"You get nothing from me," Jem mumbled. Meka merely shook her head, her eyes downcast.

"All right, then. Jem, take Dree and stand close to Buck," I instructed.

"What about Meka?" Buck whined. In a blink I shot a fireblast at Buck, rendering his body to black ash that crumbled as Jem, who stood closest, shrieked in terror.

"I have plans for you three," I pointed to Jem, Meka and Dree. "You will serve penance by cooking, cleaning and doing repairs for Garkus and Kyri in Ny-nes. Step out of line or betray anyone while you're there, they'll fry you without a second thought." I *stepped* back to the palace before I could change my mind.

Sherra

"What just happened?" Dree wiped tears from her cheeks.

"The King's justice and mercy happened," Armon said. "Be grateful you're still alive."

"I'll take them to Kyri," I offered.

"I'll come with you," Levi said.

"Thank you. But first, we'll allow these three to collect their belongings before we send them into exile."

Jem blinked in confusion as Armon *stepped* us to his cabin first.

~

Kerok

"Messengers have been sent; Armon is offering warriors and roses to retrieve any who disobey the King's summons," Hunter set a list of names in front of me. The list contained all the names of former Council members who'd been relieved of their duties by my father.

All of them were involved in the Republic of Az-ca.

"I don't want them retrieved," I said. "If they disobey the summons, my orders will be to kill on sight."

"Sounds good," Hunter agreed amiably. "I'll let Armon know."

"Send messages to all villages," I stopped Hunter before he left my study. "Tell them that clemency will be granted to all other citizens, if this group is disbanded. If any require proof of the continued existence of the enemy, we will happily leave them in one of the cities Kaakos has visited and left death behind him. They can make their own way afterward."

"I'd suggest sending a representative group first and let them see the destruction. If they still don't believe, leave them. The others can return and tell their fellow members what they've seen. I also suggest we tell them that Kaakos is collecting another army, and we are in more danger now than we ever were," Hunter advised.

"Good point. Do it and bring me the responses from the villages. I wish to see them firsthand. Send the same message to all the current Council members."

"I suggest we take the current Council to the cities Kaakos attacked," Hunter said.

"I agree," I told him after considering the wisdom in that proposal. "Shall we make that happen tomorrow? I have no desire to go back to that stench today."

"I'll see the messages delivered," Hunter walked out of my study.

Thanks, Hunt, I sent to him.

You are quite welcome, my King.

Ny-nes

Sherra

"I thought they killed you and lied to us about it," Jem told Garkus.

Garkus and Kyri looked over their new servants with a critical eye.

"I remember you," Garkus pointed at Jem. "I am in exile, just as you are, now. I am paying for my disobedience, just as you will. All three of you," Garkus crossed massive arms over his chest and glared at Jem, Meka and Dree.

"Don't let them anywhere near Soobi," Kyri dismissed all three prisoners and stalked away.

"Soobi?" Dree turned toward me, hoping for an answer.

"Soobi is working with Kyri, here in what's left of Kaakos' palace," I explained. "He destroyed it, along with all his servants before he escaped. He wants to do the same to Az-ca. Pray you never see him. If you do, you're dead. He wants to raze Az-ca and kill every Az-can he can find."

"Is that true?" Jem pointed his question at Garkus.

"It is true. We barely survived this destruction," Garkus waved an arm, indicating the state of the palace—half of which was rubble, the other half damaged in some way.

"You fought against him?" It was easy to see that Garkus was one of Jem's heroes.

"Yes. I wasn't the one who saved everyone that day, though. Perhaps someday, when your attitude improves, I'll tell you the full story of that battle."

"Levi and I have to get back," I interrupted Jem's and Garkus' conversation. "Don't let them get out of line. Make them earn their keep."

"Oh, I intend to," Garkus replied. "None of them will be allowed near Soobi. If she's harmed in any way," his eyes narrowed at Jem. "I still have my power," he said. "Neither Soobi nor any other from Ny-nes will be harmed by these three."

"Thank you, Garkus." Levi and I *stepped* back to Secondary Camp, where Armon, Caral and Misten waited for us.

~

Is it all right if I stay to have dinner at Secondary Camp? I sent to Kerok.

Of course. My appetite disappeared after I saw that village. Visit with your friends and let me know when you return.

I will.

"Will we really have *Eagle* rings?" Misten asked as we sat at Armon's usual table in the officers' mess.

"Yes. I think you'll like them," I told her, dropping a napkin in my lap. I was grateful to discuss a topic that had nothing to do with hundreds of rotting bodies left on city streets for scavengers to pick through.

"My sister asked after Dree and Meka," Caral sighed.

"They're fine in Ny-nes, and Garkus will make sure they mind their manners," Levi replied.

"I know she'll be relieved that they're still alive, but exile was a generous sentence," Caral shook her head. "If they'd just bothered to talk to my sister, they'd have known better."

"This wasn't something that would come up in regular conversations. Plus, people are allowed differing opinions," I said. "The difference comes when their opinions force them to break laws and sell out their own country. Because of Buck and his lies, they think we're living off the citizens now, who are getting nothing in return."

"So they believe we're at peace, now?" Misten sounded shocked.

"Can you imagine peacetime?" Levi's eyes lost focus. "I'd find a place near my parents, plant a garden, run errands and carry messages for my pay, that kind of thing."

"I'd like to have your parents over for dinner," Armon agreed. "I like your family. I'd like to know them better, too. I only met them once."

"I want Caral to meet my family," Misten's dimple appeared as she smiled. "I haven't seen them since I was taken away from my village."

"My village is nothing but burned and blasted rubble," I sighed. "The only family I have now is Pottles—and the people at this table."

"You have Cole, his entire village, the King, the King's heir and too many others to count who would be happy to serve as your family, Sherra," Armon reached across the table to pat my hand.

"Yes, I suppose I do," I agreed. Armon and I knew that Adahi, hidden within Hunter's body, was family to me, if you could call any dreamwalker kin.

"I'll introduce you to my family the next time we can go," Levi grinned. "They'll love you, too."

"I'd like to meet them," I said. "My mother died not long after I was born, so I have no memories of her. My father mostly ignored me from the moment a black rose was tattooed on my wrist."

"Two losses, rather than one—to him," Caral nodded. "Some people don't know how to deal with that."

"Some go so far down the wrong path it's painful to those around them," Armon said, lifting his fork to eat.

"I think that's the road my father took," I said. "Pottles raised me and taught me what I ought to know. I'm grateful for that. She never had children of her own, so she adopted me. Now she has Anari, Klete, Kyal and Laren as her children."

"See, you have even more family than you thought," Armon grinned.

"I wouldn't mind having a family—if peacetime ever happened," Levi's words were wistful.

"I didn't know you wanted children." Armon turned to his partner and lifted an eyebrow.

"It's all right, I know you don't, and we can't anyway," Levi said.

"No, that's not it at all. I'd love to have a son or daughter, but as you said, it's not possible for us."

"I think there are plenty of children living in Kyri's City right now who'd love permanent parents—parents who understand the power they hold and can show them the proper way to use it."

"The children from Ny-nes, too," Levi pointed out.

"That sounds like a dream," Armon said. "One I'd like to wish for, but we have no guarantee that any of us will survive the coming days."

"We'll hope for better times as we prepare for what we've always prepared for—war," Caral told him.

"You have the right of it, as usual," Armon told her. "Eat, now. We have plenty to do before we go to bed tonight."

Before *stepping* back to the palace, I stopped to visit with Klete. They'd had their evening meal already, so Klete and his mother, with the baby asleep in her arms, were poring over a book designed for new readers.

Klete was already helping his mother with simple words.

"Sharing," Klete tapped the book on his lap, then grinned at me.

"I read that one, too," I told him, grinning back.

You want? He sent images with his words. Two more villages had been destroyed by Kaakos, while we'd spent our day dealing with traitors.

Yes, thank you, I told him.

Dangerous, he informed me.

Too dangerous for us to help?

Yes. Too—much.

I understood that to mean that Kaakos was growing stronger. How in the first rose's name were we going to deal with him?

I have to tell the King, I said.

"Beri, you're doing very well," I said aloud. "Soon, you can teach your daughter to read."

"Yes," Beri smiled. "Teach."

"I have to go; I'll come back to visit again," I said and *stepped* away. I had news for Kerok, Hunter and Barth, and they needed it now.

Kerok

"Wine?" I poured a glass and handed it to Sherra. She'd found Barth, Hunter and me in the small dining room, having a late meal and discussing the day's events. Sherra's hand shook slightly as she accepted the glass.

What's wrong? I asked her.

Kaakos took two more villages. Klete showed me and told me that he didn't warn me beforehand because it was too dangerous for us to help.

"Bloody hell," I growled aloud. "Can Kaakos be that powerful already?"

"It's either that, or he's setting traps for us," Sherra countered.

"Damn," I muttered. "Did Klete say whether Kaakos added to his current stable of talented slaves?"

"I didn't ask," she replied. "I think I was too afraid to ask," she amended. "What if he's using a new type of perimeter divination?"

"I suppose that's possible, as he is his father's son."

"If that's true, how can we tell?" Sherra sipped her wine as she considered this new problem. "I'll have to work on it, I suppose, if for no other reason than to see if he's found a new way to trap us."

"It would be like him to do so," Hunter offered. "With a new source of power and talent to draw from, it could have been easy to accomplish. We have no idea what the levels of talent are that he's taken, or whether any of them are quite strong and resourceful."

"I'll ask Klete about that tomorrow, to see whether he knows anything," Sherra offered.

"Good. I'd like to hear what he says on the matter." I poured more wine in my glass and drank.

"I'm still afraid of what he may know about it," Sherra admitted. "Arresh has been unusually silent, too, and she is generally the first one to go whenever Kaakos hits somewhere."

"Then your dreamwalker knows better, just as Klete does," Hunter dropped his eyes. What he said made sense; Arresh appeared to know these things before Sherra did.

"I think North has accepted his fate, or become more pragmatic about it," Barth said, changing the subject. He'd seen how troubled Sherra was about our current topic.

"How so?" I asked Barth.

"He's complaining less," Barth explained, "along with eating what he's given, which is the same thing we're being served, by the way."

"The servants are probably grateful for that; I can't imagine anyone wanting to wait on someone who whines constantly," Sherra sighed.

"Marc told him if he behaved for two days in a row, he'd take him for a walk in the garden," Barth went on.

"As long as he behaves while he's there, too," I said. Sherra's mouth tightened but she didn't say anything. I wanted to ask what she was thinking. I didn't—it was probably better that way.

"You don't trust him," Hunter's eyes narrowed as he studied Sherra's reaction.

"Not even a little. All the good is sitting here at the table with us. That means all the bad is locked inside a shield in North's suite. If that doesn't frighten you, then I don't think anything will."

"He has no power," I pointed my fork at Sherra. "What can he possibly do, with Marc, Wend or another guard there to stop him before it happens?"

"I don't know, but I don't want to rule anything out at this point."

"It's always wise to be cautious," Barth said. "It wouldn't hurt to bring in more trusted guards, though; Marc and Wend have seen and heard enough of this one to last a lifetime, no doubt."

"We can give them a break, certainly," I agreed. "I'll see to it after dinner. Armon can send two pairs of warriors and roses. That should be enough for now."

"Make sure they know not to harm him; a bubble shield is all that's required," Sherra said, refusing to look at me.

"I know it well," I told her. Nobody knew better than I what would happen if North died.

~

Sherra

I watched Kerok dip his fork into the berry dessert we were served. The cursed ring he wore flashed in the lights shining above the table. Sitting on the desk in my study lay the rings Lofflin had made for me—the plain ones with no adornment, that I'd intended to use for practice. After the failure with Jubal, I considered them a lost cause.

Except now, Kerok's ring drew my attention. I'd never touched the thing, actually. Could I touch it? Would it react in some way if I did so? I'd have to convince Kerok to allow me to examine it while it rested on his finger. If there were a way to divine the construction of the spell itself, perhaps I could find a way around it.

Or move the spell into another ring.

He'll refuse to let you examine it; a part of me understood that. He'd worry it would prove dangerous—to both of us. He could be right, but I'd held spelled things before—Kaakos' gold came to mind.

First things first, I told myself. *Practice with the plain rings and see if a spell can be moved from one to another.* Perhaps a conversation or two with Cole could help formulate ideas. He and I needed to bring seawater to our distillation bubbles; we could discuss plenty of ideas while we watched our system to see whether it worked.

The other person to talk to about spells was Kyri. Maybe she knew how North's spells worked.

Particularly his blood spells.

Do you have time to talk to me tonight? I sent to her.

Of course.

Shall I bring food or wine?

Both, if you can.

I will. I'll be there in less than an hour.

"We're planning a field trip for the Council tomorrow, to one of the destroyed cities," Kerok interrupted my silent conversation. "Find one that will be suitable, where Kaakos has left no traps for us."

"I'll talk with Klete. When did you want to go?"

"Tomorrow morning."

"All right. I'll ask Cole to come tomorrow afternoon, then, so we can gather seawater and make sure our freshwater distillery works well enough."

"We'll be wrangling Council members, many of whom, no doubt, will feel quite ill after our journey tomorrow," Kerok said, regret in his words. "Otherwise, I'd like to see these first experiments. I believe this will prove to be an enormous asset for Az-ca—getting food grown with a ready water supply in hanging bubble gardens. If we weren't so distracted with Kaakos, this would be cause for celebration."

"What if we began a program for the villages that aren't near streams or lakes, to have their own distillery floating over their village," Barth suggested. "Rather than traveling miles for water, as it is in some cases, we left the distillery overhead, had regular deliveries of seawater, and a pipe or something hanging from the freshwater side, so the villagers could take water from it?"

"That sounds like a good idea; we'd have to choose one for the initial experiment," Kerok said.

"I'd say choose a village that doesn't have the Republic of Az-ca taint on it," Hunter sniffed.

"A reward?" Kerok turned to Hunter.

"I suppose you can call it that."

"Then you'll have to research the candidates," Kerok told him. "I'll look over a list if you put one together."

"I'll put one together."

"Good, that's settled," Kerok declared.

"Will we meet for breakfast tomorrow?" I asked as I rose from the table. I had to get to Ny-nes soon, or Kyri would think I wasn't coming.

"Yes," Kerok nodded. "Meet here, and we'll eat before we go to the Council chamber to collect our guests."

"They'll probably accuse you of torture after it's over," I said. "Bring something to cover your nose," I added.

"I've already prepared for that," Kerok sighed.

~

Ny-nes

Kyri

"I didn't tell him I was coming," Sherra answered my question. "Besides, he has other problems to think about. We're taking the Council to one of the cities Kaakos has destroyed tomorrow morning, so they can see for themselves that the enemy is still working against us."

"The Republic of Az-ca, eh?" I blew out a frustrated breath. "Doret told me about it earlier today. So far, Garkus is riding herd on the three former members sent here; Jem could end up being a problem unless his attitude changes."

"What an idiot," Sherra shook her head. "Don't give him any clemency. Kerok should have sent him to the poisoned lands rather than here."

"I'll let him know that I can drop him off there myself, if he fails to follow instructions."

"Do it. He's already committed treason, by violating the vows he took when he came to the army in the first place. I have no idea what he thought we were training for, if the enemy was no longer a problem."

"Some people are easily led by others, especially if the others are spouting what they wanted to hear in the first place. They show their weakness by taking the easiest way. Things are never easy, and Jem should have learned that long ago."

"Well, it's done. I hope he realizes his life hangs on a thread from now on," Sherra said. "The fool. If you think Soobi may be in danger at any time, send her to stay with Beri and Klete. She can help with the baby and be taught lessons with them."

"There's an idea. While Soobi is happy to help around here, I worry about her," I admitted. "I'll consider sending her to my village."

"Nobody has time to teach her much here, unless I'm mistaken," Sherra said. "She deserves whatever advantages we can give her."

"I agree. If she weren't already asleep, I'd send her back with you tonight."

"Then place a shield. Something about this troubles me," Sherra said.

"I'll do it. Now, what did you want to talk to me about?" I asked.

"About North's spells in those rings," she replied. "Do you know how he did it?"

"I have the words of the spells, and, as he already has kinship to Thorn in his blood, he didn't need to take any to make the spell. Besides, that spell was formed long before your Thorn was ever born."

"Too bad it didn't disintegrate with time," Sherra huffed.

"The spell wasn't activated until the King placed the ring on his hand," I explained. "It lay dormant until that happened. It's the same as being a freshly-laid spell."

"That's—good to know, I suppose."

"The words of the spell are in an ancient language—I'll write them down for you and add phonetic pronunciation," I told her. "The spell wasn't well-thought out; there's too much leeway for the spell to get snarled up, just as we've seen, with the strengths and weaknesses getting separated and going from one to the other."

"I know—I'm seeing the continuing evidence of just that," Sherra said. "While I like this Kerok, I know it's not his body beneath the disguise."

"I understand how troubling that would be. Doret says North is nothing but a bag of whining wind, now."

"I haven't seen him in two days, but I've heard the same thing. We're bringing in other guards to switch off; the ones who've been with him are sick to death of the complaining already. I have a question," Sherra switched topics.

"What is it?"

"Do the spells have to be in the language you mentioned, for them to work?"

"I don't believe so. Adahi always said that North was too full of himself. He thought he'd appear wise and learned if he used the ancient language to begin with to set his spells. As you see, they backfired."

"Good. I don't want to leave any of my experiments open to misinterpretation," Sherra wore a determined look.

"You intend to practice blood spells?"

"Not if I can do it another way. I want to find out if a spell can be redirected. Lofflin made several practice rings for me, so I can learn as much as possible about all this. I have to find a way to reverse this mess, or North could bring all of us down."

"How?" I asked, curious.

"I can't explain it—I just have this feeling that all the bad—all the deviousness—from both Kerok and North could combine and cause trouble we can't even guess at right now."

"Now you're frightening me."

"You think I'm not frightened?" Sherra sounded panicked. "One wrong move by the half we call North could kill both. Az-ca is already warring with itself; how will things go when the King dies under unexplained circumstances? Will Kaakos know if his father passes? Will he use that opportunity to attack? There are too many things that can go wrong, Kyri, and you know it."

"Yes, I do know it. I'll write the words down for you." I searched through a bureau that used to belong to Kaakos' scribe, looking for a pen to write with. "There," I handed the slip of paper to Sherra. "I hope you find a solution to this problem. If you need more help, let me know."

"I'll let you know," Sherra said and *stepped* away.

CHAPTER 14

Sherra

"Klete sent images of three villages to visit that are safe enough," I told Kerok at breakfast. "He knew we needed the information before I asked for it."

"Good. Hunter wants to go this time, rather than letting the King get away from Az-ca," Kerok didn't sound disappointed. I didn't blame him; the stench from the day before was fouler than anything I'd ever experienced.

"I think it will only take one," I said. "Armon and Misten are coming, as are Cole and Garkus. They sent mindspeak this morning, letting me know."

"I'll have Armon bring three drudges and two other pairs of warriors and roses with him; one from the *King's Eagles* and another from the regular army. It wouldn't hurt to get this information passed around quickly."

"Once, I might have warned against frightening the population," I said, allowing my shoulders to droop in resignation. "Now, that no longer holds true. Members of the Republic obviously need a wake-up call."

192

"If they'll even believe it. Some will refuse to accept a difficult truth until they die from it," Kerok snorted.

"They'll die wondering why they never saw it coming," Hunter's laugh was humorless.

"I wonder what they'd do if we disappeared—the palace and the army," I said. "Since they're fully convinced we're no longer needed."

"They'd fight among themselves, until Kaakos arrived and killed all of them," Barth said. "Then, as Hunter observed, they'd all wonder how they never saw that coming as they breathed their last."

"I still think it's a good idea to conscript some of the younger, able-bodied villagers, so they can get a taste of what war is actually like," I said.

"We could do a lottery system, drawing only a certain percentage of those able to serve from each village," Barth said. "Unless there are volunteers to fill some of the available slots. They'll receive pay, meals and housing, just as the drudges do. I think the idea has a great deal of merit."

"It could be a small percentage to begin with, and we could replace drudges and washouts who didn't want their power returned and who no longer wish to serve at one of the camps. Perhaps each officer should have a trusted citizen-soldier as an assistant, to write messages, run errands and go with them now and then, so they can see what's involved."

"Something to consider," Kerok agreed, lifting his cup of tea and drinking. "But for now, we have to gather the Council, and you have to take them to see rotting bodies." His dark eyes locked with mine. *I'm sorry you have to deal with this,* he told me in mindspeak.

It needs to be done. We have to do our best to convince them we're not freeloaders, I suppose.

I don't want to level treason charges against the general population, he replied. *That will happen if this continues unchecked. I worry that they'll become brigands, burning homes and killing anyone who disagrees with them.*

They do appear to be headed in that direction, I conceded.

"Come, let's go to the Council," Kerok rose and stretched. "The sooner you get them there, the sooner you can return."

Grumbling softly among themselves, we found the Council members gathered in the meeting chamber, waiting for our arrival.

"This shouldn't take long," Kerok raised his hand after Hunter called for quiet in the presence of the King. "You'll be transported there quickly and returned immediately, once you've seen the damage that the enemy can do."

"Where are we going?" Kull, who imagined himself the head council member, demanded to know.

"The citizens called their village M'chestr," I said. "It's far to the east of us, across the sea."

"Why should we worry about what happens so far away?" Kull insisted.

"Because Kaakos is attacking these villages, searching for those with power who live there. He takes those people, to sap their power. The rest—those without power—like you, he kills."

"What will he do with the power he takes?" Kull's closest associate, Jenner, asked.

"Attack us," Kerok snapped. The fool should have known it already. I hoped the idea penetrated what appeared to be a thick, impermeable skull.

"He got away from us in Ny-nes, when we attacked him there," Hunter said. "We took Ny-nes away from him, and he barely escaped with his life. Now, revenge against us is foremost in his mind. He will stop at nothing to destroy Az-ca, if we don't do what we can to fight back."

"What if the citizens don't believe that?" Kull spoke again. I wanted to grip his collar in my hands and throttle him, but we had worse things in store for him on this day.

"Then you'll have to tell them what you see today," Kerok growled.

"Or, failing that, we can leave you where we're going. You can decide for yourselves, once you get there."

Many Council members exchanged glances; they had no idea what Kerok meant and were now worried they wouldn't be brought back to the King's City.

"The decisions rest in your hands," I spoke for the first time. "Prepare yourselves; what you'll see won't be pretty."

Nodding to Hunter, I *stepped* him and the Council away.

Thank you for the shield, Cole sent as he and Garkus arrived at the visual coordinates I'd sent to both. Armon and Misten were already with us, in addition to the warriors, roses and drudges they'd brought with them.

Cole, Garkus and I observed as a third of the Council retched on the streets, bodies lying at their feet where they'd fallen when Kaakos killed them. In this case, he'd also blasted some of the stone buildings, making me think those with power in the city had fought back—at least for a little while. Kull and Jenner, who'd already emptied their stomachs, now held shirts over their noses and glared at us from several yards away.

'Lo? A tentative voice sounded in my head. The voice itself was a strange one, but the language was similar enough that I understood the greeting.

Who? I responded, worried that Kaakos had left a trap behind that Klete hadn't seen.

We live—lived here, he corrected. The voice was definitely male.

You survived the attack? I queried.

Only three of us. Please tell us how this is possible?

That would take longer than I can stay to explain, I replied. *Will you not show yourselves? We can talk away from the carnage here.*

We're hungry—they took all the food, he replied.

Then come forward and I'll see that you're provided for.

Three men appeared from behind a bubble shield nearby, causing the Council to gasp—those who weren't still dry heaving.

"We mean no harm," the one I'd spoken to said aloud. "We just— can't understand this," he swept an arm out at the death all around us.

"Come," I motioned him forward. "I have to touch you," I added.

"You are a diviner?" he asked. "We haven't had one in many years."

"Yes," I told him.

"Then we will allow your touch. Please hurry, we thirst, too, and there is no clean water here anywhere. He poisoned what we have before he left."

"That's close enough," Armon held up a hand as the man approached. "Sherra, are you sure?" He frowned at me.

"Yes. I think it will be all right." Reaching out, I placed my hands on the man's face. From behind a shield Kaakos hadn't seen or felt, I watched the village of M'chestr fall in Kaakos' attack.

King's Palace, Az-ca
Kerok

"At least they weren't tainted by Kaakos' blood spell," Sherra shuddered, as if the visions of the attack still troubled her.

"What about the Council?" I asked, directing my question at Hunter.

"More than half have those images—and the stench—branded on their memory," Hunter replied. "The rest—who knows whether they're convinced or not." I'm sure he referred to Kull and Jenner, specifically.

"Fools. Are our guests still eating?" I asked Armon.

"Briar is standing over them in the kitchen, making sure they eat slowly so they won't be sick from wolfing it down," Armon told me, his voice dry as paper.

"That makes sense. Sherra, did you get their names?"

"Yes. Daren, Noah and Ollie. Ollie is the one who spoke first."

"Kaakos didn't know they were there?" I asked.

"They combined their shields. At least they knew how to make them," Sherra said. "Ollie says they were the strongest, and they'd been outside the city when someone sent mindspeak, telling him the village was under attack. They returned, already shielded, and witnessed Kaakos taking those who had power and destroying the rest of the population. Some of them fought back initially, but Kaakos broke through their defenses."

"They speak our language, but with strange accents," Armon offered.

"They say the same about our speech," Sherra countered. "At least we can understand one another—for the most part."

"You found nothing in your divination that tells you they're dangerous?" I continued my questioning.

"I only found fear and confusion in them; they had no idea that anyone with Kaakos' power or desire to kill even existed until now."

"I'm sorry they had to find out this way, then," I breathed a heavy sigh.

"They're willing to work with us," Armon said. "Offered right away, when they understood we had an army. They hadn't needed one until now, and they didn't have that many with talent to begin with."

"How many talented ones did Kaakos take?"

"Roughly fifteen, at Ollie's estimation."

"Fifteen, added to who knows how many others," I shook my head. "And already he feels confident enough that he's setting traps for us in other villages."

"Is there any reason not to begin training them at Secondary Camp?" I asked Sherra.

"We can begin their training; they have no idea what a fire blast is, although their shielding is excellent."

"Armon, put them in a cabin together, and ask Levi, Misten and Caral to begin training them. Either of those three should be able to handle disobedience if it comes. Make sure you explain exactly what they're in for, before training begins."

"I will," Armon assented.

"Did you ask the Council to prepare their written reports?" I asked Hunter.

"Yes. I told them they had until tomorrow to turn them in. We'll go through them afterward and determine how effective this trip was."

"Good. Barth, how are we doing on the summons to former Council members?"

"Only a few have shown up. They're at the training camp now, where they'll be temporarily housed while the new lockup is being built."

"I can put a shield around the camp so they can't get out," Sherra offered.

"Then do it. The rest have two more days to arrive. If they fail to do so, their names will be added to a list of kill-on-sight traitors."

"I'll record the names of those who've already arrived," Hunter said and rose to leave my study.

"I'll go with you," Sherra said and followed Hunter out the door.

"More and more, I feel as if everything is spiraling out of control," I told Barth and Armon. "At least these three aren't blood-spelled by the enemy. Keep an eye on them, Armon. We don't need more betrayals than we already have."

"It will be done—discreetly, of course. One more thing, may I see the Council's reports after they're submitted? I'd like to discuss them with you, too," Armon said.

"I'll have you, Barth, Hunter and Sherra in the meeting," I said. "Keep me apprised on the progress and doings of our three guests."

"I will."

～

Sherra

Hunter stood by silently as I laid a shield around the training camp in King's City. The prisoners wouldn't be allowed outside the shield, but others could come and go to deliver food and supplies—after we made sure that the guards had done their duty and relieved the prisoners of any weapons they carried.

"I need to talk with you in private," he said. "After you and Cole finish your duties for the afternoon."

"All right. After dinner?" I turned to look at him.

"That sounds good. I'll bring wine."

"I have some things I'd like your advice on, too," I told him. "I already talked to Kyri about the spells North laid on those rings, and I intend to do some experimentation on some plain rings, to see whether the spell can be altered or redirected."

"Did she give you the words he used?"

"She did, and even wrote out how to pronounce them. I have no idea if that will help, but I do have them."

"Good. I'll consider that this afternoon, while I make notes and read any Council reports that come in early."

"What do you think we'll get in those Council reports?"

"Besides bad grammar and misspellings?"

"Besides that."

"What I'm hoping for we may not get."

"What are you hoping for?"

"Revulsion. Fear. Compassion for those less fortunate."

"You may be hoping for too much," I agreed. "I've seen little compassion in any of them, except for their own plight when they find themselves vomiting on the streets of a dead village."

"True enough," he nodded thoughtfully. "Go. Make Az-can history with your suspended distillery and subsequent hanging gardens."

"I like that description—hanging gardens," I said.

"It's borrowed, I assure you."

"Will the originator complain?"

"Not likely. I understand he died long ago."

"Then we'll borrow it for as long as we need it," I smiled at Hunter.

"I can get myself back to the palace," he told me. "Go on. Cole is waiting."

On my way, I sent to Cole and *stepped* to his village.

⌇

Kerok

I'd almost forgotten about Adahi's continued existence, so many things had happened since we'd had our last conversation.

I think it's safe to reveal yourself now, I sent to him.

No. His answer was flat and bore a finality that wouldn't be dissuaded.

At least tell me why.

Just as you have the memory of my existence, so too does your evil half. I will not make myself vulnerable to either of you.

I suppose that makes sense, but what can either of us do to you?

I am not willing to risk it to find out. If you have questions, then speak to me this way. I will answer if I can.

Then I'll put this bluntly. What do you think our chances are of surviving another attack from Kaakos?

Without more information, I cannot say. If I had knowledge of his talented slaves and what their capabilities are, perhaps I could speculate, perhaps. Otherwise, I am at a loss.

I was afraid you'd say that. Do you have any suggestions? Something we might do to combat what is coming?

Prepare your troops, in case we have to fight Kaakos with his own methods.

I suppose that's a good idea, I responded. *Any suggestions on how to deal with the Republic of Az-ca?*

I worry that a war within your own country is secretly building. This will certainly divide your army. Should that happen, I suggest taking your Eagles to fight Kaakos, and sending the rest to deal with the rebellion here.

You really think it could come to that? I've offered clemency, I began.

That would appear to be a slap in the face to those who've become convinced that the King and his army are leeches on the citizens. They'll want to destroy you if they can, and you know yourself that it will be wrong to answer their mundane attacks with power.

Yes, I do know that. Leaning back in my desk chair, I closed my eyes and pinched the bridge of my nose. *What if there were an uprising? Have we become that divided in such a short period of time?*

I didn't realize I'd passed those thoughts to Adahi, until he responded to them. *While Drenn was over the Council,* he pointed out, *there was much graft and corruption. The people were fed lies by those very Council members who were taking whatever they could from their people and their position. Now, they are lying to them again, claiming that you are corrupt and that the army is nothing more than a blight and a burden on Az-ca's citizens. You cannot fight this with your army. I am concerned that the people have listened to lies for so long that they no longer recognize the truth.*

Then I can't wait to see what reports I get from the Council after their field trip.

They will pay lip service, if they write anything. Get your diviner to see their views firsthand.

Yes, I think that would be best. I'll read their reports, and if the divination turns up something completely different, we'll have a talk.

I'd also look for connections between them and any leaders of the Republic. I dislike the notion that one night you'll wake and find the city burning, like the lockup.

Damn, I swore. You think it will come to that?

You can't fight a tidal wave of lies, Thorn. You'll drown in them before you can even get a tendril of truth to the people.

You seem to know a lot about this, I said.

Because I've seen it happen before.

When?

Just before the End-War.

∽

Sherra

"You're right—this isn't as pretty as the other inlet," I agreed. Cole and I stood on the sand near the edge of the water, looking over the area protected from bigger waves by enormous, towering rocks.

"Shall we combine shields, or do you wish to do this yourself?" Cole asked me.

"How about you take half, and I'll take half?"

"Sounds fair," he grinned at me. In the west, the sun was making its way downward, toward the horizon. We needed to get going, if we wanted to accomplish everything on our list before nightfall.

"I'll go first," I said, forming half a bubble shield over deeper water, then completing the bubble so that water below was encased inside it.

"Any seaweed?" Cole asked as I lifted the bubble above the surface.

"No seaweed, but there may be some sand in it."

"We can always bring that back, if there's no other use for it."

"Sand makes good ground cover in chicken coops," I said. "At least that's what I learned in my village when I was young."

"Then we'll offer sand to chicken keepers." Cole formed a bubble shield and did what I'd done to collect water.

"Now, it's off to our distillery," I laughed, the sound in the clear air around us making an unfamiliar noise in my own ears. I couldn't recall the last time I'd laughed out loud about anything.

"Let's go," Cole chuckled, and we *stepped* together.

Kerok

Do you have time to come see? Sherra sent.

See what?

The King's distillery at work.

Is it working?

You should see for yourself.

All right. I dropped the pile of reports on my desk and *stepped* to the bubble shields hanging outside the city's domes.

Clouds of mist were forming inside the larger of the two; someone had leveled enough fire at it to keep the seawater inside boiling for as long as necessary.

"Look, it's already dribbling into the other bubble," Sherra was so excited, she was bouncing.

Cole, nearby, appeared pleased with their efforts.

"Is that sand in the bottom?" I looked at the underside of the boiling water in the clear bubble.

"Yes, but we'll take that to chicken keepers and whoever needs or wants it. Once they have enough, we'll return the rest to the inlet." Cole replied to my question; Sherra was engrossed in watching how nature cleaned its water.

"This is going to work, isn't it?" I followed her gaze. It was a slow process, but water was already condensing and driving rivulets down the sides of the smaller bubble.

"How did we not think of this before?" I shook my head in wonder.

"It's going to be amazing," Sherra clasped her hands together. "When we get the hanging gardens in the air, we can feed so many."

I didn't disturb her excitement with the words Adahi spoke to me; there would be time for that later. Here and now, she was happy, and it was well-deserved.

Sherra

I'd like to speak with you over a glass of wine after dinner, Kerok sent to me as plates of food were set in front of us at dinner.

Of course. I'd have to let Hunter know, because he wanted to do the same thing.

I'm inviting Hunter, too. You both need to hear what I learned earlier today.

All right.

"To a successful distillery experiment," Kerok held up his glass of wine to me.

"Here, here," Barth and Hunter did the same.

"Thank you. It works so much better than I thought it might," I felt my cheeks heating in a blush. "I can't wait to get others going. The gardens, too."

"That will be a sight to behold," Barth beamed at me.

"I think so, too."

"Armon tells me the three new ones were amazed at what our troops can do, and now, more than anything, they want to attempt flight in their bubble shields." Kerok nodded at me. "They appear quite sincere and eager to learn."

"Good." A sigh escaped me before I could hold it back. I worried that Kerok would continue to see them as suspicious, when I'd found nothing of the sort in them. "Does he think he can train them to do that? If they can keep their flying bubbles in the air, someone else can fire blasts."

"That sounds reasonable," Kerok replied after considering my words for a moment. "Blasts can take more time than shields—and they already have a firm grasp on shields."

"It saved their lives," I agreed. "I love asparagus," I stared at the lovely, green spears on my plate before cutting into them. "We'll grow pears and asparagus in our hanging gardens."

Kerok made a choking sound; I turned to look at him. He was trying not to laugh.

"You know you'll have to incorporate beehives in your gardens," Hunter said, matter-of-factly.

"Oh. I hadn't thought about that."

"I think we can supply some bees for your gardens," Kerok said, the corners of his mouth still attempting to turn upward.

"Good. I don't want anything to go wrong."

"You should allow a breeze to pass through now and then, because pollination occurs that way, too," Barth said.

"We can do that; I'll adjust the shields so parts can be opened and shut."

"Like a window?" Kerok stuffed a chunk of roast in his mouth.

"Maybe like dozens of small windows," I shrugged.

"Sounds good," Hunter approved.

We discussed the gardens, future harvests and other ideas over dinner, but Kerok grew quiet at the end of the meal.

Meet me in my study, he instructed Hunter and me.

All right. I left the dining room, *stepped* to my suite to clean my teeth, then *stepped* again to Kerok's study, where Hunter was already waiting.

~

"I have news that may be difficult to hear," Kerok said as he walked into his study and shut the door. "I'm placing a privacy shield, so nobody else can listen in or barge through the door."

His expression bore pain, and I wondered why that was. Had something happened, and I wasn't aware of it? Only minutes earlier, he'd been fine.

"The first news I have is rather shocking," he said. "In recent days, I've learned that Adahi is still among us."

My eyes surely wide with shock, I turned to stare at Hunter. In his eyes, I saw what I hadn't known before; *he'd* contacted Kerok. Or North. It no longer mattered; they probably held the memory of it between them.

"The first time I heard from him, I—we—were in Ny-nes, and his words weren't complimentary," Kerok slumped onto his chair with a sigh. "Today, I reached out to ask him a question. His answer was —disturbing."

North

The promised walk in the garden wasn't during the day, but at nighttime, when everyone else was gone. They didn't want me talking or interacting with anyone else; I realized that.

My keepers weren't far away, now, as I strolled past flowers that had closed for the night, and the narrow paths were lit sparsely with artificial lamps. With so much of my time spent alone, I'd had plenty of opportunity to examine the conundrum of my life from all angles.

Plenty of time, too, to formulate a plan to free me from this place.

And from the bond that bound me to the other one. Dim light reflected off the ring I wore on my right hand. I knew the spells that created that bond; the other wasn't fully aware and had no care about them.

A weakness I intended to exploit. It only required a bit of help, from an unexpected source. If the source were agreeable, I'd provide the information I had to reform the spell and remove myself from the bond.

Once that occurred, I could *step* wherever I wanted.

Take whatever I wanted.

I'd have my power back, if all went according to plan.

Mustering my will, I sent mindspeak into the night.

Kaakos, this is King Thorn of Az-ca. I have a proposition for you, I said.

Sherra

"If you have ideas or suggestions, I'll hear them willingly," Kerok finished, after telling us of the warning he'd gotten from Adahi.

I felt numb, but it wasn't unexpected, I suppose. The time to set this right had long passed, and now we had citizens who believed whatever lies were fed to them.

"I'll think on it," Hunter agreed and rose from his chair.

"As will I," I promised, nodding to Kerok as I stood.

"After you," Hunter gestured toward the door. I followed him out of Kerok's study.

What did you want to talk to me about? I sent as we walked away together.

I've had a few—episodes—of double vision in the past few days, Hunter said.

What does that mean? Are you all right?

I am fine, Granddaughter.

Then what is it?

I believe, he hesitated for another moment before continuing. *I think, Granddaughter, that Hunter is finally waking.*

CHAPTER 15

*S*herra

He says he'll leave if Hunter regains his senses, I sent to Armon.

I understand that, but it will likely leave holes in Hunter's memory, which cannot be explained.

I know. That worries me, too.

How does Adahi feel about this?

Pragmatic.

That's easy for him; he won't have to answer to the King for keeping this secret.

I know.

Look, we have enough worries as it is. If those episodes only last for a second or two, we have time to deal with it. I hope that time is much later, after Kaakos is eliminated.

Keep that hope alive, Armon. I think it's all we have. Kerok will be furious if he finds we've kept this from him.

What about Hunter? He may be furious, too.

That's true. What a mess.

Go to bed, Sherra. Worrying about this accomplishes nothing and aids the enemy.

All right. Sorry to disturb you, Armon.
You didn't. Good-night.

Kaakos

At first, I was angry that he'd contacted me. His proposal, too, was rubbish, although it didn't surprise me that the one who fathered me would rip the Kingship from another to suit his goals. Thorn II didn't realize I wanted both dead, not just one, no matter how much he helped me. There was merit in considering it, however. If I appeared to agree to his plan, it would reveal much to me.

They'd already destroyed my source of influence, although Jubal had served his purpose well before his death—my growing power had made that connection possible. As for the rest of my plans—I only had to follow the tendrils of the rumors he'd started to learn of that success.

With a direct link to Thorn II, that connection could be employed to transport my new army to the proper place—the witch's shield over the King's City couldn't hold us back. Every day, with every new blood spell I placed, my power increased.

What delusion kept me from doing this before? Az-ca's army had been pulling power away from half its talented force for two centuries or more. In Ny-nes, I'd drained power from those who had little of it and they'd died in the process. This—pulling power from those who had real ability and the power that came with it, now rested in my hands.

Az-ca would die, and its own King would bear the ultimate responsibility for it. I laughed aloud for the first time in months.

Kerok

"One more day for them to obey the summons, and I believe that the former Council members who arrived already are the only ones who will respond to your command," Hunter dropped a list on my desk. "There have been no new arrivals since yesterday morning."

Hunter and I were up before sunrise; he'd probably had a rough night, just as I did. "In light of the information we discussed last night, I don't expect any others to come," I said, weariness coming through in my voice. I'd slept badly the night before; too many concerns invaded my dreams and turned them into nightmares.

"Is Sherra up already? I'd like to have breakfast in the garden, if possible."

"I'll send mindspeak," Hunter offered.

"Please. Then send for tea to be delivered to the table first, along with a marching draught. I think I need it."

"I'll see to it." Hunter walked out of my study to alert servants. Lifting a pen from my desk, I turned it in my fingers. How could I quell a rebellion among the people of Az-ca, when they fully believed they were in the right? The way Adahi had presented it, we were too far past a point of return.

The same thing happened before the End-War, he'd said. Was it the cause of the End-War? He didn't elaborate, and I'd been too shocked to ask the question. The next time we spoke, I hoped he'd tell me.

I'll be in the garden in a few minutes, Sherra informed me.

I'll have tea waiting. And a marching draught if you need it.

No—thank you. I'll ask Briar to brew my tea extra strong.

Did you sleep well?

Of course not.

Then take the draught.

You don't separate into two entities when you take it, she pointed out. *I tend to do just that.*

I've often wondered what that felt like, I admitted. A part of me recalled asking Adahi, far in the past, about that very thing. He hadn't explained it to my satisfaction, but then he'd never been affected by marching draughts as Sherra was.

It's confusing, Sherra replied. *One moment you're awake; the next, you're no longer completely solid and doing things you wouldn't normally consider doing.*

I find this fascinating. Have breakfast with me, my love. We'll discuss things with Barth, Doret and Armon.

What you told us last night?

Yes.

What about Adahi? Will you keep that secret?

If you think I should.

I think we should.

Then it will be so.

Thank you.

~

Sherra

Kerok hadn't slept because of the news of unrest within Az-ca. That had kept me awake for a while, until my mind turned to the other issue only Armon and I knew—that of Hunter's brief awakenings.

What if he wakes suddenly, and Adahi is forced to remove his spirit from Hunter's body? That would leave a tangle of confusion behind, with no ready explanation for it.

What would I do if that happened?

Shaking myself, I went to find a clean uniform. Perhaps it was time to let Cole know what was going on; if anyone could keep a secret, it would be that man. It would be good to have another mind working on the problem from a different angle, and he would not be judgmental in the matter.

Once I was dressed and my hair brushed and pulled back in a knot, I *stepped* from my suite to the garden.

Kerok rose from his seat at the table to smile and greet me. I was shocked when he lifted my hand and kissed the rose on my wrist as he used to. Heat formed in my belly at the gesture; it had been too long since we'd been together.

That's not Kerok's body beneath the disguise, I reminded myself. "I think it's time to change the law regarding *stepping* into or outside the palace," I pointed my thoughts away from the obvious. "Since we're all breaking it anyway. I say that residents of the palace should be permitted to do either, along with the General and the *King's Eagles*, perhaps."

"Interesting idea," Kerok nodded, gesturing for me to sit next to him. "Have Hunter write it up; I'll review the proposal."

"Thank you. I weary of breaking the King's law in that respect."

Kerok chuckled. Briar approached with a laden tray; tea was poured for us, and napkins with utensils were set out. Not long after, Barth, Hunter and the others began to arrive. Breakfast was carried out on trays and we were served quickly.

Kerok dumped the marching draught in his tea first thing and drank half the cup before stopping.

"Now," he said, lifting his fork to eat, "What shall we do about the coming civil war in Az-ca?"

Kerok

"What about Kaakos?" Armon asked immediately. "Should we ignore that coming disaster, for another that won't be nearly as bad?"

"I agree with Armon," Sherra said, her voice soft.

"As do I," Barth agreed. "Hunter informed me of your discussion. I appreciate the full night's sleep rather than knowing it before this morning."

"Suggestions, then? I don't want them burning down the King's City, or their neighbors' huts because they disagree."

"I say we split our resources," Hunter suggested.

"In what way?" He'd been thinking about this, I could tell.

"Take a small portion of your army and assign them the task," Hunter advised.

"How many warrior and rose pairs, or pods, if you will, should be required if the rebellion begins?" Armon asked. "I have an estimate, but you were commander of the army far longer than I've been."

"At least twenty," I said after considering the problem for a few moments.

"I agree. Twenty should be more than enough, and I'll make sure they won't be aligned with the rebellion before we send them out."

"I dislike the idea of citizens being blasted," Doret spoke up.

"As do I. Shields will be employed first, and traitors will be brought to the training camp for divination before sentencing," I said.

"What sort of punishment?" Barth asked.

"It depends on their crime," I answered. "If they've committed arson and treason, banishment may be a consideration. Anyone adding murder of fellow citizens to their crimes will die—either by blasting or being left in the poisoned lands."

"I see you've been thinking about this, too," Hunter nodded his approval. "Will you authorize distribution of this notice? Will you change the laws to include acts by normal citizens?"

"I think it's a necessity," Armon sat back and lifted his teacup to drink. "We've had this problem in the military before, but not with the untalented, general population."

"I'll entertain thoughts and notes on changing the laws," I said. "In the meantime, I'd like a draft of the notice to be sent to the villages on my desk by this afternoon."

"I'll take care of it," Hunter said.

"We still need to find the former Council members who disobeyed your summons," Barth said.

"You know they've gone into hiding by now," Sherra pointed out. "And probably are being protected by their followers, wherever that is."

"I can send a few into their villages to ask questions," Armon volunteered.

"Make your choices carefully—I have no idea whether they'll be met with civility or violence," I said. "I'd suggest sending the village's current Council member, but that could be a mistake."

"From here on out, everything could be a mistake," Hunter shook his head. "First, the villages were cut off from the King and the Council through Drenn's efforts, or lack thereof. Then, Merrin and Ruarke came along, many former Council members aligned with their efforts, they murdered their way through the country and lied to the population. Now, the rest of Az-ca isn't willing to listen to anything we say, particularly the truth."

"I can't banish the entire country, Hunt," I said wearily.

"I know this. Unrest is growing; I can feel it."

"They're not all aligned with this movement," Sherra said.

"How do you know?" I frowned at her.

"Arresh says so."

"That number may be growing smaller every day," Hunter turned toward Sherra.

"I know. She told me that, too."

"When did this happen?" I asked.

"Last night, when I was so tired I almost didn't notice her standing next to the bed. She'd been somewhere after I'd drifted off to sleep for a while. She let me know that she couldn't get much accomplished if I didn't at least try to sleep."

"Accomplish what?" Barth asked.

"She wouldn't tell me that. She just told me that Az-ca was close to exploding, because some thought to fuel the fires of unrest and dissatisfaction. Now that they believe the enemy is conquered, they want us out of the way."

"They think we're useless to them unless we're protecting them from an enemy?" Armon's anger was building.

"I believe we can add jealousy of your talent to the causes of this growing rebellion," Hunter observed. "We currently have two classes of citizens in Az-ca—the talented and untalented. All the talented are taken for the army, and none are left behind to work or serve in the villages. We've sent guards, but those have been temporary in the past, and they've always been isolated and viewed with suspicion."

"What would they do if we were out of the way?" I asked, feeling my own anger rising.

"They think to form their own government, which will likely be subject to as much graft and favoritism as they believe ours to be. I can't say they're wrong as far as the Council is concerned, or Drenn and his Council before them."

"Armon, send your warriors and roses to search for our traitors.

Bring them here if they're found. I wish to have Barth and Sherra do divination before sentence is passed."

"I'll see to it." Armon's mouth was drawn in a straight line of anger and determination.

"Hunter, I want you and Barth with me this morning. I wish to look into Drenn's records of the Council—if there are any."

"I'll bring what there is; he wasn't good at writing or keeping records on anything, and his scribe was often in a tavern outside the palace, drinking and complaining about Drenn."

"Is he still alive?"

"I suppose so."

"Find him. I want to talk to him."

"I'll find him," Barth said.

"I'll go to Secondary Camp to speak with the *King's Eagles*," Sherra said. "I'll ask Pottles to bring Klete, Anari and the others. We need to find Kaakos before everything blows up around us."

"Go then, and make sure I have reports regarding all ideas and decisions."

"It will be done, my King," Sherra dipped her head as she rose from the table.

Sherra

We have a problem. I received mindspeak from Kyri only moments after I arrived at Secondary Camp with Armon.

What problem? I replied.

I should have taken Soobi to stay with Beri and Klete yesterday, but I got distracted. Last night, Jem attacked her in the kitchen while she was cleaning up. Garkus killed Jem afterward, but Soobi has cuts and a broken arm.

I wanted to curse. I didn't. *Take her to your village now, and make sure she's cared for. Will you join me at Secondary Camp afterward? I want to know more about laying spells—especially blood spells.*

I'll be there in an hour.

Thank you.

"What are you thinking, Sherra?" Armon frowned at me as we stood inside his office.

"There has to be a way to deal with all of this, but I can't say what it is." Anger and frustration threatened to overwhelm me. "Pottles used to say you can't fight lies, because there are always more of those than there are truths."

"Levi's father used to tell him that a lie flies like a bird, while the truth pokes along like a turtle," Armon's laugh was grim.

"Armon, I think you should bring Levi's family here. On the Queen's orders. Give them one or two cabins. Things are starting to happen that I fail to understand. Jem attacked Soobi in Ny-nes. He cut her up and broke her arm. Garkus killed him, but this tells me that things are about to happen that we may not be expecting."

"You think Kaakos may be behind this in some way?"

"If he is, then he's found a way into Az-ca that we haven't detected, yet. If he managed that, then he's found a way to dig into the minds of the Republic and set them on a sudden path of destruction. A month ago, I wouldn't have said it was a huge worry. Now, it is."

"He can't get past your shields," Armon pointed out.

"He did it once before, when he attacked Hunter," I said. "If he's gathered enough power, and then found a way to infiltrate someone's mind," I didn't finish.

"Bloody hells," Armon swore. "Could he have started this through Jubal?"

My breath caught at Armon's words. Jubal. He'd spent his time in the lockup talking his head off and pulled Buck and the lockup physician into his web of lies.

"Yes." My shoulders sagged as the possibility became more reasonable the longer I considered it.

"What if he's found another, to take Jubal's place?" Armon asked.

"Those men from L'on-Alberr don't even speak our language," I said. "Plus, they're shielded all the time—except that probably won't keep Kaakos' powerful thoughts from ripping into their minds."

"It may not be them—they're obvious," Armon growled. "It could be anyone in Az-ca with latent mindspeaking talent, or some such.

Once he'd reached Buck, Jem and the others, he can reach anyone, talented or otherwise."

"I'll let Kyri know to sequester those two women Kerok banished," I said. "Armon, Kaakos has been three steps ahead of us since he was forced out of Ny-nes, and we may not be able to catch up in time."

"Are you saying you think the people of Az-ca who are involved in the Republic are innocent?"

"No. I think he's taken their dissatisfaction, hatred, jealousy and anger, and raised those things to their highest levels, that's all. Those basic feelings are their own."

"He's forming a mob of our own citizens to rise against us, likely knowing we won't blast them out of hand before we know their crimes."

"Exactly. Kerok let Jem, Meka and Dree live, not knowing that they could still cause trouble. A part of Kyri knew, I think, because she told Garkus to keep Jem and the others away from Soobi."

"You did a divination of Jubal before he died. Did you find anything that would indicate all this?"

"No, but Arresh shoved me out at the last. I had no idea what her concern was, then, and that troubles me now. I saw that Kaakos had infected Jubal's blood—all of it—and I knew quickly that removing a blood spell like that one was impossible. I didn't dig through his mind like I did after he first arrived."

"Then Kaakos has certainly formed these new bonds after he began taking the talented from those cities and adding their power to his own."

"Yes."

"What are we dealing with, Sherra?" Armon breathed. "We only thought he was a monster before."

"Send a message to Kerok; I have to think about this," I said. "I need to see Klete, too."

"For now, I'll hold back on sending warriors and roses to look for those miscreants. The King will decide whether we pursue them farther than this."

Kerok

"How?" I said aloud after Armon explained his conversation with Sherra. How had Kaakos done this to us? It all made sense, but it was terrifying in the extreme. A foreign entity had sent tendrils of lies into the country and wrested it away from us.

He was destroying Az-ca—one citizen at a time—with words. The only thing he hadn't done yet was set himself up as a savior, but I imagined it was because he was only interested in killing the entire country.

Hunter, I sent, *I need to see you and Barth now.*

Sherra

"Yes, you—right," Klete said with a solemn nod the moment I appeared inside Kyri's home. The boy and his family were having breakfast. Klete had taken one look at my troubled face and agreed with everything I'd come up with in the last hour.

"Sit," Beri rose and touched my arm while pulling out an empty chair at the table. "I get—tea."

Burying my head in my hands, I moaned at the current state of affairs.

Arresh had felt it; so had Adahi. He'd warned Kerok that an uprising was imminent. *Adahi, has your dreamwalker been among the villages? Arresh has, and she's kept the information from me until last night.*

I have been among the villages, granddaughter. I am meeting with the King to discuss these new developments. We will speak later.

Thank you.

Beri set a mug of tea at my elbow. Dropping my hands, I gave my thanks and lifted the cup of warm tea to my lips. The taste, flavored with honey, calmed me.

"What we do?" Klete asked, pointing from me to himself.

"I don't know yet," I told him, before drinking more tea. "I have to think about all this, sweetheart. Good tea," I lifted my mug to Beri, who smiled as she took her seat again.

"I—think on it too," Klete put his words together carefully. He was learning so fast, now. It was a small joy in a sea of chaos, in my opinion.

Kyri arrived at that moment, with Soobi right beside her.

"She can have my chair," I scooted back so Soobi, whose arm was wrapped in a sling, could sit at the table.

"I'll get her some tea," Kyri waved Beri back into her seat.

"Soobi, how are you feeling, now?" I placed a hand on her shoulder.

"All—right. Kyri heal," she whispered.

I could see the healing cuts to her face and the arm that wasn't broken. *Dree and Meka are terrified that they'll die like Jem did,* Kyri sent as she set a cup of tea in front of Soobi.

Do you think Kaakos will use women like he has the men? So far, I've only seen men leading the charge in this, although they've pulled their women into the whirlwind with them.

I can see there are new developments I haven't heard, yet, Kyri's sending was dry.

Come to Secondary Camp, and we'll explain as best we can.

"I come?" Klete asked, his eyes full of curiosity.

"Do you want to? I'm taking Anari and the boys back with me," I replied.

"I do."

"Then we'll go when you finish breakfast."

"Beri, will you see to Soobi while I'm gone?" Kyri asked.

"Yes. Care—for her."

"Thank you."

"What can we do?" Armon paced inside the officers' mess. "I don't know how to begin to combat this kind of attack."

"If we knew the one or ones he's infiltrated, it would help a lot," I said.

"In what way?"

"I'd like to think we can use his own tactics against him—sort of. If we pool the power from enough people, we may be able to use the method Barth and I developed to find things."

"You mean like the gold Kaakos and Ruarke spread among the villages?" Armon was interested in this idea.

"Yes. If we knew who was infected by Kaakos' mind, then we could wait until he was in direct contact, spring our trap and follow the thread back to where he is. I'm hoping we can kill him remotely, like using a small tube to send a blast."

"You may be talking about a very long tube," Caral shook her head.

"I'm still working this out," I told her. "If we can't send a blast, maybe we can pull him to us instead?"

"If you succeed with that, you'll have an immediate battle on your hands; one you may not win," Armon pointed out.

"I know. That's the major flaw in that plan."

"We'd still have to find the one he's connected to—or the ones, as you said."

"Only one will do, if we can find them," I said. "It should only take one."

"Do you intend to reexamine those from L'on-Alberr?"

"I will, although I don't want to go in without backup."

"I think we can arrange to augment your power before we do that," Armon nodded.

"Good. We'll try that tomorrow. I also want to examine the one who almost died. He's recovering and learning a little of our language. I doubt any of those, as Armon says, will be involved. That would be too obvious."

"Then where will you start, if that proves true?" Levi asked. "By the way, we thought it best to collect my family after dark. It may be easier on all of us that way."

"Good thinking," I agreed. "In the meantime, I'd like to pull power from as many as possible to reinforce the shields around Secondary Camp and the domes of the King's City."

"I think you can have that whenever you want. Let me know and I'll alert the troops," Armon said.

"Tonight, then, after dark. Those going for Levi's family will be excluded from the pull."

"That will be Levi, Misten, Marc and Wend," Armon decided. "In case there is trouble. Caral and I will help Sherra."

"I'll let Kerok know," I said. "Kyri, are you willing to come to the palace with me? I need someone who can speak to the injured man from L'on-Alberr. Klete, I'd like you to be there while we talk to him."

"What about us?" Laren asked. Behind him, Anari and Kyal nodded their agreement.

"Would you like to come with us?" I asked. "There may be some difficult questions and answers."

"We know," Kyal shrugged. "We've seen difficult already. Besides, we can provide support for Klete."

"All right, then. Let's go."

~

We found Jean sitting beside a window in his suite, a glass of juice on a small table nearby. Although Kyri had done as much as she could for him, his healing skin would always show signs of scarring from his burns.

He and Kyri spoke for a few moments; she was asking him how he felt, most likely.

"He wants to know your questions," Kyri turned to me.

"What does he remember about the attack?" I asked.

Kyri translated my words. Jean closed his eyes for a while, as if the recollection pained him a great deal. I realized after a few moments that it was true.

"The first he knew of the attack was the fireblast leveled in a field nearby. It caused the ground to shake and everyone ran out of their homes and businesses to see what happened."

Jean spoke again, and Kyri continued; "He says that the man appeared in the square, near where we found him after Kaakos left him for dead. He says that Kaakos drew those with talent toward him by killing everyone in the square."

"But they showed no signs of burn marks," I objected.

"Jean thinks he killed them with his mind."

"What?" I couldn't align that sort of talent with what I knew or understood.

"Sherra, he killed the people in Ny-nes like that."

"But that involved a blood spell," I argued.

"Jean," Kyri turned back to him, before asking a question of her own. He replied. She drew in a ragged breath before telling me what she'd heard.

"I asked him if anyone had turned up missing before the attack. Jean says that two families who'd gone to visit friends in another village never came back from their trip. He was considering going to the other village to ask after them when Kaakos arrived. I believe that most of the people in L'on-Alberr were related in one way or another —think about it. If there was a small population left alive after the End-War, it makes sense that they'd intermarry. If Kaakos took a handful, then he'd have a line on all the blood in the city."

"Then why not just take the talented ones and leave the rest alone?"

"Because this is Kaakos we're talking about," Kyri's voice filled with anger and emotion. "He kills for the pleasure he finds in it."

"Is Jean the only one who fought Kaakos?" I asked after digesting Kyri's words.

"The others fought, too, but Kaakos overcame them quickly. Their talent gave them some sort of shield, but eventually, they succumbed. Jean was the only one who continued to fight."

"Was he connected to the others by blood?"

Kyri turned to relay my question.

"He says that he came to L'on-Alberr three years ago."

"So not connected by blood, then." I squared my shoulders. "Shall we go talk with the six held at the training camp?"

"I'd say we need to," Kyri agreed. "Let's go. We'll get a snack for the young ones afterward."

I *stepped* us to the training camp, where the six I'd taken from L'on-

Alberr were held. "Shall I ask them what they recall of the attack?" Kyri asked me.

"Yes."

They were more than happy to speak with someone in their own language, that was evident, and there was much conversation between all of them before Kyri nodded and translated their words.

"They tell me that at first they attacked the invader, but felt themselves getting weaker and weaker as they fought. Until they were eventually pulled close enough to Kaakos for him to touch. Once he touched them, they were his and couldn't refuse his commands."

"He already had enough of a connection to them to pull their power?" That was terrifying.

"Yes," Klete, who'd come to my side, hugged my right arm to him and verified my fear.

"Is this why you didn't want us going to those other villages and cities?"

"Yes. Afraid."

"Do you think he has a connection to my blood? I don't have any blood relatives left," I argued.

"But others do," Kyri pointed out.

"Even you?"

"Perhaps not me. Or Doret. Those in the army do, however."

"That's true, I suppose, but how would he get to them?"

"They can walk outside the shields over their villages. Jubal managed to spread his lies and form connections with others in Az-ca, while Kaakos has been gathering power to him like a squirrel gathers nuts. What if blood is no longer a requirement?"

"Yes," Klete hugged my arm tighter.

"That's why you didn't want me to go."

"Yes."

"Sweetheart, what are we going to do, then?"

"Think about."

"You let me know about that, all right?"

"Yes."

CHAPTER 16

S*herra*

The bulk of the army arrived outside the domes of the King's City after nightfall. Armon had already told them what was required and reassured them that I knew where to stop in drawing power away. Already, I'd formed a giant bubble around the entire city, which included the catacombs underneath, and the water pipes to and from the sea.

With borrowed power, those shields would become so powerful that Kaakos would have difficulty getting past them to attack the city. I worried about the mind or minds that he'd invaded already, however, and whether I could keep him away from those contacts.

At Armon's nod, I began the process of pulling power from the gathered army to reinforce my shields. Secondary Camp would be less of a challenge, as it was far smaller than this.

Kerok

It's done, Sherra reported. *I'll be back after we finish Secondary Camp. I want a meeting with you and Armon, if you're able.*

I'll let him know.

Ask Cole if he's available, too.

I will.

"Are they coming?" Hunter asked. He and Barth sat in my study, discussing what we'd learned over the course of the day.

"Yes."

"Good. I hope we find a way to determine the contacts in Az-ca. This troubles me a great deal."

"I'd say that's an understatement, Hunt." Several seconds passed, while Hunter blinked rapidly. Then, his eyes unfocused before he spoke.

"Whu?" Hunter's response sounded slurred.

"Hunt?" I was on my feet as he slumped in his chair. Only the chair's arms kept him from falling off as Barth and I rushed to his side.

"Get my physician," I shouted at the guards outside my door.

"Th-Thorn?" Hunter tried to straighten himself and failed.

"Hold on, Hunt," I begged. "The physician is on the way."

❧

Sherra

"Well, that's done, for as much good as it may do," I sighed as Armon and I stood inside the huge bubble shield surrounding Secondary Camp. It was now as strong as we could make it, but if it couldn't keep Kaakos from invading minds with the power he had at his command, then we could still be lost.

Granddaughter? Adahi's voice sounded in my mind.

Adahi?

Hunter has wakened, and I have left him, Adahi informed me.

"Oh, no," I whispered. Armon heard.

"What?"

Hunter is awake, and Adahi is only a dreamwalker again, I sent.

"Do you need assistance getting to the palace?" Cole appeared at my side.

"If you wouldn't mind," I shoved hair back from my face. Too many things were happening at once, and I felt more than weary.

"I can't remember anything," Hunter croaked. Briar's eyes were wide with fear as she set a tray on a table inside Hunter's suite.

"We were just talking, Hunt—in my study," Kerok sat on the side of Hunter's bed, concerned for his heir.

"I—only remember that you said something to me, I don't know what it was," Hunter's hands trembled as a mug of tea was given to him.

Adahi's exercising of the body will eliminate the need for regaining his physical strength, Armon informed me. *The mind will take longer to mend, although the physical activity may have aided the brain's recovery.*

I know. At least we have Hunter back.

At a dangerous point in our history, Armon grimly reminded me. *Ever since you destroyed his army and the bombs he sent to eliminate us, Kaakos has been working to destroy us from the inside out.*

Drenn had a hand in this too, as did Merrin. Corruption from the inside, meet corruption from the outside, I responded.

True, and an uncomfortable aggravation to admit, Armon agreed.

"We'll bring you up to speed, Hunter," I said aloud. "Welcome back."

Kerok

"There's nothing physically wrong with him," Collin replied to my question. I'd asked my recently-appointed Royal Physician to join me in my study after we left Hunter's suite.

"Mentally?" I asked.

"There's evidence of past trauma, but we knew about that already. I'm unsure as to the cause of this episode—or the memory loss."

"He may complain, but for the following week or two, I'd like you to examine him frequently, just to make sure."

"Of course. I was thinking the same. Hunter smiled at the Queen when she said *welcome back*, it took no effort and both sides of his mouth were symmetrical. This leads me to believe he has full control of his body and it wasn't a stroke."

"How quickly will he be able to go back to work?" I asked. "I depend upon him so much."

"Whenever he feels up to it, although I wouldn't tax his brain too much—the memory loss may be more than frustrating to him until he catches up."

"Hunter is my best advisor," I sighed. "This is a hard blow in troubling times."

"I've been hearing things from the staff. They're worried."

"I can't blame them."

"Is there a reason for the secrecy? They understand that there are some citizens who are working against the Crown, but they don't know how bad it really is. That causes rumors to run rampant."

"Do you think it's a good idea to tell them that the enemy has infiltrated citizen's minds—either through their neighbors or those ex-Council members who've started the Republic of Az-ca? The enemy is selling them lies as the truth, and we don't have a way to combat this."

"It's that bad?" Collin breathed.

"It appears so. This has hit us hard, as it wasn't apparent until recently. It's enough to make most people either harden their convictions or question their sanity."

"And it won't be a good thing to tell the servants, because they'll start looking at those around them with suspicion," Collin guessed.

"Yes. Exactly that. We have good people here at the palace. I don't want this disease introduced artificially."

"I fully understand," Collin agreed. "If only there were a way to keep them all safe."

"Sherra has employed the power of the entire army to strengthen the shields around all the domes of the city," I explained. "This keeps them as safe as we can make anyone in Az-ca."

"It's sad that it has come to this," Collin shook his head. "Thank you for speaking with me. I'll make sure Hunter is in good health as he recalls his memories."

"Send regular reports to me," I said, walking him to the door. "We all need sleep, and I doubt anyone will rest easy tonight."

～

Sherra

Are you awake? Kerok's voice interrupted my thoughts.

Yes.

May I talk with you for a little while?

Where?

I'll come to you.

All right. There's something I need to tell you anyway.

What's that?

When you get here, I held him off. Now that Hunter was awake and seemingly himself, there wasn't any need for the subterfuge. It was right and fair that I tell Kerok the truth.

I'll bring wine, he said. Moments later, he appeared inside my suite, two wineglasses hanging from his fingers and a bottle in the other hand.

I watched him open the bottle with practiced ease from years of experience. Once the wine was poured, he handed a glass to me and sat on the chair opposite my small table at the window. "What do you have to tell me?" he asked.

"It may make you angry, but I had valid reasons for holding the information back," I said. "Thank you for the wine; maybe it will make this easier for both of us." Lifting my glass, I drank a generous swallow before speaking again.

"I know what happened to Hunter," I said.

"Did you do a divination after I left?" Kerok asked, sipping from his glass.

"No. I didn't need to," I sighed.

"Then what happened?"

"Adahi left him," I said.

"What? I don't understand what you mean." His face bore a puzzled expression.

"It means that when Hunter first awoke, it wasn't his awakening. It was Adahi's. Somehow, Adahi's dreamwalker had remained inside Hunter's body after Kaakos almost killed us, and he ah, woke first."

Kerok had gone still, his fingers frozen on the stem of his wineglass. "That's—are you sure?" Carefully, he set the glass down on the table and blinked at me in confusion.

"Yes, I'm sure. At the time, I was afraid to tell you, because we were terrified that Hunter was truly gone, and you were in such a bad place then that it could have pushed you over a precipice."

"Then how—where?" Kerok tossed a hand in the air, still struggling to understand.

"Hunter is back; you witnessed his awakening. Adahi is where he was before all this happened—wherever his dreamwalker decides to go, as invisible as the wind unless he wishes to be seen."

"May the first King have mercy," Kerok breathed and passed a hand over his face. "Thank you," he added after a moment.

"Huh?" I couldn't understand why he'd be thanking me for any part of this. He should be angry, instead, that we'd kept this from him.

"I'm grateful that the knowledge and the wise counsel hasn't disappeared," Kerok dropped his hand to lock eyes with mine. "Hunter—he seems himself, but all those memories are gone. Will Adahi come back to advise us again—at least until Hunter catches up?"

"I think so—if you ask him."

"No wonder he wouldn't tell me where he was or who else knew about his existence," Kerok lifted his wineglass again. "Who did know —besides you? He told me there were two."

"I don't want to get anyone else in trouble," I stated flatly. "I made this decision; he merely bowed to it."

"Who? Barth?"

"No. Armon."

Kerok sagged in his chair. "Barth would have told Doret. Armon can keep a secret until the end of days."

"He is a worthy commander of the army," I said. "And a trusted friend."

"To trusted friends," Kerok lifted his wineglass.

"Trusted friends," I agreed, and tapped my glass against his. Before I could stop him, he'd risen from his chair to kiss me over the small table. What happened afterward I couldn't have stopped with all the army's might behind me, nor did I want to.

I woke to someone pounding on my door, my heart kicked into a painful gallop and I *stepped* to the door before I recalled that I wasn't wearing anything.

"What is it?" I cracked the door open to peer out carefully, my heart still pounding too quickly to draw even breaths.

Briar stood outside my door, fear clouding her features. "The King isn't in his suite," she sounded almost as breathless as I did.

"I'm here," Kerok called out from the bed. Relief flooded Briar's eyes. "Thank the stars," she whispered. "I'll bring breakfast here if you want it."

"We want it," Kerok said.

"I'll see to it." Briar turned and walked away quickly. I shut the door and leaned against it, still trying to get my heart to beat in a normal rhythm.

Kerok had the nerve to laugh.

"Ass," I flung his shirt at him. "I'm going to clean up."

He was still laughing when I slammed the bathroom door in indignation.

Kerok

"Hunt, I didn't expect you to be up and about," I told him when he walked into my study after breakfast.

"I feel restless," he said. "I questioned Barth when he joined me for breakfast, and then I went through the pile of notes on my desk. I've been busy, even if I can't remember it."

"I'm just grateful you're here. Could have been fatal," I told him. "Pull up a chair and ask me anything you want."

"About North," he said promptly.

"What do you know already?"

"He took your power? You're switched? I don't understand any of this."

"Hunt, this is going to sound strange—as in nobody could dream of this strange," I prefaced my explanation. "I suppose I ought to start with the attack on Ny-nes, first."

~

Sherra

"I told him," I stood inside Armon's office at Secondary Camp. "He was strangely accepting of it—relieved, actually."

"Thank the first warrior," Armon breathed. "I had visions of a court martial, or worse."

"It would have been worse if he'd known it before the switch happened."

"True enough. Anything new on how else to combat Kaakos and the civil war in Az-ca? By the way, Levi's family is here—we gave them two empty cabins side-by-side. They were worried and had no way of getting private messages out of their village. It appears that the Republic has taken the tactic of demanding all messages before they're given to the messengers. They're read before being sent out, and anyone who references the Republic, unless it's going to another member of the Republic, are forbidden to send messages."

"They're cutting off communications?"

"Yes. Levi asked me to invite you to dinner tonight, so you can meet them."

"I'd like to ask questions, if they're willing."

"They'll tell you whatever you want to know, but their knowledge is confined to their village."

"I understand. I'll let Kerok know, in case he wants to come."

"I think he'll want to come," Armon agreed. "I have to tell you, something is coming."

"Are you getting uneasy, like Kerok used to, when the enemy was up in arms against us and preparing to strike?"

"I suppose that must be it, although I never felt it before."

"I feel it, too. In fact, I think I'll pay a visit to Klete this morning. He may know something. It's like it suddenly got ramped up, didn't it?"

"Yes. I was about to make the same observation."

"This is frightening. If I learn anything, I'll let you know. I may ask Cole to meet me in Kyri's City."

"Good. I'll see you tonight at dinner."

"Thank you." I *stepped* to Kyri's City.

Cole met me on the mosaic rose image outside the city, and together we walked to Kyri's home close by. The door was opened by Klete before we arrived; he was expecting us.

"Come," he took both our hands and led us inside. Beri had already made tea for us; another indication that we were expected.

"What's going on, sweetheart?" I asked Klete.

"Move. Here." He pointed in a circle. "There." He pointed at Cole.

At first, I didn't understand what he meant, until the sudden realization made me draw in a breath. "He knows, doesn't he?" I gasped.

"He know," Klete bobbed his head. "Danger."

"What?" Cole was concerned.

"We have to move Kyri's City—and your village, Cole. Kaakos knows where they are."

Cole rose from his seat in a blur. "Where?" He included Klete in his question.

"Camp," Klete pointed at Cole. "City," he circled his hand again.

"Do they have time to gather their things?" I spoke in a hushed voice, as if Kaakos could hear me speaking.

"Little," Klete held up his thumb and forefinger, which were very close together.

Kyri, I sent, *we have to send the people in your city to Az-ca, and we have an hour to get them ready to go. Klete says Kaakos knows where they are. Cole's village, too.*

I'm coming. Take Klete and his family with you. Send the message to Cole's village and tell them to get out now.

Cole is here with me. He'll carry the message. I'll send his people to Secondary Camp. Your city needs to relocate to the King's City. There's enough room at the King's City training camp to house them, I think. I hope this is temporary, too.

As do I. Make your preparations; I'm on my way.

"I'll take you to the palace," I told Klete. "Beri, do you need help gathering your things? Do you need anything else for the baby?"

"I fine—ready now," she nodded toward Klete. Lifting the baby, who was doing her best to stand by holding onto her mother's leg, Beri nodded to me.

"You'll tell Armon we're coming?" Cole asked before stepping away.

"Of course. Hurry, Cole, I'm beginning to feel more uneasy with each passing minute."

"I'll hurry." He *stepped* to his village, while Klete gripped my hand. "Go," he said.

I went.

~

Kerok

"Those villages have shields, but not like the ones we have around the King's City or Secondary Camp," Sherra said. "Kaakos can probably destroy everything there if he wants."

She sounded more than upset; Klete, who sat beside her in my study, nodded at her words.

Beri and the baby had been taken to an empty suite by Briar, who was more than happy to play with the baby.

"How did Kaakos get this information?" I asked. "I thought both those places were hidden from all but a very few."

"Someone must have leaked the information," Adahi appeared behind Sherra's chair and placed a hand on her shoulder.

"Who, then?" I demanded. "Are the supplies sufficient in Secondary Camp to provide for them?"

"Armon says they'll be fine for a few weeks, although dried beef and such isn't his favorite food," Sherra told me.

"I hope it doesn't come to that," I responded. "How long has it been since you sounded the alarm?"

"Not more than an hour; we went to Armon, first, and then here."

We're at the training camp, Kyri sent to Sherra and me.

"Kyri's people just arrived," I said for Adahi's benefit.

"She included me in her mindspeak," Adahi said.

"Ask her and Cole to meet us here," I told Sherra. Sherra relayed the message; Cole arrived first, Kyri moments later.

Cole dipped his head to me, first, then stiffened. Klete grabbed Sherra's arm as if it were a lifeline.

"Cole's village has just been destroyed," Adahi rumbled.

Sherra

"So. We are faced with an imminent attack, no doubt, and someone has given secrets to the enemy," Kerok paced inside his office while the rest of us watched. Armon, Barth, Hunter and Pottles had joined us; I'd asked Klete if he wanted to stay. He opted to go to his mother's suite.

Kyri hadn't spoken since she'd felt her city die far in the north. Cole was grim-faced and as angry as I'd ever seen him.

"Do you think he'll go to Ny-nes?" I hesitated before asking Kyri the question.

"I don't know," she tossed out a hand.

"I know he's been exiled, but tell Garkus to come back here, now," I said.

"Yes," Kerok agreed. "We don't want another talented warrior caught by that evil and used against us."

Bare moments later, Garkus appeared in Kerok's study, making the room seem overfull by his presence.

"I left Dree and Meka at the servants' entrance," Garkus said. "They were the only ones who didn't have another place to go. I sent all the others away from the palace."

"None of us may be able to hide from that monster any longer," Kyri's sigh was mournful.

"The question still remains, though—did someone tell Kaakos how to find us?" Cole asked.

"The only ones who know are trustworthy, and most are in this room," Kyri answered.

"Let's make a list," Hunter suggested. "Thorn, do you have paper and a pen?"

Kerok opened a desk drawer and pulled out both, handing them to Kyri. "Leave none out; be thorough," Hunter instructed as Kyri began to write.

Kerok and Hunter stood behind Kyri's chair, watching her put pen to paper, naming all who'd known where to find her city, or knew of it at all. She began by listing all those from her city; as it turned out, there were fewer than two hundred, including the children from Az-ca.

I ordered tea and something to eat while the list grew. The last names to be added to the list were the people inside Kerok's study.

Except for one. The very last name Kyri wrote.

North.

CHAPTER 17

*S*herra

"He hates Kaakos as much or more than anyone inside this room," Kyri argued.

"That was before," I pointed out. "After the separation took place, can you say that with absolute certainty?"

"I can't," she raised her hands in exasperated surrender. "What can we do about it, anyway? We can't harm him, for obvious reasons. We can't accuse him—if he is communicating with Kaakos, then that will tell him we've figured this out, when we're not prepared for the onslaught that may arrive. If we banish North, either of those things is a possibility, and we're where we were at the beginning, only with a dead King."

"That is unacceptable to me. We will not place the King in danger," I snapped. "We have to find another way to deal with this—one Kaakos won't expect. Bloody, flaming hells, I wish there were a way to tie North and Kaakos together with those fucking rings instead of Kerok and North. Fuck North and his fucking blood spell."

"You know the blood is connected—mine to his," Kerok growled. "The ring that cannot be removed makes the spell unbreakable—because of the blood connection."

"You hold those memories, do you not?" Adahi asked.

"I do. I see the recollection of it, as if it were a dream long past."

"And you recall how it was done?"

"I do, for as much good as it does us. Sherra says that all of Jubal's blood was affected, and the blood would have to be removed to remove the spell."

"Also not an option," I said.

"How much time do we have, you think, before Kaakos comes calling? If North is his connection, Kaakos can employ the power he now has to flow straight through the bloodline that binds them and pass in this way through the shield surrounding the King's City." Adahi pointed out what I'd been too afraid to consider; that North was leaving us open and vulnerable to Kaakos' attack.

It didn't matter whether North was in his own body or Kerok's; both bore a blood relationship with the bastard, although one was closer than the other.

"Once he gets here, he can destroy the city with what he's gathered. He won't even have to think about it; it will all be blown to bits in seconds," Kyri wiped tears away. I understood those weren't tears for the King's City, but for her own, already lost to Kaakos' hate and anger.

"Should we empty the city?" Hunter asked Kerok.

"We need enough time to think of a response to this threat, and we may not have that," I said. "Barring that, we need deception and a massive illusion."

"What are you talking about?" Kerok demanded.

"We need to hide," I told him plainly. "Until we can come up with a way to deal with this."

"What do we do with North? As long as he's with us, he can lead Kaakos straight to us."

"I think I may have a solution—at least a temporary one," I said. "Yes, it's worrisome, and Kerok's life will be in danger, but he's already in danger, as are all of us."

"Let's hear this, and then we'll decide," Kerok said.

"First, I'll need to close off and sever the pipes that go to and from the sea to the King's City."

"Granddaughter, are you suggesting we move the entire city?" Adahi asked.

"And Secondary Camp. It may be the only way," I replied.

Kerok

"North will still be a problem, no matter where you place him in a bubble shield," Armon said. "If Kaakos doesn't know already how you two are connected, it won't take much to figure it out."

"There's no chance that he'll let either of you live when he does attack—he wants to raze Az-ca to its bedrock," Kyri huffed.

Sherra had gone with Cole, Adahi and Doret to the kitchens to have a short meal with Anari, Klete and the boys. Adahi wouldn't eat, but he could distract the young ones. Impending doom had left a sour pit inside my stomach and I wasn't hungry. Armon, Kyri, Barth and Hunter had stayed with me for further discussion.

"If the worst comes, I hope you know to sacrifice both of us," I said, meaning North and myself.

"I believe your Rose Queen said that was unacceptable," Hunter said, finality in his voice. "If Az-ca falls, we fall together."

"Kyri, your people don't have to stay here, waiting for doom to fall," I turned to her. "Sherra will allow you and Cole to take your people elsewhere, to save their lives."

"Were you listening to your Queen, Thorn? I believe Sherra is right. If there is a way to pool our strength and remove the domes of the King's City, perhaps we should consider it. If it takes separating North to remove Kaakos' connection to the city, then do it."

"You're all dancing around the basic truth in this," I said. "Beneath this disguise I wear is North's body. Beneath the disguise North wears is the King's body. Does Kaakos not have a connection to both of us?"

"It doesn't matter what body or disguise you wear," Hunter said in the ensuing silence. "Your mind and your words make you King of Az-ca."

"But what if I still draw Kaakos like a moth to flame? The blood in these veins is closer to his than the blood North holds."

"I don't know how to change any of that, no matter which body you're in," Kyri shook her head. "Please, allow Sherra to move the city and Secondary Camp."

"Where? Where should she move it?" Anger and frustration boiled inside me. I wondered if North could feel it, or whether we'd been separated completely after the switch.

"How about moving it nowhere?" Sherra had returned and now stood just inside the doorway, after *stepping* to my study.

"What the hell does that mean?" I asked wearily.

"We can float the city—and Secondary Camp, Kerok. You remember your lessons, don't you? That it's more than difficult to destroy a moving target?"

"What about the villages left behind?" I demanded.

"Mirror shields," Sherra shrugged. "I think Kaakos will be focused on finding us, first. We have to stay ahead and out of reach if we can."

"Sherra's right," Kyri rose and nodded at me. "He can always come back to destroy Az-ca. If he doesn't know where we are, he won't know what we're planning, and that will worry him. We have to be eliminated first," Kyri's voice was growing stronger as she recognized the merit in Sherra's idea. "Both the King's City and Secondary Camp. How much power will it take, and how quickly can we pull them into the air and set them on a moving course?" Kyri asked Sherra.

"I can have the troops ready to lend power any time," Armon began.

"Cole and his people will help," Sherra said. "The question remains; what should we do with North?"

"I have an idea," Adahi appeared beside Sherra. "We should get the bubbles into the air, first, and make Kaakos chase after us."

"I suppose you discussed this over dinner?" I frowned at Sherra and Adahi.

"In mindspeak; we didn't wish to alarm the servants," Adahi replied. "The children participated, and they agreed with Sherra."

"These aren't ordinary children," Kyri pointed out. "I believe Klete would object if the idea wasn't sound."

"Klete says we need to go soon," Anari arrived, sounding breathless.

"Armon, prepare your troops. We take to the skies," I said.

Sherra

"He's still inside a bubble shield within his rooms; his view won't change and he won't know that we've done anything," I said as Adahi and I moved toward North's suite.

"Then I will render him unconscious, once we are in the air and moving."

"What is this idea of yours?" I asked.

"One that you will have to execute. If it works, then we may be able to remove or confuse the spell North set. If it doesn't, we are no worse off than we were before."

We stopped outside North's suite. Adahi smiled and tucked loose hair behind my ear. "Your blood to mine, isn't that what Kaakos said?"

"That's what he said."

"Bears thinking about, doesn't it?" Adahi walked through North's door. *Go raise the domes*, he sent. *I'll deal with North.*

I *stepped* away.

Kerok

"I'm not joking. Send all of them to the nearest village and leave them there."

"What if they wish to argue?" Hunter asked. "What am I saying?" He pinched the bridge of his nose. "They're the Council, of course they'll argue."

"There's no time to listen to their claptrap. Tell them Kaakos is coming, and he intends to destroy the city. That should motivate them."

"Claptrap? That's something I haven't heard you use before," Hunter blinked at me.

"Stop worrying about metaphors and get things moving," I ordered.

"I have two-thirds of the army in your gardens," Armon appeared as Hunter walked out of my study. "Including Cole's people. The other third, with Caral and Levi in charge, are still in Secondary Camp. We're prepared to raise the bubble shields on your command."

King, I received a message directly from Klete. *Go now.*

"Thorn, the hair on the back of my neck is rising," Armon hissed.

"Mine, too. Get us in the air. Now."

❧

Sherra

I'd barely placed a shield around both ends of the severed pipes to and from the city before Kerok ordered us into the air. Swiftly connecting to the troops massed in the King's garden, we pooled our strength and lifted together.

Fly, I sent to all of them, once we were high enough. *Fly swiftly*. We set the enormous bubble shield in motion, traveling toward the east as the massive cavern that once held the King's City disappeared behind us.

We're in the air and following, Caral reported from Secondary Camp. *Sherra*, she sent only to me, *Kaakos just destroyed the crater we left behind*.

How long could we stay ahead of him? Would we exhaust our troops and become vulnerable to Kaakos at the end of it?

Time to find out what Adahi meant when he'd repeated Kaakos' spell; *your blood to mine.*

❧

Kerok

"If we keep traveling in a straight line, we'll be an easier target," I told Armon. "If we shift course now and then, it will be more difficult to fire blasts at us."

"I'll put us on a zig-zag course," Armon agreed and sent instructions to Caral and Sherra. Sherra could send the message to all troops; Caral could provide a connection with Levi in the flying version of Secondary Camp.

"It's too bad the King's City is so massive, that we can't see the planet flying by," I shook my head. "All we can see is the sky overhead and how it's changing."

"We can *step* to the outer domes," Armon suggested. "If you wish to see it."

"How long do you think we can keep this up before we reach exhaustion?" That was the real question plaguing my mind.

"Once we were in motion, I divided the troops into thirds in both cases. One third at a time can keep the shield moving while the others eat and rest. Shifts will change, with fresh troops coming on duty. As long as the food and water hold out, we can stay aloft."

"Good thinking," I patted Armon's shoulder. "Exceptional thinking," I amended.

Sherra

"I didn't leave the distillery behind; it's half full of fresh water," I told Kerok. He and Armon came to find me after speaking to supervisors in the outermost domes. They now understood that crops and livestock needed water, and the city was no longer connected to a ready supply.

"We need more of them," Kerok told me. "Perhaps several, for the farms alone."

"I'll find Cole," I said.

"Can you pull seawater in, rather than going to collect it?" Kerok gripped my arm.

"I think so, although we'll have the issues of kelp, fish and sand to deal with."

"I'd rather deal with those things than allow you outside this shield," Kerok breathed.

"Cole will help me," I said. "We'll have more distilleries set up in no time." I didn't tell Kerok that I needed time alone with Adahi, so I could hear his plan. If we had enough food and water to supply the city, and could rotate the troops needed to keep the bubble shields flying, then perhaps we'd have more time to deal with the issue of North's drawing Kaakos to us.

Kaakos attack, Klete sent images to me. The hole we'd left behind after removing the King's City had just been obliterated. I'm sure all of Az-ca felt the massive blast—how could they not?

Soon enough, Kaakos would be flying after us, with murder on his mind. Would the Republic of Az-ca now believe that the enemy wasn't dead, or was it too late for all of us?

∼

Kaakos

The connection was traveling away from me; I could feel it. Since it was moving, I couldn't get a lock on it to *step* there.

My army of ninety-two milled around me as I stood on the edge of the massive, blasted crater where the King's City used to be.

They'd moved the entire thing. Secondary Camp, too. This turn of events infuriated me. I hadn't attempted to fly a bubble shield before; my army was drained and needed to rest and eat. Well, I had those I'd connected with, through Jubal and those he'd pulled into my clutches.

They would serve me and my army, or they'd die. Then, I'd perfect the art of flying bubble shields and I'd go after them, using my army to provide needed power.

"We're moving," I snapped at my minions. Heads jerked up and all turned toward me. Using power that I pulled away from them, I *stepped* us toward the nearest collaborators in the Republic of Az-ca.

Kull

"Your lies have come to visit," Shon hissed as he carried a tray filled with plates of food toward those who'd barged into the village Headman's house, where we'd gathered to discuss the Republic's next moves.

We'd felt an earthquake; it shook the entire village for a few seconds before subsiding. Then, *he* came.

Kaakos, who introduced himself as Supreme Leader of the Republic of Az-ca, had come to find us. Jenner attempted to argue; Jenner was now a pile of ash on the stone floor. We were forced to step through Jenner's ashes to deliver food to Kaakos and his foreign-speakers.

Kaakos' army spilled onto every chair and empty floor space, then out the door, onto the porch and some even sat on the ground while we emptied every home in the village of food to serve them.

"There's nothing left of the King's City and Secondary Camp except massive holes in the ground, so don't threaten me with the King's army," Kaakos shouted at the Headman's daughter across the room, before firing a blast at her and reducing her to cinders.

"Is this what your vision of the future showed you?" Ban, the Headman, choked on his grief as he rushed past me toward the door.

It wasn't supposed to be like this. The people should be in charge of their future—the people who supported the Republic of Az-ca. Not some powerful assassin who named himself our Supreme Leader.

"This is the enemy from Ny-nes," Shon was back and shoving a plate of precious berry tarts into my hands. "Serve him yourself, bootlicker."

Sherra

"Klete says Kaakos is still in Az-ca," I told Kerok as we stood in one of the outermost domes. Cole and I had set up five water distilleries in the five largest farming domes, to provide fresh water.

Currently, the seawater bubble shields were boiling, and fresh water was condensing into the smaller bubbles connected to them. "We'll have to do this round the clock to build up a reservoir of water that all the farming domes can use," I added. "Later, we'll put more distilleries in the main dome, to supply the city. Cole thinks we can connect those to the pipes we severed, so it can be business as usual."

"We won't have to go through the filters—we can hook them directly to the pumps," Kerok pointed out.

"You're right," I agreed. "This way, when you turn on a faucet, you'll get water. We set up another bubble and hooked it up to the waste pipes. That can be disengaged periodically and dumped somewhere."

"How long will it take to fill?"

"Probably two weeks."

"Reasonable. We could all be dead before two weeks pass. We'll let Kaakos deal with the mess." He moved toward me; pulled me against him and wrapped his arms tightly about me.

"We'll get through this," I mumbled against his shoulder.

"I hope you're right."

～

Az-ca

  Kull

"Take this message to as many villages as you can. He'll empty this one fast enough, and come for their food and daughters next," Ban hissed at the three men he'd chosen. *Men who'd refused to join the Republic.* We'd learned the hard way that any member of the Republic was now tied in some way to Kaakos, and he'd kill us if we attempted to escape.

"Will the King's army not come to help?" One of the men sounded terrified.

"They're dead," I snapped at him. "Kaakos said he destroyed them.

This is our life from now on, unless you warn the other villages so they can escape."

"Go now. We may not be able to stand against this enemy, but we have to try," Ban patted the man's shoulder. "I'm sorry for the mistreatment, Adem. I didn't know what I was doing."

"For as much good as an apology does us now," another man hissed. "I'll go, but it'll be to save those I can, and not because you asked." He took off at a dead run into the night. Adem and the third man followed quickly.

"Swallow your pride and admit you were wrong. Extremely wrong," Ban hissed at me and stalked away, his boots crunching on the loose, rocky soil beneath our feet.

"Difficult, isn't it, admitting you were wrong." The voice at my ear made me jump and stifle a shout.

Jerking around, I saw what looked like a man, but he was —transparent.

"I'm not a ghost. Not specifically—although you'd consider me just as dead as Kaakos does."

"Who?" I took a step backward from the spirit or whatever he was.

"That's not important. I can't keep Kaakos from killing you or anyone else in this village; he's grown too strong."

"Then why are you here?"

"I just wanted to rub your mistake in your face, and tell you that all the subsequent deaths at Kaakos' hands are charged to the Republic of Az-ca. For centuries, the Kings of Az-ca and their armies have kept that monster away from you and your ancestors. You've delivered the entire country to Kaakos by tearing it apart from the inside. Pleasant dreams, Kull."

He evaporated into the night, leaving me shaking and feeling ill.

Sherra

"I can give you something to help you sleep," Collin offered. It sounded tempting; I was exhausted but too terrified to sleep.

"Granddaughter, it would be a good thing if you accepted the help," Adahi appeared inside my suite. Kerok had *stepped* to Secondary Camp with Armon, to speak with Levi and Caral. He'd told me to get some rest, so I could take over and allow him to sleep later.

His decision was sound, but too many things whirled through my brain, and sudden death for all of us was at the top of that list.

"But," I argued with Adahi.

"I need to speak with Arresh," Adahi said. "Allow me this, Granddaughter."

"Then give me a marching draught," I turned to Collin.

"That's not," he sputtered.

"It works for her," Adahi confirmed. "Bring it quickly. Time grows short."

Collin was back in less than ten minutes, with a cup of tea and a marching draught. "Here goes," I dumped the powder into the tea, stirred it with the spoon provided and drank it down.

"Lie down; Collin will watch over you," Adahi led me toward the bed. "See that no one disturbs her," Adahi told the Royal Physician.

"I'll see to it," Collin agreed.

I laid back on the bed; Adahi covered me with a blanket. "Let your body rest," he told me, and everything went black.

Arresh

"The time has come, hasn't it?" I studied Adahi's face. Lines were drawn deeper than I could recall as we'd worked together throughout Az-ca and beyond.

Each of us could pinpoint those who hadn't followed the Republic with sufficient accuracy. Adahi would be the one to draw them away, however. I had another duty to perform.

One that Adahi couldn't.

"Pull power from the sleeping troops when you need it," I told him before he disappeared. He nodded and faded away from Sherra's suite.

Collin, his eyes wide, watched our exchange from his chair in the corner. "Physician, one day, if you live, I want you to record what you have seen and heard."

He didn't speak; he merely nodded.

"Good. I will return soon. This is of the utmost importance; guard Sherra with your life and see she is not awakened."

With that warning, I disappeared as Adahi did, although our errands were vastly different. He was headed to Az-ca; my first destination was L'on-Alberr.

Kerok

"Sherra and Klete are asleep, but they think Kaakos will rest and feed his troops in Az-ca, until he masters flying bubble shields and comes after us. That could take a day or three days, we have no way of knowing. As long as North is with us, he has a connection to follow. What we need is a battle plan, in case he's forced to fight us rather than blasting us out of the air."

"Then we'll move Secondary Camp behind the city, to prepare for Kaakos' arrival. Do you want one battle pod or several?" Armon asked.

"He'll have one pod, because he'll have to direct it; I don't believe for one minute that he'll leave any of his army in charge of their senses," Caral sniffed.

"Good point, and I agree," Armon said. "I think we can be more effective with several pods, all attacking him from different directions. It could give the city time to escape if we can hold Kaakos back."

"If we scatter the citizens currently inside the domes, we might be able to save their lives," Levi suggested.

"That's a thought," I conceded. "If it comes to that, I'll ask Sherra to send them somewhere safer."

"Kyri can help with that; she has seen more places than Sherra has." We all turned to Misten, who'd offered the sensible suggestion. "She may point them to L'on-Alberr—the city is still intact and all the bodies were taken away and burned."

"A very good option," I said. "I'll tell Sherra and Kyri. The final decisions will be theirs."

"Good enough. Do we have large pods that can work together?" I asked.

"The *King's Eagles* already know how to work together," Armon said. "We can run through some exercises and put similar pods together. At this point, I'll take whatever works."

"What about those men from M'chestr?" I asked.

"They can drive a flying pod shield with no trouble," Caral said. "Still weak on blasts, but they haven't been at it for long."

"Then let them drive one of the pods and allow the warriors and roses to work on keeping the blasts and shields working."

"Draw up a battle plan for our pods, showing them how to attack a single, larger pod," I told Armon. "We'll discuss it when you're done."

"I'll have it ready in an hour."

"Good. Send the others to bed. They need sleep."

"It will be done, my King."

~

"North is asleep in his suite; we have two palace guards and a rose-and-warrior pair outside his door," Hunter reported when I called him into my study.

"Good. If he wakes outside his normal sleep time, or begins to act strangely, it could mean Kaakos is on the way."

"I worry about that, too. We have eyes on him all the time, although the rose and warrior are behind a mirrored bubble shield."

"Good. I want regular reports."

"You'll have them."

~

Adahi

Kaakos had built a shield about himself and his army as they slept;

I worried that nothing might crack it. That meant another way would have to be found. I hoped Arresh knew what she was doing.

The first part is done, Arresh informed me, as if she were listening to my thoughts. *Bring them away; I think they'll be safe enough here until other arrangements can be made.*

Pray that Kaakos won't feel their absence; that will upset everything.

Then tread lightly, Grandfather.

I waited so long for you to reach the one descendant who could hold you— who was worthy of you, I told her. *So many generations have come and gone, and she arrives at just the right time. Sherra was a gift to both of us.*

I know. Take care in gathering them; a single cry in the night could bring everything down.

Let me know where you take it, I said. She'd understand what I meant.

I will. It will be safe, Grandfather. I promise.

Good. Go, now, and do what you must. I will begin my work here.

CHAPTER 18

*A*z-ca
 Kaakos

They hadn't wakened me. Yes, they'd have died—the first few, anyway. Somehow, those I wasn't connected with in Az-ca had slipped away in the night, leaving all their belongings behind.

If I didn't know better, I'd have said the witch was responsible, but there wasn't a trace of her anywhere. After the third village was searched with no clues left behind, I turned my anger on the Headman and his family and blasted them into oblivion. It was a pleasure to hear the youngest's screams as I killed her parents first.

Kull, whom I'd brought with me, looked ill. I slapped him for his concern and transported us to his village. He and his Headman would feed my army today, while we went about practicing our skills at flying bubble shields.

I saw this in a dream before I left Ny-nes, I recalled. In that dream, I'd been flying over the King's City to attack it. How convenient that it was a premonition of better things to come.

Arresh

It is done, Grandfather, I sent, along with images of the location.

That is a fine choice, he told me. *I am grateful. Do you have what we need?*

I do. Just small bits, with the best samples within.

You have to do the first part. I suggest beginning with the one they now call North, as he'll still be sleeping.

You'll have to perform the other half, I reminded him.

I know. Let us hope that I can hold on until it's done. I'll dispose of the remains from your procedure when I'm done, at the same time I dispose of what is left after I do what I must. Leave yours where I can find it.

They'll be where you asked, just as we planned. Call for me if there is trouble. You know there will be if Kaakos discovers only one connection rather than two, until both can be eliminated.

I will, Granddaughter. Do not fear. There are times when breaking laws become a necessity.

His mindspeak ended as I gazed down at the man who wore Thorn I's disguise over Thorn II's body. If this failed to work, we were all dead. Opening my palm, I studied the pale dust lying there. *Would it work?*

"Do this for me," I whispered to it, and began.

Kerok

"Don't drink too much tea; you'll never be able to sleep," Barth warned as Briar set a mug of hot tea at my elbow. "Sun will rise shortly," he added.

"You're awake early," I pointed out.

"Doret had to get up and make sure the children went to breakfast. If I wanted breakfast with her, then I had to get up, too."

"Is this a new development?"

"Relatively new. We're getting along. That's why I feel it's necessary for all of us to come out of this alive."

"You don't need to remind me about incentive, Barth."

"Here are the battle plans," Armon *stepped* into my study.

"I'll take those," I held out my hand. "Go to bed, Armon, before you fall over."

"Are you saying something about my appearance?"

"You look like hell. Now go get some sleep."

"I could say the same to you. Is Sherra awake yet?"

"I'm here." Sherra *stepped* into my study, set a mug of tea on a corner of my desk and frowned at me.

"Sleep well, my King." Armon gave me a sardonic grin and *stepped* away.

"Did you get some rest?" I quizzed her as I stood and stretched.

"I did. Now you do the same."

"I'm going. Don't let me sleep too long."

"All right. Go. Let me know if you need anything."

"If you promise to do the same. We have no idea how much time we have before Kaakos comes after us."

"I'll wake you if that happens."

"Good."

"Oh," I said before *stepping* to my suite, "If we survive, we'll definitely change the law about *stepping* in and out of the palace. Otherwise, I'll have to send all of us to the lockup."

Sherra

Somehow, I knew Arresh had been up to something while I slept, but I didn't know what it was and had to trust that she was right to keep her secrets.

I took Kerok's chair behind his desk and gazed at Barth, who sat nearby, sipping tea and looking as if he needed another night's sleep.

"These are the battle plans Armon delivered?" I unrolled the paper and studied it.

"Yes."

"This looks good," I went through ten pages of tactical plans that

Armon had drawn up. "Let's hope we have enough power to force him back."

"I have a suggestion," Barth cleared his throat. "Actually, Doret and I though of it last night."

"What's that?"

"We still have the six prisoners from L'on-Alberr. Kaakos may be able to lock onto their presence, too. I suggest sending them elsewhere until this is over."

"That may be a good idea. Let me ask Kyri where she thinks they'll be safe."

"My Queen, Lofflin wishes to see you," a guard at the door announced.

"Lofflin?" I waved him inside.

"I don't know where it is," he began, the lines on his face indicating the depth of his concern. "I was working on the *Eagle* rings, and one of the rejected rings was on my work table before we left Az-ca. It is now missing."

"Oh, no. How important was it?" I asked.

"I have all the drawings, and, as it wasn't the chosen design, its value was in the gold used to make it. Therefore, it was a significant theft. Only two servants have access to my work room, and they've never taken anything before. I don't doubt their innocence in this, either. That means that someone else learned of it and got past the locks on the door."

"Lofflin, I promise when the current threat is eliminated, we'll find the culprit. Keep working on the other design in the meantime and put everything in the safe when you're done for the day."

"I will. Thank you, Queen Sherra." He bowed and walked out of Kerok's study.

Kyri, I sent, *where can we put the six from L'on-Alberr temporarily, until this is over? Kaakos may still be able to lock onto them.*

What about the palace in Ny-nes? I'll take them; put some food together and I'll come to transport them in half an hour. There's nobody else in the palace, now, so they'll be all right.

I'll have them ready in half an hour.

~

Kyri

"This is only temporary," I told them in their language. Sherra had put a generous box of food together for them, that should last a week if they were careful. "If things go well, we'll come back for you in five days or less. If we don't come back by that time, then there's nothing we can do to save you."

"We understand," Louis dipped his head to me. "Where can anyone be safe in such troubled times?"

"*Bonne chance*," I told him and *stepped* back to the King's City, which was now floating over the southern continent.

~

Kaakos

"What is that?" I demanded as the gold flashed on Kull's hand.

"My r-ring," he stuttered.

"Your ring?" I lifted an eyebrow, which should have told him his life hung by a thread.

"I st-stole it from the King's jeweler before they l-left us."

"Give it to me. Now." Kull almost dropped the ring when he pulled it from his finger—it was too large for him. His hand shaking, he laid it on my outstretched palm. "This is good work," I turned the ring in my hand, examining the craftsmanship of the carved eagle on the crest. "What was this for?"

"F-for the *King's Eagles*—his flying tr-troops," Kull said, attempting to back away.

"Well, then," I closed the ring in my fist before stuffing it in a pocket. "We'll see who survives to claim that title, won't we? Go—we'll want a midday meal in an hour."

"Y-yes, Supreme Leader."

I watched him walk away swiftly, knowing he'd prefer to run, instead.

Sherra

"You know he'll empty every one of his slaves to defeat us," Pottles told me at lunch. She, Caral and Cole had come after I issued the invitation. We were discussing Kaakos' imminent attack, and how soon it might come.

Armon and Kerok were asleep; I'd verified that before putting this meeting together. North appeared to be subdued; his guards had heard no rumblings from the rose and warrior who'd come on duty to guard him, or from the ones they'd replaced.

"How is Klete doing?" I asked Pottles. So far, I hadn't heard from the boy. I took that as a good sign.

"He's fine for the moment; he appears to think that everything that can be done is being done. That's what he told me, anyway, only in about three or four words."

"Even if that child learns every word that exists or ever existed, I believe he'll still use the fewest words possible to get his meaning across," I said.

"Sounds good to me. I've heard some windbags in my time who could take a few pointers from Klete."

Caral stifled a laugh; Cole chose to duck his head to hide a smile.

"How much time do you think we have?" I turned to my next question, which was far more serious.

"I doubt it will be long; Kaakos, when he is motivated, can achieve results in a minimum amount of time. If he feels confident in the power he has with him, he'll come after us once he's successfully in the air and moving forward. Everything else can be set aside for later; killing us is his primary objective."

Pottles sounded grim and convinced of her words. I had little doubt that she was right. Kyri could know more, but I'd already asked enough of her for today.

Sherra? Kyri's voice.

What is it?

I'd like to take my people to L'on-Alberr if that's all right with you. Kaakos will hit here first, you know that.

I do. Go ahead; just be careful.

I will. I'll be back later.

Kyri, why don't you stay with them? They may not know what to do if Kaakos manages to destroy us and then starts looking for others who survived.

Are you sure?

Very.

All right.

When will you go?

In the next half hour.

Good luck to you, then. If we survive, I'll send a message.

"Kyri's taking her people to L'on-Alberr," I sighed aloud. "I told her to stay with them."

"Probably a good idea," Cole nodded. "They aren't suited for war."

"What about your people, Cole?"

"Why do you think Kyri separated us from her city? She took those of us who came to her and wished to learn to use our talent to fight and defend ourselves. She placed us elsewhere, so we could learn away from the others."

"I never thought of that," I shook my head. "I thought maybe you just wanted to live closer to the water or something."

"That was an unexpected benefit," he said, lifting his teacup and saluting me with it. "The people in Kyri's City were better adapted to growing vegetables and fruits, rather than practicing war maneuvers, or hunting and raising animals for slaughter. We traded with Kyri's City for what we lacked. We received vegetables and tea; they'd get meat from the trading."

I didn't point it out, but we were discussing things that had no purpose for the coming battle, and I felt it was our way of separating ourselves from the worry and burden of it—at least for a short while.

"Did you do much hunting?" Caral asked Cole.

"No. We had others who were better at it and enjoyed the solitude of tracking through the woods more than I. Those same men and women will fight beside us when needed, but they'd rather *step* onto the crook of a tree and watch for game animals."

"So their strengths are taken into account," Pottles said with a nod.

"Yes. Most definitely. Somehow, I ended up in charge of the village, because I was good at listening and sorting problems."

"You are certainly good at those things," I agreed. "I depend on you for that. Caral, too."

"Should we survive the next two days, I suggest new titles for your assistants," Pottles said. "Queen's Advisor, with a pay increase and appropriate authority, would be a good place to start."

"Kerok has Hunter and Barth—I think Queen's Advisor sounds like a wonderful idea."

"But I still want to be part of the army," Caral said.

"I think we can work that in," I told her. "Plus, we haven't survived the looming confrontation, yet."

There it was—the truth behind all the small talk and false happiness—our survival, or the conceivable lack of it.

"I want all of you to know," I wiped moisture from my eyes, "that you are my family, and I love all of you. Others, too, but they're not here right now. If nothing else is true, and nothing of us survives, we will all die knowing how to love. I don't think Kaakos understands any part of that or knows how to love."

"To those we love." Pottles lifted her cup of tea. The rest of us did the same.

Adahi

So far, the plan had fallen into place. Would it continue to do so? When Arresh and I decided on this course of action, we understood that if the smallest part of our plan failed, all would die.

Standing beside Thorn I's bed, I watched him as he slept deeply. What I had to do involved urgency, accuracy, and a great deal of speed.

On the table beside the bed lay Thorn's Book of Divination, its torn halves lying one atop the other. Between those, Arresh had placed the small packet that I'd need, and shielded it heavily.

As noiseless as I could, I lifted the top half of the book and set it aside. The paper wrapping looked innocent enough, but had it not been shielded, so many things could go wrong. In this, every movement I made had to be done in a precise order.

The sharp knife I'd taken from the kitchen appeared in my hand. I studied it for several seconds, examining the edge on the blade. It had to be quite sharp to make the cut, such that a second would pass before the pain would be felt.

I needed that time to release what was in the packet left by Arresh.

May the skies be merciful to all of us, I thought, and lifted the small packet.

Arresh said that the dust within the square of paper would be released when I squeezed it in my hand. With my right hand, I held the knife over the King's skin. As swift as a snake striking, I readied myself.

Cut!

Squeeze!

Perhaps I shouted afterward; I couldn't recall, as too many things happened at once.

z-ca
Kaakos

I'd almost perfected flying a bubble shield, even with the lack of understanding through a language barrier between my slaves. Preparation would begin soon for our attack on the flying city and its army camp.

An evening meal before we left would be appropriate; night was a better time to attack anyway. I'd kept note of the connection with my contact within the King's City; it thrummed within my mind, a background noise to my present endeavors.

Soon enough, my desires would be reality. Reaching out, I felt the strong connection between us, until it evaporated like a drop of water on a hot day. "No," I shouted aloud as the connection was broken. "No," I shouted again, while all my minions, floating within the bubble I'd created, cowered around me.

"Those fools. They've killed my connection," I began with a shout, before trailing my words into a whisper.

Was this how they intended to hide from me? They'd learned I was connected, somehow, and killed their own King?

I still have six others there, I told myself, and began searching for their blood signal until I found them.

In Ny-nes.

"No!" I screamed again into the air inside my flying bubble. This was too much. It was unacceptable. They'd killed my first targets, leaving the bitch Queen in charge. Well, we'd see who was in charge at the end.

"We go." I began moving the bubble shield forward, gathering speed as I went. They couldn't fly the city even a quarter this fast. I knew where they were when the contact was lost; I intended to get there quickly, and I'd find them soon enough, once I did.

Sherra

"They're dead? Both of them?" I stared at Hunter through my tears as he delivered the news.

"We have both bodies in the infirmary, but yes, my Queen, they are gone from us."

"H-how?" My words, like my hands, were trembling.

"Throats cut. There's something else."

"What else could there possibly be?" I sobbed.

"The fingers—the ones wearing the rings? Both are missing." Hunter was now wiping away tears of his own.

"Hunter," I stood and bowed to him, "You are now King. We follow your command."

"Why would they take the rings? Sherra, we have a murderer—or murderers, in our midst. Who would do this?"

"Sherra," Pottles appeared in the doorway. Klete stood beside her, his hand held tightly in hers. "Kaakos is on the way."

"We will mourn later," Armon released me from his tight embrace. "Today, we fight the evil that is Kaakos, to the bitter end."

"Yes," I agreed. I'd *stepped* to Secondary Camp to tell Armon the news myself. Hunter, with Barth's assistance, was combing through the palace, looking for the one who'd killed Kerok. He promised not to rest until the culprit was found.

How did they get past the guards? Caral sent to me. She and Cole had come with me to Secondary Camp, as we had to make ready for Kaakos' arrival.

No idea. Barth is doing divination, but so far, the guards know nothing about it.

"How long before Kaakos gets here?" Levi asked.

"I can't say for sure, but Klete said he can travel much faster than we can fly the city."

"That makes sense—the city is massive."

"Yes, it is. Secondary Camp, on the other hand, isn't. We'll move into position to fly between Kaakos and the city and send out our battle pods from there. Pottles will stay in the city with Klete and Hunter. If she has updates, I'll get them from her."

"Do you suppose Kaakos is following blindly, now, since his connection is dead?" Armon asked.

"I think he's heading for our last known location," I admitted. "He'll run after us past that point, so it's only a matter of time."

Hunter

"Why did they cut their throats, then take the rings? Taking the rings would have served both purposes," I asked Barth and Doret.

"I don't know, Hunter," Doret shook her head. Barth, sitting beside her in Thorn's study, wore the saddest expression I'd ever seen him wear. Still, I was attempting to come to grips with this.

Barth had finished his divination of all the guards and all the servants with access to both North and Thorn. None of them were guilty or had any involvement in the deaths.

"The only thing this accomplished was to turn off the connection between us and Kaakos, but that could have been achieved a different way," Doret complained. "None of this makes any sense, and to my knowledge, nobody outside the ones we trust knew that Kaakos held a connection to North."

"What does Klete say?" Barth turned to Doret.

"Wait. Just that one word." Doret shook herself, then shuddered. Barth put an arm about her shoulders and pulled her close.

"I—don't know how we'll go on without Thorn," I sighed. "He knew how to fight the enemy, dispense judgment and handle the military. I can only keep records and provide advice on the making of laws."

Kaakos has been sighted in the distance, Sherra informed me. *We're preparing for battle.*

"Kaakos is on our tail," I said aloud. "Sherra and Armon are preparing the troops."

❧

Sherra

Cole, Anari, Kyal and Laren formed their bubble shield, and welcomed sixteen others aboard. Already, we had fourteen other pods ready to be released against the coming menace.

"Wait for my command," Armon told them, from his position beside me. "Sherra, are you sure you want to do this?"

I wanted to say, *what do I have to live for, except these?* and include all the bubble shields with a sweep of my hand.

I didn't; Armon would suspect I was on a suicide mission, rather than one to protect the King's City. In a way, I suppose I was on a suicide mission.

Once Kaakos was busy swatting at all our attacking pods, well, I wanted to give him a surprise of my own.

Either way, one of us would die. With Kerok gone, I no longer cared which of us it would be. My heart had been ripped out with his death and there was little left to do, except this one thing.

Somehow, Kaakos was tied to these deaths, and I wanted to show him what dying felt like, with no mercy given—only pain.

"He's within range," Caral shouted to Armon.

"It is time, warriors of Az-ca," Armon shouted. "Time to attack the enemy. Remember your training and may the first warrior be with you in this battle. Go, now. The shield window is open."

I watched as bubble shield after bubble shield lifted higher and flew toward the hatch I'd placed in the outer shield. Soon enough, they'd be given the order to attack. Forming my own shield; one that even lightning couldn't crack, I was the last bubble outside the shield before I closed and locked it against Kaakos.

Hunter

Sherra asked me to send visual images, Caral's mindspeak sounded in my head. *If the others are lost, Armon, Levi, Misten and I will make the last attack. I'll notify you if that happens.*

What about Sherra? I responded, almost afraid to ask.

She's flying alone in her own bubble shield, Caral replied. *Armon and I tried to convince her otherwise, but she refused to listen. She's with the other troops, preparing to attack Kaakos' flying bubble.* I received images then, of what Caral was seeing outside Secondary Camp's shield.

It's half the size of Secondary Camp's shield, she explained, as I gasped at what followed us. *Armon and I think he's put all his slaves aboard and is prepared to empty them to kill us.*

How adept is he at flying it? I asked, while wondering what the hell Sherra thought she was doing, going out on her own.

So far, I've seen no mistakes, but the true test will come when Armon commands our pods to attack. I'll show you as it happens.

Thank you.

Sherra

He know—you come, Klete's sending informed me.

Just me, or the others, too?

Others. Not see—you, Klete rephrased his statement.

At least the unseeable status still worked in my favor. I only waited for Armon to give the command to attack, and I'd carry out my plan. *Thank you, Klete*, I told him.

Welcome.

We didn't fire the first blast; Kaakos did. Armon's order to attack came immediately after, as we watched the bubble shield hit by Kaakos fly backward at an astonishing rate of speed.

From where I was, I had no way to know whether the shield had been breached, or if any of its occupants were alive. Suddenly, the darkening sky around us was lit with blasts from maneuvering pods, seemingly engaged in a dangerous dance with death.

Fire and retreat; fire and retreat. That was the game they played with Kaakos, who fired blindly at first, but once he realized their blasts were hitting his outer shields and only shaking his bubble, he began to fire back with more accuracy.

Time for me to act before he killed them all.

~

Drenn's Quarters

Adahi

I'd come to Drenn's suite because it was locked, mostly empty except for the bed and other furniture, and the perfect place to hide while I considered my next move.

Sherra had shielded it against anyone coming inside, but Arresh told me how to get past that.

And so I did.

I'd cast two small bubble shields of my own, which floated before me. Inside each was a finger bearing a ring—both of which I'd taken from the fingers of Kings of Az-ca. It was a gamble that I took—a desperate one that Arresh and I had made together. If the last bit of our plan failed, then all were doomed, and not only the two dead men in the infirmary.

If we failed, then the planet itself would belong to evil, because

Kaakos would see to it. He would control everything, including the minds of his slaves.

"You brought this on us, North," I accused the air. "You deserved this."

Was it truth I spoke, or was it only a way to assuage any guilt I might feel? Across the room, the mirror that Drenn used to check his stylish appearance every day, now showed my reflection. It sighed with me. "It is done," I told myself. "With no way to take it back."

Sherra—inside, a young voice informed me in mindspeak. *Be ready.*

So. There was another who knew of my guilt in this, and he was now telling me what I should know to carry out the last part of the plan.

Thank, I replied. *Much.*

Sherra

Kaakos was distracted.

Very distracted. I'd slipped through his shield as if I were water flowing over smooth stones. From his position at the front of the bubble, he fired continuously at the pods attacking him. Silently, I made my way forward, to reach him.

North tried the same thing, I reminded myself. He'd taken Kerok's power and then attempted to take Kaakos down from behind. I had to be more cautious.

Hiding within the smallest mirror shield I could place around myself, I floated along a scattered path between Kaakos' slaves, who hung haphazardly in midair throughout the bubble while he pulled their power away.

If any of these men raised the alarm, Kaakos would begin searching for me, and if he found me, I'd die. If it came to that, I intended to make the most of my death and the distraction it would cause.

For now, all the remaining pods were still dancing about Kaakos' bubble, firing and retreating. Kaakos cursed aloud; a direct hit from a combined fireblast, closely followed by another, shook his bubble and caused it to judder to one side. Fear engulfed me as I came within a hair's breadth of bumping into a floating slave.

Was this a method of protection for Kaakos—scattering the slaves inside the bubble like this? In places, the space was so tight I was forced to go far out of the way to find a clearer path. I was sure that contact with any of them would give an alarm of some kind.

Send others—away, Klete told me.

But, I wanted to argue.

Do. Please. Work.

Armon, call a retreat, I sent. *Klete thinks it's important.*

Where are you?

Inside Kaakos' bubble. Armon, call a retreat. I think it's important.

We just lost two more pods, Armon cried out as Kaakos shouted with glee and shook his fist in the air.

Call. A. Retreat.

We only have seven pods left, Armon said—*and we've just lost another.*

Call a retreat, I repeated.

Sherra, I—all right.

I'll never forget the sound of Kaakos' laughter as the remaining pods disappeared from view, leaving a clear path to Secondary Camp's flying bubble. "Now, who's the eagle?" he shouted, shoving a hand into his pocket and withdrawing—was that the missing ring that Lofflin reported?

"No!" My anger was white-hot as I cast my mirror shield aside and shouted at Kaakos. He laughed at me and shoved the ring on a finger before pointing his hands to fire a blast at me.

Leave, Klete's mindspeak was shouted.

Still laughing, Kaakos released a blast that would fry me if I stood still. As I *stepped* away, the laugh became a scream.

Adahi

Drawing in a breath, I grasped both bubble shields before me, breaking them. They were never intended to keep me out. The fingers, still bearing rings, floated before me.

Hurry, Klete begged. I grasped both fingers and blasted them with my fire, rendering them to ash. The rings, smoking and heavy, dropped to the floor of Drenn's suite, ringing as they hit.

Hunter

"What's happening?" I shouted aloud as I received visions and mindspeak from Caral. For some reason, Armon had called a retreat, bringing all remaining pods away from their attack on Kaakos.

That left us vulnerable to Kaakos' blasts, and those would come any moment. *Wait*, Caral shouted into my mind, as the vision she sent showed me Kaakos's bubble slowing behind Secondary Camp.

Then, it lurched forward again, only to stop again.

And then, with none of our pods around it, an enormous blast was fired upon it from the outside. That was followed by a second blast, and then a third, until Kaakos' bubble burst into a massive fireball. The next blast fired upon it blew it skyward, where it climbed so fast Caral had a difficult time keeping it in her view.

Far and high into the night, another blast lit the sky, and then another, until the bubble exploded in such a violent burst of light that it looked like daylight outside. The darkness that fell when it snuffed out was like Kaakos' eyes closing in death.

And so it was.

*H*unter

"Armon, she's been gone for two days. What are we supposed to think?"

"I won't willingly mourn her until I know she's dead. And I suggest you find out who took those bodies from the infirmary. We can't mourn the death of a King if we don't have the King in question."

"This is impossible," I raked fingers through my hair. "I'd give anything to walk away from this responsibility. I'd planned to abdicate in favor of Sherra anyway. It's just—where the hell is she, if she's not dead?" My frustration had built up for two days, and now Armon was bearing the brunt of it.

"At least Kaakos is dead. I'm pretty sure of that one," Armon said quietly.

"As is half our army," I said, bitterness in my voice. "We've lost so many." I shook my head as mist gathered in my eyes.

"I know. Levi and Caral are putting the lists together, so we can create a memorial to those who died to defeat the enemy of Az-ca. We'll add Thorn's name at the top, and Sherra's, if and only if, I have final proof of her death."

"I still don't know what happened there at the end. Do you?" I searched Armon's eyes for an answer.

"No idea. The only person who might explain what happened is Klete, and he's not speaking to anyone right now."

"Probably lost in grief," I muttered. "Leave the boy alone."

"As you say, my King." Armon dipped his head to me and turned to leave my study.

"Armon, ask Cole to report to me in four days, if he's recovered from our losses enough to work as my advisor," I said.

"I'll do that," Armon agreed and walked through the door.

Swee'n

Sherra

I'd been away for two days, living in a borrowed house in the deserted village outside the picturesque lake. I'd wondered what it would be like, waking to that beauty every day. I'd wakened to it for two days, now, and only managed to see it through eyes reddened and swollen from too many tears.

I should go to the high village and let the people know they can come back, I reminded myself for perhaps the fiftieth time. Lethargy and sadness had prevented me from going earlier.

I sat near the edge of the lake, the sun creating spikes of light on ripples of water as a grey heron flew past. The beauty and perfection of its slow, graceful flight was lost on me; my vision had turned grayer than the bird's coloring.

"Don't you think it's time to stop crying for me?"

Kerok's ghost knelt in the grass before me.

Behind him stood North's ghost. Perhaps I deserved the rebuke— and the haunting. I still hadn't solved their murders. Rubbing my eyes with the heels of my hands, I worked to clear my vision of apparitions.

Instead, when I moved my hands and blinked, both were still there.

"We're not apparitions, Granddaughter," North said.

"And neither are you my Grandfather," I snapped at him. This wasn't a haunting; it was a nightmare and I was still dreaming in a borrowed bed.

"Hmmph," North sounded as if he wanted to laugh, but didn't.

"Sherra," Kerok reached out and gripped my wrists in his hands. Absently, I noticed his right ring finger was missing. "Adahi did what he had to do—to save us. You, me, the others, too. He and Arresh did this together. I hold them blameless, although they broke the King's laws."

"You're not real," I told him, although his grip on my wrists tightened.

"Yes, I am. Perhaps a bit different in some ways, but the same."

"But you were North," I accused. "And he was you," I jerked my chin up, indicating North. I blinked when I saw that his right ring finger was also missing.

"He is Adahi, now, Sherra, although if you wish him to take North's name, he will."

"Why would I do that? It makes no sense. None of this makes sense." Pulling my arms away from Kerok's ghost, I stood and began walking away from them.

"Hunter is losing his mind, wondering whether you're dead or alive," North informed me. "Armon and Caral aren't sure what to believe, although Armon refuses to accept your death unless there's proof."

"Armon has always been an intelligent man," I said, quickening my steps.

"Sherra, you can't outrun us; we can *step* just as well as you can," Kerok was suddenly before me. He'd moved unexpectedly, driving me straight into his waiting arms.

"I can *step*, too," I said, although the warmth of the embrace threatened to undo me.

"Shhh," Kerok breathed against my hair. "Let us take you home, and we'll explain everything."

"I've never been carried by a ghost," I whispered as I was lifted and transported a short distance.

"She hasn't eaten in two days," Collin announced. When had *he* gotten here? I wasn't aware that he could *step*.

"Collin *steps?*" I mumbled.

"No, my rose. Collin doesn't *step*."

Armon

"Tell me Kaakos is really dead, then," I demanded. Thorn, accompanied by North, requested my presence in the King's study. Had Hunter not sent mindspeak only moments before, shouting that Thorn was alive, I would have been even more skeptical.

"Kaakos is truly dead, and Sherra is being tended by the Royal Physician in my suite," Thorn replied. Hunter, who sat beside Thorn's desk, nodded enthusiastically.

"I fail to understand any of this," I said.

"I don't blame you," Thorn said. "Have a seat, and we'll do our best to explain all of it."

"How are you—you, and North? Are you ah, yourselves, now?" I demanded.

"North is no longer North," North answered. "Thorn is himself."

"Armon, meet Adahi," Thorn indicated North.

"How is that even possible?" I snapped.

"Because for several months, I was Hunter, too," North replied smoothly.

"And that's why my memory isn't complete, and why I managed to do all kinds of things which I couldn't remember," Hunter agreed. "You knew about that, didn't you?"

"How—are you all right with that?" I turned toward Hunter.

"I think you know how much time and effort Adahi saved me, by exercising my body and getting my brain to come back to itself," Hunter said. "Collin confirmed it, actually, after he was told what happened."

"All right, then, tell me how North is Adahi, now, and how you're fine and sitting in front of me as if nothing ever happened," I told Thorn.

"We never said nothing happened," Thorn said. "Do you want to tell this? I only have most of it second-hand from you anyway," he asked Adahi.

"I broke the King's laws," Adahi said. "And before you ask, the part of this brain that was North—no longer functions."

~

Sherra

"We have oatmeal with brown sugar, bacon and eggs," Briar informed me. I suppose she knew—or someone did—that the smell of warm food would bring me around faster than anything else.

"You've been asleep for twelve hours," Collin announced from the other side of the bed. "The King is on his way to check on his Queen. He says to tell you that he's not a ghost and will explain everything while you eat."

"I've been to the edge of the King's dome," Briar told me as she poured fresh tea in a cup and added honey. "It's a miracle to watch the city just floating along. We've passed green fields and forests, rivers, lakes, even the oceans. At least Doret says there's more than one ocean."

"What about Az-ca?" I struggled weakly to pull myself up in bed so I could eat.

"The King says they're waiting for you to help make those decisions," Briar fluffed my pillows, making it easier for me to sit up.

"Sherra?" the door opened and Kerok's head appeared.

"Please explain how you're suddenly all right," I leaned back and shut my eyes.

"Eat your breakfast, and I'll tell you."

"Fine. Get in here. Why am I in your suite rather than mine?"

"Because this is where you belong."

Briar pulled a chair to the side of the bed so Kerok could sit.

"Adahi and Arresh came up with this plan together," Kerok began, while urging me to eat with a hand gesture.

"She didn't tell me anything," I accused and dipped into the oatmeal first.

"For good reason," he said. "Adahi says that without your ideas, they'd never have developed the plan."

"All right, what was the plan?"

"Remember when you did the last divination of Jubal?"

"Yes."

"You said that the blood would have to be drained—or changed—in order for the blood spell to be removed."

"I did," I nodded and ate more oatmeal, with a bite of bacon in between.

"Arresh and Adahi did their own version of a blood spell, to change the blood—mine and North's."

"How?" I blinked my concern at Kerok's face. The familiar scar ran down his cheek as he grimaced at my tone.

"By taking something from Adahi's body in Ny-nes and performing a second blood spell on North and me. Arresh then took Adahi's remains from Kaakos' palace and buried them in a place only they know about."

"She used Adahi's blood or bone for the blood spell? You mean to tell me that you are now enslaved to Adahi?"

"No. They changed the words of the spell for me. I'm back to myself, now."

"How?" I chewed more bacon—forcefully.

"Arresh knows those words, and she won't tell anyone, not even Adahi."

"And the spell placed on North?"

"They used the same one North performed to entrap me. Only now, North has been entrapped by Adahi."

"Then what happened to North? Is he still in there, somewhere, waiting to cause more trouble?"

"Adahi says that this next part is what he begs your forgiveness for. If you don't give it, he will exile himself."

"I'm not going to like this, am I?"

"I have no problem with it," Kerok shrugged. "But you may find me partial to my own existence in this case, and grateful to Adahi for making it possible."

"Tell me," I said, biting off more bacon, although it was suddenly tasteless in my mouth.

"Adahi spent time in Hunter's body, and in his mind. He knew the part of Hunter's brain that was damaged, preventing him from being in control."

"Understood," I nodded, lifting my teacup to drink.

"Adahi burned that part of North's brain. It's as if North is truly dead, only his body isn't."

I choked on the tea and hurried to set the cup down. Kerok handed me the napkin, so I could wipe stray drops of liquid from my nightclothes.

"Adahi says that this is his penance—to live the rest of North's days, trapped in that body. It's a disguise he'd never have taken, if given the choice. North burned his bridges with Adahi, after his lies and blood spells resulted in disabling me, harming you and allowing Kaakos to go free the first time. North then committed the ultimate treason against Az-ca, when he contacted the enemy and offered him a deal. For that, he would have been sentenced to death anyway."

"Does Kyri know? That North is dead?"

"Doret told her. She doesn't blame Adahi for what he did; it freed us from Kaakos forever."

"Tell—my grandfather that he has my thanks. For bringing you back. Too many times I was more than willing to kill North after what he did to you. Only the blood spell and your mutual deaths held me back before. There's more to this story, though, isn't there?"

"Yes. It has to do with two rings blood-spelled by North, and another, blood-spelled by Arresh and Adahi."

"I watched Kaakos put the *Eagle* ring on his finger—and he screamed that he was the eagle, after Armon called the retreat."

"I waited for that moment, most earnestly, Granddaughter." North—Adahi—appeared inside the suite. "Everything hung upon that event. I stole the ring from Lofflin's workbench, but then I had to find a way to get it to Kaakos without raising his suspicion. It was easy enough to do so, once Kull learned what he'd invited into Az-ca."

"You passed the ring to him, didn't you?"

"I did. Kaakos went straight to Kull, like a moth drawn to a flame. Kull was immediately ordered to serve Kaakos, and it turned out he didn't have the stomach for watching his friends and fellows get burned to death if they displeased the bastard."

"So. You got the ring to Kaakos through Kull. Then what?"

"Arresh and I substituted two dead villagers for Thorn and North, making you believe they were dead. The blood spells were performed on the King and on North, and they were then hidden in Drenn's old suite. Their ring fingers, bearing the rings, were removed before the blood spells were done, so they'd maintain their blood connection."

"How did you get the *Eagle* ring to affect Kaakos?"

"Again, the original idea was yours. You were searching for a way to transfer the spell. The only way to do that would be to perform another blood spell. North had a direct connection to Kaakos, didn't he? I commanded the *Eagle* ring to connect with related blood, and with the other two rings. If any of them were removed from the finger of the wearer, all would die. It was a closed loop North formed in the beginning; I merely added another section to the loop."

"How did you know what to do?" I asked.

"Thorn's book was mentioned not long ago, and I wondered if there were any others he'd written. I wasn't aware of any at the time, but it sent me into the catacombs to search. I found this." Adahi held out his hand; a tied leather cover containing a sheaf of papers appeared there.

"Thorn I's personal notes," he presented them to Kerok. "Keep or destroy, I care not."

I blinked as Kerok gingerly accepted the leather-covered bundle as if it contained a poisonous snake within. If he kept it, it would be hidden within the strongest shield I could place around it; it was far more dangerous than it appeared.

"What are the plans for us—and Az-ca, now that Kaakos is dead?" I asked Kerok as his hands gripped the notes tightly.

He considered my question for several moments. "I think," he hesitated slightly before continuing. "I think it's time to give the regular citizens of Az-ca what they wanted—self-government. Let them lead themselves." Kerok shook his head, as if this saddened him. "I think—we can be self-sustaining as we are now."

"What if they put people like the former Council in charge—they're not fond of the truth, you know."

"I'd suggest providing supervision until their government is stable, and then gradually pulling away. I'll be interested to see what they do when we tell them they'll be responsible for protecting themselves from now on." Adahi crossed arms over his chest as if he were looking into the future.

"We'll think on that," Kerok slapped a knee. "Finish your breakfast. When you feel rested enough, come find me. We have a new, smaller Council to form, and it will include Armon, Barth, Hunter, Adahi, Caral, Wend, Marc, Misten, Doret and the Royal Physician. When they are old enough, Anari, Kyal, Laren and Klete will join them." Kerok rose, nodded to Collin (who beamed from his seat in the corner), and *stepped* out of the suite.

"You don't have to ask my forgiveness, Grandfather," I told Adahi. "You did what needed to be done, and, as Kerok says, I hold you blameless. Welcome to the world of the corporeal," I said.

"Granddaughter, you make my heart young again." He laughed and *stepped* away.

CHAPTER 21

*K*ull "Grandfather, why did you bring me here?" Fraya shaded her eyes against the relentless sun as we stood on the edge of the crater. Even now, the edge was burned, and molten rock was mixed with the sandy soil from the powerful blast aimed at it decades earlier.

The pit was so deep it was difficult to see the bottom, even when the sun was high. "This is a lesson in hubris, Granddaughter," I told her. "When this happened, I wasn't sure what that word really meant. I've paid more attention to words since then."

"Because you became a teacher, and taught people in Ny-nes?" she asked.

"That is part of it, certainly," I said. "It salvages some of my pride to know that we've brought Ny-nes back from the brink in the past seventy years. Now, we trade with them; they plant and build, because we taught them how to start."

"You still haven't said why you brought me here," she reminded me.

"Because this was where the King's City stood," I replied. "Built of massive, clear domes connected together, it would shine in the sun, almost blinding anyone traveling toward it from the outside."

"What happened to it? Was it destroyed by the great enemy?"

"No, Fraya. The great enemy was destroyed by those who lived here. The King's City was almost destroyed by us."

"Almost destroyed? Where is it, then?" Her eyes, squinting in the bright sunlight, bore the uncomfortable question which pained me to answer.

"Gone," I shrugged. "The Queen and King managed to float it away. They drew the great enemy after them, trapped him and destroyed him. I thought they would return, but that didn't happen. Some have seen a few from the King's City now and then, but they only appear when it's prudent, and never stay long."

"You make it sound like they had—magic," Fraya's voice sounded hushed and curious at the same time.

"It isn't magic," I said. "It's power. Talent, they call it. They could move from one place to another far away, in the blink of an eye. They could form fire to combat the enemy. They built shields of protection around themselves and around entire villages."

"Why didn't they come back?"

"Because we began to believe that they served no purpose—that they were a blight on Az-ca and were mistreating the people to provide for their own comforts. Most of those lies were told by the enemy, who was determined to provoke a civil war within Az-ca— between those with talent and those without. If Az-ca were at war with itself, it would be so much easier for the enemy to take it.

"We listened to those lies because we wished to believe them. Some of us went so far as to commit treason against the King. That's why they didn't return. I often think that they're floating the King's City overhead now and then; we just can't see it, because they keep it hidden from us."

"You make me want to see it, Grandfather."

"I would like to see it again with you, Granddaughter. I doubt they would accept my presence, if I were able to go. What I brought you here to tell you, however, is that you may be able to see it one day."

"How can you know that?"

"Because of something I received shortly after your birth. I feel it was given to me because in some small way, I was instrumental in the downfall of the enemy."

"What did you get?" Fraya now sounded breathless.

"One day, when you woke early, fussing to be fed, I lifted you from your cradle and found this." I pulled the object from a pocket. For fourteen years, I'd kept it hidden, knowing what it meant all along.

"But it's a rose, Grandfather. A fresh rose. How could it have survived since I was a baby?"

"Because it was gifted to you by the Queen of Roses, Granddaughter. It means you have within you something that neither I nor your parents ever did. You will be given the choice someday soon, whether to stay here in Az-ca, or go to the floating city to find your destiny."

"When will that day come?"

"The day is now, Fraya," a woman appeared before us, standing over the void of the crater as if it were solid ground.

"Queen Sherra," I bowed my head to her while tears formed in my eyes.

"Hello, Kull," she said and smiled as I straightened. "Fraya, you are one of only a few who have been chosen to develop your talent in the King's City. If you come, you will be taught many things."

"Will I see Grandfather, and my parents again?"

"We no longer keep our people from seeing their relatives—that is an old mistake that has been corrected. What we ask is that you spend a year in training before you return for a visit. And, if you determine that a life among the talented is not what you desire, we will let you go. Reluctantly, of course, but we don't force anyone to do something they abhor."

"Is this true, Grandfather?" Fraya turned to me.

"You can trust what Queen Sherra says."

"What about my things?"

"If your family has them packed and ready in two days, someone will retrieve them for you."

"I'll see to it," I said.

"What do you think I should do?" Fraya asked me.

"I think it would be a shame if you didn't find out what you truly are."

"Kull," Sherra turned to me. "Klete tells me to extend the invitation to you, as well. You'll be given a place to stay, and Fraya can live with you while she learns."

"Klete? The boy?"

"He's a grown man, now, and he's been waiting for Fraya to come to the King's City for a very long time."

"I am overjoyed," I whispered. "I wish to come."

Fraya's hand reached out and gripped mine while tears ran down my cheeks. I closed my eyes to clear them, and when I opened them again, I found we'd been transported to the King's study. There, King Thorn, with several others standing beside him, waited for our arrival with a smile.

The End

CHARACTERS AND PLACES

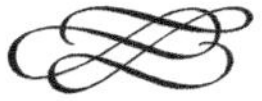

haracters and Places Appearing in this Series:

Adahi: AKA the phantom; well acquainted with former King Thorn. Dreamwalker, who has a long history with Kyri and events in Ny-nes.

Adem: Villager who refused to join the Republic of Az-ca.

Affa-Gannis: Mountainous area where Kaakos gathers his new army,

Alf: Worker in the berry farms under Az-ca's southern domes. Spy for Ruarke and then Kaakos.

Alun: New hire for the King's palace in Az-ca. Spy for Kaakos, sent to kill Thorn II.

Ana: North Camp Instructor, Second Cohort.

Anari: 17-year-old black rose girl with mindspeaking and *stepping* talent.

Armon: Elevated to General of Az-ca's army. Chosen by Caral.

Arresh: The name chosen by Sherra's dreamwalker.

Aspe: Warrior-priest and favorite of Kaakos.

Az-ca: Desert country now ruled by King Thorn II; always at war with barbarians from Ny-nes.

Balsom: Village in eastern Az-ca, roughly twenty miles south of Sa'wann. There, the terrain is relatively flat.

Ban: Village Headman, Az-ca.

Barth: King's Chief Diviner.

Beckley: Warrior, chosen by Reena.

Beels: Warrior-priest; mindspeaker and spy among warrior-priests for Kaakos.

Bela: Former washout.

Beri: From Ny-nes; Klete's mother.

Barney (Barna): Escort trainee and former washout.

Blane Grove: Former Council member and Merrin's ally.

Bones of the Prophet: A drug given to those in Ny-nes' army and its clerics, to ensure their compliance.

Book of the Rose (The): A book in the King's library, describing talents and duties of Black Rose escorts.

Bray: Barth's secondary Diviner.

Briar: Servant in King's palace, Az-ca.

Buck: Member of the King's Council and a leader of the Republic of Az-ca movement.

Bulldog: A nickname used by Yasa, North Camp Instructor, Sixth Cohort.

Calli: Escort who, with her warrior, deserted the army and joined with Merrin.

Captain Indus: Officer in Az-ca's army; chosen as one of the King's elite troops.

Captain Neele: Ranking officer often left in charge of Secondary Camp.

Caral: Fourth Cohort trainee at North Camp, now Captain in Az-ca's Army and an Advisor to Queen Sherra.

Claude: Former sergeant in Az-ca's army. Mindspeaker who worked as a messenger after his retirement.

Cole: A refugee from Ny-nes. Born with power, he was tortured as a child until he escaped by stepping to Kyri's City at her invitation. Now serves as an Advisor to Queen Sherra.

Collin: Royal Physician.

Colonel Kage: Training Instructor for warrior trainees in the King's City—becomes a King's assassin.

Colonel Weren: Training Instructor for warrior trainees in the King's City; becomes General of the Army.

Commander Alden: Post Commander for Secondary Camp.

Dar-den: Caral's former village.

Daren: Former resident of M'chestr—has talent and joins Az-ca's army.

Daria: Doret's sister, killed by Ruarke.

Derissa: Caral's older sister, from Dar-den.

Dayl: General Linel's personal messenger.

Derk Beadl: Former Council member and ally of Merrin

Doret: Former Queen of Az-ca; more than 200 years old

Dree: A drudge at Secondary Camp; one of three hidden members of the Republic of Az-ca.

Drenn Wulfson Meris Rex: Former Crown Prince of Az-ca (deceased).

East Camp: One of four training camps for black rose trainees.

End-War: Crippling event that changed and destroyed nearly everything on the planet.

Enzo: Resident of smaller city near L'on-Alberr.

Falia: Instructor at North Camp.

Ferni: One of two young troublemakers at the training camp for girls.

F'nexscot: AKA the King's City.

Fraya: Granddaughter of Kull.

Gale: Armon's former escort.

Garkus: Drill instructor at Secondary Camp—became a King's assassin. Defied the Crown and was exiled.

Garth: Outpost Commander.

Gaull: Far northeastern village in Az-ca. Jubal lives outside the village.

Geb: Retired warrior—now works as a traveling instructor for all trainees.

General Linel: Chief Commander of the army in the Prince Commander's absence (deceased).

General Tern: Officer in Ny-nes' army.

Glindi: Rose in Az-ca's army; bonded to Warrior Samm.

Giles: Instructor from Cole's village.

Grae: Kerok's deceased escort.

Gram Plicton: Former Council member, who became Merrin's ally after Drenn's death.

Harel: Messenger who was burned by Merrin's warrior allies before escaping to take the news of Merrin's location to the Crown Prince (deceased).

Hari: Escort abandoned by her warrior (Narris).

Harnn: Bela's warrior.

Hayla: Black rose trainee.

High Commander Finn: Supreme Commander of Ny-nes' army.

Hunter Lattham: King's advisor, Uncle to Merrin, Drenn and Kerok.

Jacob: Council member for Dar-den, Caral's former village.

Jae: Black rose trainee—Sixth Cohort, North Camp (deceased).

Jean: Former resident of L'on-Alberr; wounded in Kaakos' takeover of the city.

Jeen: One of two young troublemakers at girls' training camp.

Jem: Warrior washout and one of three traitors at Secondary Camp belonging to the Republic of Az-ca.

Jenner: Kull's second-in-command in Republic of Az-ca (deceased).

Jerr: Council member from Wildtree Village.

Jubal Raime: Disabled warrior and mindspeaker, who became a spy for Ruarke and then Kaakos. Convicted of treason and executed.

Kaakos: The name taken by the Sovereign Leader of the Free Nation of Ny-nes.

Kage: See Colonel Kage.

Kerok: AKA Thorn Wulfson Kerok Rex, King Wulf's youngest son and Prince Commander of the army—becomes Crown Prince upon Drenn's death, and then King upon his father's death.

Ketchi: The village where Cole and many other refugees from Ny-nes live. All were born with power and were sentenced to death by Ruarke.

King Wulf Carlson Alexander Rex: King of Az-ca (deceased).

King's Eagles (the): An elite force within Az-ca's army, proficient in flying bubble shields and forming pods to combine blasts against the enemy.

Klete: Formerly of Ny-nes; a nine-year-old who has formidable divination skills—a dream diviner.

Kull: Council member who imagines himself to be chief of that body; Leader in the Republic of Az-ca movement.

Kyal: 11-year-old warrior boy with mindspeaking talent. Now trains troops to fly bubble shields.

Kyri: Female Diviner—believed to be a legend or myth.

Laren: 16-year-old warrior boy with mindspeaking talent. Now trains troops to fly bubble shields.

Lera: Escort abandoned by her warrior.

Levi: Elevated to rank of Colonel. Chosen by Misten.

Lewus: Council member for Merthis and five other villages.

Liam: Kaakos' Chief of Technical Sciences.

Lilya: North Camp Instructor, Fourth Cohort.

Liri: Chief instructor from Cole's village.

Lofflin: Jeweler to the King of Az-ca.

L'on-Alberr: Foreign city, whose non-talented citizens were destroyed by Kaakos.

Louis: Former resident of L'on-Alberr; victim of Kaakos' blood spell. Rescued by Sherra.

Luc: Resident of village near L'on-Alberr.

Lusern: Resident of a city in Swee'n.

Marc: Captain in Az-ca's army. Chosen by Wend.

Mari: Black rose girl; Romma's daughter.

Marra: Daria's chosen warrior.

Marta: General Weren's wife.

M'chestr: Foreign city taken by Kaakos.

Meka: Drudge from Secondary Camp; one of three traitors belonging to the Republic of Az-ca.

Mendacium: Ny-nes' capital city, renamed after Kaakos took over rule of the country. He named it that in a private jest.

Merrin: Nephew of Hunter and King Wulf; cousin to Drenn and Kerok on mother's side (deceased).

Merthis: Small village where Sherra was born.

Miri: North Camp Instructor, Fifth Cohort.

Misten: North Camp trainee, Sixth Cohort.

Narris: Warrior-turned-traitor who left his escort behind (Hari) before deserting army.

Narvin: Deserter who, with his escort Willa, chose to follow Merrin.

Neka: North Camp trainee, First Cohort.

Nguyen-Mei: Resident of Kyri's City—caretaker for Mari, a black rose girl.

Niles: Cleric who became Ruarke's second-in-command upon Ward's death.

Nina: North Camp Instructor, First Cohort.

Noah: Former resident of M'chestr. Joins Az-ca's army.

North: Healer in Ny-nes—changed his name to hide a past identity. Formerly King Thorn I of Az-ca.

North Camp: One of four camps where black rose trainees are taught.

Ny-nes: Formerly ruled by Kaakos. Was considered the land of barbarian enemies by those in Az-ca.

Nyra: Levi's deceased escort.

Olan: Chief Diviner for the army.

Oren: Messenger for Crown Prince Thorn.

Pa-sen: Small village in southwestern Az-ca.

Phantom: See Adahi.

Pierre: Resident of smaller city near L'on-Alberr.

Pottles: Blind pot seller and friend to Sherra (see Doret).

Poul: Assassin for King Wulf (deceased).

Querl: Army deserter and Merrin's chief ally.

Reena: Former washout.

Republic of Az-ca: Subversive group determined to fight those with power and bring about civil war.

Reva: Escort who, with her warrior, deserted the army and joined with Merrin.

Romma: Resident of Dar-den, mother of Mari, a black rose girl.

Ruarke: Chief Cleric of Ny-nes, and Kaakos' second-in-command. Former Crown Prince of Az-ca (deceased).

Salik: Petitioned the King to get the dowry from his fiancee after she ended their engagement. A member of the Republic of Az-ca, he intended to expose Kerok's lack of power (deceased).

Samm: Lieutenant, warrior in Az-ca's army. Bonded with Glindi.

Sa'wann: Village in eastern Az-ca, nestled in a hilly area prone to predator attacks.

Secondary Camp: Location for final escort training after warriors are chosen.

Sherra: Black Rose trainee from Merthis. Bonded to Thorn Wulfson Kerok Rex; Doret considers her an adopted daughter. Became Queen of Az-ca when Thorn II ascended the throne.

Shon: Member of the Republic of Az-ca.

Soobi: Kitchen servant in Kaakos' palace.

Stave: Resident of the far northeastern village of Gaull in Az-ca; Jubal's closest neighbor.

Swee'n: A foreign city.

Tera: North Camp trainee—Sixth Cohort.

The Rose Mark: A forbidden book. That decision was overturned by Crown Prince Thorn, and copies were provided to all trainees.

Thorn's Book of Advanced Divination Techniques: A forbidden book.

Thornson: Kaakos' given name.

Ura: North Camp trainee and one of the Bulldog's pets (deceased).

Vale: Northernmost supply village for Az-ca's army.

Varnon: Village elder in Merthis.

Venge: Top General in Kaakos' army.

Vengeance: Raver created by Kaakos, after taking over Merrin's mind.

Veri: North Camp trainee and one of the Bulldog's pets (deceased).

Ward: Cleric and Ruarke's second-in-command (deceased).

Welton: Chief Physician, military post.

Wend: North Camp Trainee, Sixth Cohort.

Wendal: Assassin for King Wulf (deceased).

Weren: Former Colonel and warrior trainee instructor. Becomes General of the army (deceased).

West Cana: Area where Kyri's City is located.

Willa: Escort bonded to warrior Narvin. She and her warrior deserted the army to follow Merrin (deceased).

Wulf Tadson Ruarke Rex: See Ruarke.

Yasa: AKA Bulldog, or the Bulldog.

Zis: Warrior-priest in Raver/Merrin's entourage.

www.ingramcontent.com/pod-product-compliance
Lightning Source LLC
Chambersburg PA
CBHW060953120726
47910CB00002B/614